THOSE
Pink
Mountain
-NIGHTS-

ALSO BY JEN FERGUSON

The Summer of Bitter and Sweet

THOSE
Pink
Mountain
NIGHTS

JEN FERGUSON

Heartdrum
An Imprint of HarperCollins Publishers

Heartdrum is an imprint of HarperCollins Publishers.

Those Pink Mountain Nights
Copyright © 2023 by Jen Ferguson
All rights reserved. Printed in the United States of America.
No part of this book may be used or reproduced in any manner whatsoever without written permission except in the case of brief quotations embodied in critical
articles and reviews. For information address HarperCollins Children's Books, a
division of HarperCollins Publishers, 195 Broadway, New York, NY 10007.
www.epicreads.com

Library of Congress Control Number: 2023932496
ISBN 978-0-06-308621-0

23 24 25 26 27 LBC 5 4 3 2 1
First Edition

To those who are still learning
to bend but are done with breaking.

To the stubborn ones,
the ones who fight back, who fight loud.

To the ones who laugh.

To the ones who make mistakes.

A Few Things About This Book

This book is about a small-town independent pizza shop and the teens who run the place. They are going through a lot because teens go through a lot in their lives. Like pizza, this story can comfort and satisfy, but it's also about a perfectionist with undiagnosed depression, a teen coping with trauma by laughing at everything, a teen living with the late effects of childhood cancer treatment in an abusive home, the fallout of a friendship breakup, and other intense true-to-life situations that teens face.

In this book, teens make mistakes and those mistakes hurt: specifically, there is an insidious anti-Blackness in Indigenous, POC, and otherly marginalized communities that exists, and one aspect of that is represented here.

As well, this book centers the traumas faced by Indigenous women, girls, and Two-Spirit people, and one narrative of the ongoing human rights crisis happening now in the colonial nations of Canada, the United States of America, and Mexico.

There is one animal death in these pages, but our characters help her pass well. The rest of the animals in this book are happy and healthy and thriving.

Take care of yourself while reading, first and foremost. If you're not ready to read now, that's okay because books are forever, and you matter more than books. This is truth, always, until time runs out and books are no more, so basically forever-ever. <3 Jen

Friday Afternoon

Calgary Herald *headline: "Promising" Indigenous Teen Reported Missing First Week of School*

BERLIN

No one had noticed her new cat-eye glasses, bright red, with very faux diamonds spread across the rise like perfectly positioned stars. Not a single person had said a thing. All morning long. And now the other members of the First Nations, Métis, and Inuit Student Association—the FNMISA for short—were too busy arguing about their upcoming fundraiser to notice that Berlin wasn't fully present. She sat at a desk, her body oriented toward the circle, tracing a rough sketch of a pipe on the grimy surface with her finger.

"But should we really be calling them Indian tacos?" Darcie asked, then promptly took a bite of her bologna sandwich.

She was a year younger, Métis from Lac Ste. Anne, whereas Berlin's family was from Treaty 1 and the Red River region. Berlin had recruited Darcie for the FNMISA. It was lunchtime. They were meeting in Mr. MacDonald's classroom. They used to meet in the library, but nobody was allowed to eat in the library. When Mr. MacDonald's offer of space came with a co-conspiratorial wink and a reminder that he didn't enforce silly rules like no food in his space, the vote had been unanimous.

Across the circle of desks, SarahLynn exhaled loudly. The stage-worthy exclamation ruffled her bangs. "If you're arguing for calling them Îyârhe Nakoda tacos, I'll take it. For my people, for my Nation. But I don't think you are. So what exactly are you arguing for? Navajo tacos? Or like Indigenous tacos? If you say FNMI tacos, I'm going to cry. Literally. And if I cry, I'm going to eff up my mascara, and if I eff up my mascara, I'm going to give up on life today. Do you want to shoulder that burden, Darce?"

A bit over-the-top but it fit. If Berlin could cry, she'd probably be crying too. Out of frustration. They had this discussion at least twice a semester. Once, she cared.

"Can we not?" Vincent wasn't eating. An unopened can of Coke sat on the desk in front of him. "It's way important to get this fundraiser going and not important to worry about the words."

He wore his hair in braids and was the only guy in FNMISA. His family was from the Piikani Nation. He was also the only other member who had firsthand experience with missing and murdered women. He'd been part of the National Inquiry when he was a kid, telling stories about his mom. That is, he'd been the only other member with firsthand experience until five months ago, when Kiki disappeared. Seemingly without a trace. The first week of school she'd been alongside them in the library skipping out on lunch, working on drafting a non-cringe-inducing land acknowledgment for the AAA hockey home games, and the next she wasn't.

They all missed Kiki.

No one glanced over to the faded National Poetry Month setup on the back wall. No one needed to reread Kiki's winning poem from last year. It had been an elegy for the missing and murdered, for her mother, for all of them. Now it read like a foretelling.

Even though Berlin was unable to cry and beyond consumed with that famous pipe they'd talked about in French class last semester, she knew that this fundraiser mattered too much to be obsessing over words. The organization was local and Indigenous-owned, and they needed a boost if they were going to offer their self-defense program for youth again.

Darcie covered her mouth with a hand so she could keep talking and chewing. "But we didn't come to consensus. Not last time. Or the one before that."

This was where Berlin should weigh in.

Last year when they'd had this discussion, Kiki had been wearing her go-to neon pink legwarmers layered maximalist-style against big patterns. She'd said something sharp and funny, and in such a kind way that they'd moved on. She'd gotten them thinking beyond the words. But as much as Berlin tried, she couldn't remember exactly how, and even if she could, Berlin couldn't do it like Kiki.

The group fell silent. They ate, attempting not to make a mess. After all, they could lose this privilege. And skipping lunch weekly so they had time to meet around class schedules and after-school obligations was not fun.

Even if Berlin wasn't hungry these days, she knew that.

SarahLynn's older sister, Tashie, who exclusively wore the color black and was their unofficial leader, cleared her throat. "Vincent is right, yo. We're sticking with Indian tacos. We have too much to get done to have this thing up and running before March break to get stuck all up in here."

The school needed to assign a president, VP, and treasurer to every student group. And while FNMISA was a mouthful, it, too, was what the school insisted upon. To meet Canadian standards. They didn't have an Inuk member yet, but Tashie was ever hopeful.

"Okay, so like ten bucks for a taco. And a toonie for pop," SarahLynn suggested.

Vincent finally cracked open his Coke. "We should up it a bit."

This was where having a treasurer would help. Someone to figure the monies. That had been Kiki's role.

Even after the Royal Canadian Mounted Police had stopped looking, after the missing posters were torn down, the school hadn't pressured them to fill the treasurer spot. Everything was on pause, as if waiting for Kiki Cheyanne Sound to show up and for life to start again around her. At school, it was obvious. Where she was missing. At community events too.

As VP, Berlin could do both jobs. At least the tracking-expenses part, she could do that.

Vincent continued, talking slow: "Say we add in dessert. Go full-on combo. If Berlin can get a donation of supplies, flour and sugar and shit, from Alpine Natural Foods & Chinese Grocery again, I'll make butter tarts—with raisins. I say we aim to get everyone to spend fifteen."

If . . .

It would be a challenge. Berlin nodded her consent anyhow. They needed her to do this, no matter how complicated it would

4

be. She'd figure things, like she always did. If they wanted to ask the art club to design a poster, they needed to sort the details out fast. Mr. MacDonald's countdown at the top corner of his dry-erase board made her anxious: 20 weeks left! Including March break! A weird sketch of a yellow-haired man with visible abdominals wore nothing but swim shorts and held a surfboard.

While the FNMISA assembled a detailed grocery list, Berlin continued half-heartedly tracing that famous pipe on her desk, as if by doing so, she'd understand it. Solve for x. Find the lost piece of the puzzle. Remember how to cry, or laugh, or even feel hunger.

Hours later, the heavy exit door by the gym clicked shut and Berlin's glasses fogged up. She placed one mukluk on the iced sidewalk, refusing to glance backward. She'd never cut classes before.

Not once.

Not that escaping a few minutes early was technically cutting. And she only cared in a faint cerebral way that she was breaking the rules. A girl had to do what a girl had to do. More often than not. In this ever-spinning world.

It was something Quinta, her best friend since kindergarten, said all the time. Only, these days, she wasn't saying it to Berlin.

Red mittens rubbed against the wool of her coat, cutting into the careful quiet. It wasn't 100 percent silent. The silence was a metaphor. It was lush velvet, and the people, the birds, the predators, all that noise, they were beads stitched onto its surface.

Before the silence, there had been music. At least Berlin thought there had been something else.

It was hard to remember.

She sighed.

She hated sighing. It sounded too much like giving up.

Now, almost to the stoplight, she'd successfully avoided another awkward run-in at the lockers. School would be out soon. And like Berlin had done since the first day of winter break, when her very best friend had "asked for space," she remembered every little thing about them, searching for the moment where she'd effed up enough to crush a lifelong friendship. Even before Quinta got her driver's permit and the Jeep, it had been routine: they went everywhere together. Before winter break, they'd worked the same shifts at Pink Mountain Pizza too. Quinta was Bee's ride. Literally and figuratively.

Now Berlin walked.

The release bell sounded with an off note, like someone in the office had yanked a power cord from the wall. It fit her mood. Her forever mood these days. She couldn't look at health foods or Quinta's sunny, painted beehive boxes or 4x4 Jeeps, purple or otherwise, the same way. Even geography was ruined. Maps of the world too. The whole alphabet. Because they weren't Quinta and Bee any longer, brought together by their place names and united by what Berlin had thought were unbreakable bonds.

On the street, a vehicle slammed on its brakes, gliding over the thick white line. She peered up, eyes hard, both hoping and not hoping it was her best friend. After all, she now had to ask if Quinta's parents would donate a bunch of baking essentials for the fundraiser. She really had to do it.

"Heeey, Berliner, want a lift? It's cold, woman. You're gonna freeze your tits off."

She and Jones weren't friends. They'd been in the same home-room class since forever, and these days, he only half-heartedly teased her over her weird name. This from someone named John Jack Jones III.

She distanced herself from the truck, its rank weed and greasy-boy smells, and pointed toward Ninth Street. "Work tonight."

"Oh shit, wish I could." Jones leaned toward her conspiratorially, sliding on the bench. He wasn't wearing a seat belt. "I'm in deep trouble with the overlords."

"Again?"

Earnest Berlin didn't talk like this. If she'd been able to talk like this at lunch, and if SarahLynn hadn't crushed her, they'd have gotten to the grocery list sooner. Maybe Berlin could have even told someone else to deal with the donation request.

"You're lucky." Jones laughed, on a slight delay, leaning hard toward the passenger window. He was high. "Yours are hardly home."

His mom had an unhealthy obsession with her only child. Berlin was pretty sure Mrs. Jones had her son's cell tapped. Jones Senior was RCMP. They'd have access.

Someone in the line of vehicles honked once, twice, then laid down a long angry note. The light was green. Behind the small two-door car making all that noise sat a purple Jeep.

"You'd better get," Berlin said.

Green light and all, Jones stalled. "I'm ordering tonight. You'll make it with extra cheese, right? Like a bucketload. Don't skimp!

For me? That Sound chick used to do it." He smiled as if that would cinch things.

The car honked again.

Before she could respond, Jones took off, his window still down, the smells still leaking out. It was like he hadn't been asking for a favor at all. First, he'd tried to charm her. Then followed that weak attempt with a comment about Kiki, like it would cement things. Stepping out into the intersection, Berlin lifted a mitten as the purple Jeep passed.

But Quintana-Roo, her hair loose and coppery, fixed her eyes on the road.

She thought her legal name beyond ridiculous. Some real settler BS. Blamed her white hippie mom for the screwup and her Chinese Canadian dad for being a pushover. Quinta had even worked some administrative magic in the principal's office and had wiped it from the attendance rolls.

On the day she'd rent Berlin's world in half, Quinta had said what she needed to say, calm and collected. But it seemed any acknowledgment of each other's basic humanity was off the grid.

For how long?

To finish crossing the road before the light turned, Berlin walked faster, losing traction with each step under the weight of her schoolbag. It wasn't that she wanted to fall—but that might be enough reason for her best friend to pull over, for the two of them to talk, to figure out what went wrong. To make it better.

Or Berlin could just text, inquire about the baking supplies and hope that would connect them again.

She should do it now. While she felt this almost-motivation.

Only it mattered that her phone would have some juice left for tonight's walk home. Even in a quirky tourist town, street harassment was a thing. News tickers at the bottom of the TVs on campus and the hard-copy newspaper her parents subscribed to but never had time to read both said violent crime was getting worse. Housing prices were skyrocketing too. Minimum wage couldn't compete. The numbers told a story. But no one counted the near misses, how last week, after closing the shop, Berlin was followed almost all the way to her house by three drunk white men, her phone about as useful as a doorstop.

Not that she would have called the cops. The RCMP claimed otherwise, but they weren't looking out for people like Berlin. For people like Kiki and Kiki's mom.

If Berlin's phone had worked, if she'd been able to borrow a charger from her least favorite coworker without suffering public humiliation, she kept telling herself that her best friend would have answered, even though they weren't talking, and she'd have faked a conversation long enough for the men to realize they hadn't found an easy target.

Instead, dignity intact, Berlin had outsmarted the drunks, slipped into a neighbor's fenced-in yard and waited, pressed against that sleeping house, nails clawing through mittens into her red phone case.

Her small inner voice said maybe the best thing to happen that night was that she hadn't called Quinta. Hadn't tested if they could fix what had unknowably gone wrong between them. Relief, in a way. But Berlin hated walking around, that sharp French Revolution guillotine hovering, waiting, ready to drop. It was primed.

And Quinta held the release trigger.

The purple Jeep long gone now, Berlin's maddening obsession returned. It was like if she could figure out its riddle, she'd figure out friendship too.

But maybe the painting lied. Maybe it wasn't something more. Maybe it was only a pipe after all. And if that was fact, Berlin worried what it meant for her and Quintana-Roo.

JESSIE

Long and wildly curly, Jessie's mop was a mega mess. With free period last, she should have gone to the big old family house and bathed herself. Maybe even resurrected the straightener from that middle school phase. Ha. When piglets grow their wings. Finger-combing her hair, yanking on knots, her leased Land Rover idling in the tiny parking lot that curved around Pink Mountain Pizza's corner storefront, Jessie laughed.

Her first shift. Her first job.

And it was a solid one. A real two-four-K-gold one. Something to be proud of. Not that her parents got it. Had even tried. Or ever would. To them, Jessie was a fairy child, snuck into their home after that first scary overnight hospital stay while their real daughter was eaten by the sharp-toothed fae. She was a broken fairy child at that. Nowhere near a perfect girl, in body thanks to one of the late effects of childhood cancer treatment, or in what her parents thought should be comportment. With cancer, the treatments could be as bad as the disease. You had to destroy good cells to smash the bad. After all that chemo, Jessie couldn't ever pass for a Disney Princess when their one job was to marry young and breed. It was why she preferred fairy tales—the gritty, gory ones where toes were chopped off, where Bluebeard's latest wife divorced his murdering behind and saved the day—to Disney in most things. But that didn't mean that Jessie couldn't enjoy a straight shot of high-fructose corn syrup on occasion too.

She contained multitudes. Even if her ovaries were like irradiated toast.

When her leg started to shake again, she knew Monday's family dinner wouldn't go gently into that good night of forgotten things. The quickest way to confirm what she suspected her father had done was to straight-shot ask Pink Mountain's owner, Joe. But she didn't see his big truck in the lot.

At mandatory family dinner, Jessie had dropped news of her job. That she had one, but not its specific whereabouts. With her parents, Jessie always behaved as if she were conducting the world's least interesting disinformation campaign.

Her father had pushed his armchair back a dramatic inch. The wood creaked. "Select a current Poseidon Group business if you feel the need to work outside the home. One of our in-town holdings."

From across the table, like way across, as if they were the bloody Victorians, Jessie's mom added: "Oh, that sounds nice. Doesn't that sound nice, Jessica?"

Her younger brothers—Junior, Spence, and Chad—snickered. Because they were boys, they got away with it.

"But it will be over the school break so as not to interfere with your studies." Jessie's father cleared his throat. "And if you require summer schooling, there will be no job."

Smiling like she always did, a little zombie-land meets too much wine, Jessie's mom said: "Oh, but if the sale goes through with the Italian place, that might be a good summer job for our—"

"I said current holding. Jessica does not need additional burdens to successful graduation." Her father stared her down. "You'll call immediately after the meal and explain you're not allowed to accept employment."

Now Jessie couldn't tell her family that Cs got degrees or that she wouldn't be quitting her job. Her father hadn't threatened to belt her in a long while. But he would with statements like that . . . at the family table. Jessie ate another mouthful of limp carrots, a not-great feeling settling up in her bones.

Her father went on: "She'll work in an air-conditioned office. Answering phones or sending follow-up emails or even filing invoices."

"Oh!" her mom exclaimed. "That's better than food service. What was I thinking?"

But for Jessie, the bad seed had already cracked. She had on-purpose, no-take-backs interviewed at Pink Mountain because it wasn't part of her father's portfolio. And now she had a sinking suss that wasn't true anymore. Or wouldn't be for long if her father was truly acquiring "the Italian place."

In the Land Rover, Jessie glanced murderously at the stack of homework weighing down her passenger seat. She'd have to find time for it this weekend, and that, as much as remembering any of her family dinners, soured her. The satellite radio was playing real pump-up music but her right leg continued shaking hard. Tight black jeans normally made her feel all badassery. Even that wasn't working today. Plus, she needed to smoke.

Her teeth chattered.

Nerves sucked.

The job at Pink Mountain was supposed to be step one in her grand escape: secure external funding her parents couldn't touch and apply to trade school to become a welder. That plan would crash and burning man if her father was purchasing the place.

She'd have to do the dirty and ask Joe to confirm or deny. One blink for *Baby, bad news is the only news*, two for *Nopeses*. Or they could use Morse code, but then Jessie would have to google Morse code and that seemed overcooked.

Out of the corner of her eye, Jessie's new coworker, walking the way she walked everywhere, direct and with a mission in mind, swung into view. The girl didn't even glance about the parking lot. She owned it, all rolling hips, powered full up.

It was hot.

For a microsecond, Jessie rethought her *no smoking in the Land Rover* policy.

Watching Berlin Chambers disappear into Pink Mountain, Jessie tucked rebel curls behind her ears and willed her hands, which were now in on the party, to still. She reached for the door. Confidence was alluring, Jessie reminded herself. The other option was to freeze into a Popsicle and grant her father the win. So it was exactly no pancake-flipping option at all.

CAM

In the quiet before the dinner rush, Cam inhaled a Coke, legs dangling from the metal prep counter, almost touching the floor, but not quite. The Coke was a balm. So was the chance to rest. His feet hurt from standing all day in worn sneakers.

The staff doorbell trilled.

Cam's mom's best friend's rule-thumping daughter had arrived. And she hated him like it was her prime directive. He offered Berlin a two-finger wave.

"Hello, Cameron," she returned icily.

Her glasses were brand spanking new. Her cheeks were flushed. Wind-chapped, not colored with drugstore product. That was Berlin. Always completely authentic. Shrugging out of her handmade parka, she traded it for one of the shop aprons.

And those glasses suited her. Terribly. His favorite color. Coke red, studded with diamonds. Or probably more like Swarovski crystals, the kind his littlest sister, Sami, wouldn't stop talking about wanting for her regalia. Just last week, he and his twelve-year-old twin sisters, Tanya and Callie, had caught Sami playing with her favorite stuffed toy—the buffalo Cam gifted her when she was born—telling it about how good those crystals shined when a dancer moved.

Everyone assumed because of Sami's Down syndrome she wouldn't be a strong dancer. But that was garbage. Like one thing had anything to do with the other.

Across the prep room, Berlin muttered to herself, "These aren't clean."

While she spoke truth about the aprons, Cam knew it was a dig at him too. He shouldn't rile her but couldn't help himself. "You complaining?"

"Yes, I am. These are . . . unpleasantly sticky."

He had to know: "Is there a good kind of sticky?"

She froze. She'd been doing that a lot lately. Like her programming needed a second to catch up. "I am not answering that."

"It isn't a trick question."

But with a flutter of her hand as a dismissal, she was already ignoring him again, aggressively brushing flour from herself, drawing his attention back to how she was short and curvy, and to the very dirty apron with the PMP logo in electric pinks, yellows, and oranges—exactly like the neon sign out front.

Sometimes the laundry didn't get done. Either things were too busy, or Joe, PMP's infamous owner, would be in one of those moods, quit doing business in the office, and tell stories about his early days in town—what it was like being one of the first Black businessmen in Canmore. Or ask questions about Cam's family, the kind that gave a guy the sense that someone really cared to know. The way that Joe had been there for them after—

The door alert went off again and the new girl walked in. Jessie Hampton lingered by the exit, fidgeting with the hem of her Canada Goose jacket. "Hi. I'm looking for Joe . . ."

Break was officially done.

Cam sighed in his head so as not to give Berlin additional

ammunition. He didn't believe she'd drawn blood last year on purpose. And the kindergarten incident was past, not present. Still, he'd protect himself.

"Joe's not here on weekends." Berlin pointed to the tight-squeeze hallway that led to the washroom. "Grab an apron and hang your stuff up. Yeah, on the hooks. I'll orientate you as soon as you're ready."

Jessie stepped one foot farther into the store. "He made it seem like he'd be here . . . at my interview. I mean the tryout."

The Hampton family owned half of town and a mountain with five chairlifts in the national park. Jessie was rich enough she didn't need a job, rich enough she could tame that hair if she wanted to. At a salon. With those good chemicals. Laughing quietly to himself, Cam choked on the last sip of Coke.

Berlin stared.

He wiped his mouth on the sleeve of his fitted *Star Wars* T-shirt. Would she say something about it not being clean either? The shirt wasn't. Not after a day's hard work. Even covered in the dregs, Rose Tico was powerful.

The new girl's eyes buzzed between him and Berlin. It was obvious Jessie Hampton was out of her element.

This wasn't the high school. It was so much better.

"Joe's gone." Berlin spoke like that was that and there was nothing else to say.

Her tone majorly bummed Cam out.

So he smiled. Yeah, it wasn't his job to train new staff. It was his job to do the laundry. But he could offer a friendly assist. "Boss left midday, like he usually does to kick off the weekend. Heads up to his cabin. It's nothing personal."

Jessie nodded.

In truth, Cam kind of liked laundry. It was a peaceful task. Warm, smelled good, made his insides want to curl up under a wool blanket with Sami's in-progress regalia. With their mom in Calgary, getting her BA and sleeping on a friend's couch all week, Cam was doing close to everything at home. He was the eldest, with three siblings who depended on him. And everyone in the house knew their dad was a little lost right now. Now a lost taxi driver . . . That was a lark!

Cam cracked himself up. Out loud.

And Berlin, standing by the dish sink as if Jessie needed supervision taking her parka off, fired him a look. Even after months, working side by side, she hadn't warmed. Not a degree. Why Cam thought working together would change things, he couldn't figure. Because he'd known her forever. The lore between their families was that he'd been present at her birth, strapped to his mom's frontside in one of those baby-wrap getups.

"Yeah, don't mind the dirty aprons," Berlin said as Jessie tried and failed to find a cleanish one. "Tonight, after close, you and I will throw on a load. It's not our task, but we'll get it done."

"I can start one now," Cam offered. "I'm hydrated so break's done."

Berlin blew air out of her mouth noisily. "Cameron," she scoffed. "We might as well do things right, wash everything at once. Instead of half finishing the job."

"Only offering, Bee." She was so stiff—about everything. He threw up his hands. "But we'll do things your way."

17

"It's not my way. It's just the right way." Berlin was like a flight attendant doing the safety demo who really believed a seat belt would do its job if the plane got into real trouble at thirty thousand feet. "Clock in here. Be sure to remember to do it at the start of every shift. It's key to getting paid."

Yet even in the dirty apron, she somehow seemed put together. Maybe she didn't ever unclench. Maybe she couldn't. Some things were beyond a person's ability. Cam had his troubles, sure. But at least he could laugh.

Her mom was all hard work, but sunshine too. The perfect pediatrician. Sami loved appointments with Dr. Chambers, loved running into Dr. Chambers at the grocery store, or pulling up next to her Prius at a stoplight—and generally, Sami didn't think much of doctors, what with them poking her, measuring her, telling her what she supposedly couldn't do because of an extra chromosome. Dr. Chambers only ever encouraged Sami, had even gotten her started with sign language. Berlin's dad, the other Dr. Chambers, was real smart, too, in that super-intimidating way. But he also belted out tradish folk songs while gliding along the cross-country trails.

Berlin was, as far as Cam could tell, all work.

No play.

She was a dull, tiny, curvy human with a ponytail sticking out of her PMP ball cap, her bangs swept to the side and crushed.

She stressed him out. By breathing. By the no-nonsense way she wore those glasses when another person would have been wearing them to cosplay sexy librarian. Pushing off the prep table, Cam

18

abandoned his empty Coke can. He rushed to the front of the shop. Hoped it hadn't looked like he was trying to beat her.

It was the small things. Tâpwe.

A few emptied inserts were stacked by the handwashing station. Pizza pans hung out on the bottom track of the oven. Cam wasn't the kind who did dishes while making dinner. Tuning out Bee's detailed instructions on how to answer a phone like it was rocket science, he grabbed the neon chalk and, checking the notes on his phone to be as sure as he could to transcribe it all without mistakes, in his best hand, he started with the twenty-four-hour special.

Pizza of the Day:
  The Pupperoni
  Saltwater crust, our homemade heirloom tomato sauce, crafted charcuterie* uncured pepperoni, fresh mozzarella rounds. Each large Pupperoni comes with a small bone-shaped pie for your pup(s). 32

* DO NOT write shark coochie—last time, nobody thought that was funny.

He appreciated his own jokes. Cam's sisters thought he was a riot. His mom too. His dad used to laugh the hardest, before—

The Before place was too rocky. Cam pulled himself back to the now.

Tonight, locals would eat this up and tourists wouldn't be able to hold back either. A pizza for the fam and one for the pupper. Or

19

the kids. It was pure brilliance. And as this was Cam's brainchild, he'd earn an extra $3.50 per sale, on top of the already fair hourly wage Joe paid.

Another cord of wood was due at the house. After tonight, Cam could throw in for the bill. It had been ages since he'd scored this honor, and his bank account was feeling it. Since Berlin started in early December, Joe had been granting it to her, over and over.

Cam erased his call sign on the staff board and triple-checked he hadn't misspelled anything, shifted the letters. As best he could. He'd learned techniques, not in school but from his mom, who had the same difficulties. But like always, after trying hard, Cam had to hope that when he screwed up, someone would point things out nice-like. Joe always did—but he was a great boss who understood what it was like to stand out for things a person couldn't help. Berlin, she didn't abide mistakes, errors, the moments when people showed their soft underbellies.

On Shift:
 The Dropout.
 The Gray City.

And Introducing . . .

Clutching the chalk, checking his letters against the note app on his phone for the fourth time, searching for the signs that they were shifting on him, he wondered if Jessie Hampton, their grade's wealthiest student, had what it took to make it at PMP.

Except, it wasn't his grade anymore.

Hadn't been for going on three and a half months.

Even he should be able to find this all a little funny—his mom getting her BA in her forties while her teenage son dropped out of school. It was ironic or something. But, as it turned out, it wasn't at all funny. It was just what it was.

That wasn't saying it would always be this way.

Things turned funny all the time.

BERLIN

It was such a bad look. Good old Cameron was loitering, making it seem as if he was working but not actually doing anything productive. This time, he held a piece of orange chalk, staring at the boards, a silly grin on his infuriating face, while the shop was disordered.

Berlin *hated* his pointed eyeteeth.

They reminded her of a painting. A nightmare-scape. That, at first glance, appeared hauntingly normal.

The mess around the kitchen, it proved how much Cameron didn't care. That was why after five days at Pink Mountain, she was given a key and, as the official closer, a security alarm code. Why she trained new employees. And that was why, even though she'd only worked at the shop for ten weeks, she was the boss when the boss was out.

Like her perfect score on that last French test, falling into this role was effortless. It fit like her very skin. Berlin passed what completed the Pink Mountain Pizza uniform to Jessie Hampton. "Here's your ball cap."

"Um, thanks." Her hand shook the littlest bit. "But I'm positive like panini that my hair, and therefore my head, is not going to fit under this."

From his place by the boards, Cameron laughed, like he always did—easy. "What about bobby pins?"

A hand landed on Berlin's hip. She didn't mean to do it, but this one got off on pushing her buttons. "Do you honestly think pinning it to the top of her head like it's a bow is a valid solution to the current situation?"

"They used to do that . . . back in the day . . . across the largeish pond . . . in the English Old Times."

She could hear the capital letters in his voice, held off on rolling her eyes by the smallest of degrees. Another thing she'd never have thought to do back when she had been earnest. Before she'd started studying surrealist art like it would save her.

A fur-covered teacup, saucer, and spoon.

"You know what I mean," Cameron said. "Those hats? They still wear them to weddings and to the sport with horses and sticks."

When Jessie smiled, she exposed a lone dimple.

"You do know what I mean, Bee. The only way those hats could stay on would be with pins . . . or glue? Could we try glue? Does that really come from the insides of horses?" He paused, pseudo-thoughtfully. "I ate a large quantity of glue in my early years. It started in kindergarten."

She couldn't stop herself. Her eyes rolled almost on their own.

A reference to her one childhood mistake, as if he meant to poke at that tonight. Worse, Cameron didn't ever consider how his own bad behavior reflected on all of them: what he did or didn't do. Like dropping out of school when high school was the easiest thing. Or acting as if his entire life was for laughs. Baiting her. What he said. How he said it. Both of them, Métis and Cree, were guests of the Îyârhe Nakoda, Siksika, Blood, and Kootenai First Nations on whose land they lived. And since they were surrounded by settlers—mostly white people—and tourists from around the world, Berlin and Cameron stood in for every Indigenous person, in the whole corrupt colonial country of Canada, all the freaking time.

She tried to be a good representative.

He did not.

Berlin took a ragged breath. Even if lecturing Cameron wouldn't change anything, she couldn't help herself. "They're called fascinators. The hats."

"Cool word." His skinny shoulders rose to peaks. He passed off the neon-orange chalk.

Jessie's hand wavered. At school, she was bold, brash even. Surrounded by half of their grade, but a decent chunk of the Grade 12s, too—as if she were the epicenter of school social life.

When the printer by the dough station started to buzz out an online order, Cameron stepped closer to Berlin instead of closer to the printer.

She retreated.

It was a reflex.

He ignored her. "You need to throw your call sign up. It's

23

something we use to keep track of sales."

"I've been plotting this all week." Jessie's voice was strong, not shaky, her handwriting all caps. Under Introducing . . . she wrote: THE TEASE.

Like he was struggling to read the board, Cameron cocked his head. It was only a part of his bit. Eventually, his lips pushed up and his once-broken nose shifted to the side hard. "That's feminist shit, right?"

"Creator help us." Berlin rolled her eyes again, the movement dizzying her.

Jessie only laughed. "It's what everyone at school calls me and I own to it."

"So I'm right," Cameron said without any inflection at all, looking at Berlin, taunting her. "It's feminist shit."

She stared back. She could outlast him, could get the high score, even in this. But with Cameron around, acting the fool, nothing was quiet anymore. Nothing was vibrant either. A simmering, bitter taste flooded her mouth as she glared at his floppy hair, how it didn't stay stuck under the ball cap, how the ball cap was worn, its brim shaped into a hard upside-down U, throwing shadows across his face.

The printer ejected another order. While Cameron broke away, laughing quietly, like he found something particularly amusing, Berlin gathered a blue washcloth and, leading Jessie around the kitchen, she cleaned Cameron's dirty counters because if there was one thing Bee was good at, it was perfection.

If only that were enough.

JESSIE

This working thing was fucking grand. Grand slam with extra bacon, crisp. It had been hours of constant, absolute mischief. She curled her dirty-dog nails into her palms. No matter how often Jessie pressed the foot pedal at the tiny sink behind the pizza oven, the grit stuck. It was everywhere. On her person. Spread across the floor of the shop. Berlin even had a wisp of flour on her left cheek. Ye gods, it was adorable. Like a dusting of the freshest snow. Or powdered sugar.

Jessie had the urge to lick it clean.

But no matter what her father thought, she had some self-control.

Glancing around the shop, tapping a foot unconsciously, the unconfirmed rumor became more toothsome the longer it remained so.

Her father would ruin this messy, excellent place.

Ball cap backward now, Cam was turning the pizza oven off, and Berlin, still moving as confidently as ever, even with flour marring her cheek, carried the final pizzas of the night to the cash register.

"Pupperoni, dude!" One of the crew of snowboarders milling inside the shop, goggles slung around their necks, their coats unzipped, cackled. He gathered all six big and six small boxes.

His buddies let him.

"Have a good night!" Berlin hollered, still friendly and upbeat after all these hours.

Grand or no, Jessie's abdomen pulsed. She'd needed to pee an hour ago. And her hands wouldn't quit with the micro-shakes. Almost more than she needed to pee, she desired a smoke.

She'd never admit that out loud.

Against the big front window, a couple sat on high-back bar chairs, eating slices, their heads close together, their words soft. No one was booting them out even as Berlin climbed onto one of the chairs to extinguish the neon sign. The girl could fit in Jessie's jeans pocket. But she was also voluptuous. Small and curvy. Jessie hadn't quite realized that was another of her weaknesses, until tonight. Not women. That was well documented. But usually, when Jessie was crushing on a girl, she admired hockey players. She had a thing for mouthguards and that missing-front-tooth gap while awaiting a falsie.

It was delicious.

And, more than anything, Jessie wanted to live deliciously.

Cam sauntered over. He surveyed the kitchen, a grin on his face. "This place is a disaster zone, even with Bee obsessively trying to keep her half tidy. But she can't win at this game."

Not a piece of counter space, except the cutting station, was clean. Red sauce stained half of Jessie's apron from when she'd tried her hand at building pizzas. Red sauce tracked in a smear across the floor toward the tiny sink. Combined with flour, it congealed into a blotchy, no-fun slip-and-slide.

The pizza oven, though, was shiny, gorgeous. Jessie admired the welds, the way they were functional but also beautiful. "A good three-quarter of this is my fault and you know it."

"Fair." Cam laughed. "I'll claim the rest. So Bee doesn't have to admit to being only human."

Across the kitchen, at the register Berlin counted cash, ignoring him. It seemed her go-to move for dealing with Cam. But Jessie couldn't figure why. He was downright likeable. Devastatingly funny, in that dry way of his. *Feminist shit.* Since he was the only other cis guy in his family, and Cam's dad ran a taxi service that exclusively served BIPOC and queer and trans people, Cam got intersectional feminism, even if he wanted to play it that way.

Last year, the two of them had been in shop class together, and in Grade 9, they'd been on a course at the Outdoor Learning Center. Jessie had always admired how Cam didn't seem to care about his acne scars or that his nose had very obviously been busted more than once. How he was, at his core, a good and decent dude. How she'd caught him goofing off at the playground with his kid sister. Not caring a lick who was watching.

This was Jessie's best opportunity to put a bad feeling to bed without dinner. "Can I cross-check out a rumor with you?"

"Yeah, but I'm better with TV and movie recs."

"Noted," she said, her stomach tight. "So, I heard something and I need to know. Like need, not want."

"It's important, eh?"

Jessie nodded. It really was. "Do you know . . . ? Is Joe selling Pink Mountain?"

Cam pulled her farther into the corner with the tiny sink. "No, he would never. Like even at the end of the world, Joe would show up here and make the survivors dinner. This place, making people good food, is like a part of the man's soul."

"Not even for bucketloads of cash monies? You sure?"

"Positive."

That was godly news.

"Hey, why are we whispering?" Jessie asked.

Cam ran a hand through his hair. It flopped back into place. "Berlin's already in a mood. It's not even a little true, but this rumor would turn her sour."

"Wouldn't want to upset her."

"Yeah, it's no fun." Cam replaced his ball cap, washed his hands at the sink. "Hey, you need a break? I meant to ask earlier when we had a minute. And then we didn't have a minute at all."

Bless him, he was a bloody mind reader.

"Desperately," she replied with fervor.

"Take fifteen. You worked hard tonight." He paused, cocked his head to the side. "Okay, real talk. It's like this a lot. Most shifts, breaks are a luxury item."

She did not care. Truly. Jessie fucking adored it. She wasn't some introvert. She was a by-the-book Aries.

In the little employee washroom, she peed for the longest time. Her legs were weaksauce. She knew it was the honest truth, she'd never worked so hard in her life as she had in the past eleven hours. Okay, that wasn't exactly accurate. Cancer treatments had been the hardest work. But Jessie had been freed of that Cruella de Vil for more than half her life now. Sometimes, she forgot.

Until her father or mother reminded her.

After washing her hands under dank fluorescent lighting, she had the time to taste a cigarette. That would power Jessie up to finish strong. Even if it was also like simultaneously shooting herself in the foot. She tried not to think what her doctors at Alberta Children's would say if they knew.

Pushing out of the staff door, she sat her butt on a flipped milk crate. Her lighter clicked. It was almost instant, the way Jessie's strings loosened. Cigarettes were magic. Poisonous, addictive magic. Three drags, she told herself.

When the door swung open and somebody joined her, she decided to sit a while longer. She was surprised when it wasn't Cam. But not unhappy.

Berlin propped the staff door open with an insert pulled from the dish-drying rack. "Do you mind? I need to cool down. Working in that tiny room with that big oven all night is . . . a lot."

It was.

This girl, she was an introvert. After an entire shift—always gabbing with the customers the way she did—she'd struggle.

"Want one?" Jessie offered with a wave of her hand. "Mine are inside. Help yourself."

Berlin sat on her own milk crate. "I don't smoke."

The way she said it, it almost sounded like she regretted the fact. With a free hand Jessie reached out, brushing the flour from Berlin's cheek. It was gritty. Underneath, her skin was soft.

Girls were so soft. Jessie licked the corner of her lip.

"Thanks." Berlin wiped at her own cheek self-consciously. "I hadn't noticed."

It could be the cold, the way that even if they'd overheated in

29

the kitchen, winter was consuming and sharp-toothed, but Berlin's cheeks were pinking.

Jessie smoked, destroying and rebuilding herself at the very same time. She wanted to tell Bee that it was the worst, that she needed to quit but every time she tried, she flopped. The moment felt right. Personal. Like they could go deep. Like Jessie could be vulnerable for a hot-buttered second. Instead, smoke calcifying her cells, Jessie didn't say a thing.

BERLIN

No part of her wanted to smoke. But a radical part of her wanted to sit in the cold for five minutes. Until her skin began to freeze. Now the silence was almost everywhere. The bars had only just hit last call, but people would nurse their drinks for at least another hour. If they could lock up the shop before that happened, it would be for the best.

Berlin *really* did learn from her mistakes.

Timing mattered. One minute things were safe, the next three drunk men followed you home. One minute your best friend was laughing with you over her parents' crunchy lifestyle, and the next she was asking for a break.

"How exactly do you tightrope this and school?" Jessie's voice ruptured the silence like a car backfiring. "You're an A student, right?"

"It's not always this bad."

"Not how Cam tells it."

Berlin huffed. Her breath emerged as a small, misty cloud. "I'm more efficient. Usually, I find a half hour to eat and work on my assignments. Joe knows school comes first."

"I'm a hopeless tomato when it comes to school." Jessie smirked. It was good-natured. She wasn't putting herself down. "But I might have to switch things up, start using my free period to finish worksheets instead of flirting. Quelle horreur!"

Her accent was truly terrible. "Points for the French."

"I know, eh? I got a solid C last year. And I can match it, if . . ."

"If you study during your study period. Almost like it was intended for that purpose. With its name and all."

"I'll do it. Most likely. Maybe . . . I mean, it could happen."

To stop from brushing her cheek again, Berlin tucked her hands under her arms. "Well, don't make too many sacrifices. Flirting is a life skill."

Jessie laughed. "Too, too true."

Across the street, the convenience store parking lot was awfully bright, its lights almost pulsing. The store catered to the crunchy granola types as much as the hard-core weekenders. Hemp bites in one aisle, alcohol down another. Like most of town, it was styled with wood accents and pine-green trim. But it was a twenty-four-hour shop that sold liquor. In the middle of the night, it wasn't the best place to be. A yellow taxi idled out front, exhaust puffing up from the tailpipe like dry ice mixing with water. The surrounding snow appeared fresh and soft. It was exactly the kind of scene that would have enthralled the surrealists—on the surface it seemed fully normal. But underneath, in the swirl of exhaust, in the reflection of the night on icy pavement, it echoed, completely haunting.

Berlin leaned back on her milk crate. She could see the stars tonight. They were brilliant, as if sharper in the cold.

Eventually, Jessie stubbed out her cigarette.

Now Bee was alone.

Work waited. Cameron would at least make mention of how he had been at it the whole time. But something, one of those inexplicable things, told Berlin to stay, to wait, to sit a while longer. And she listened.

She stayed, she waited, she breathed.

Then: the hum of the universe, the one that matched her heartbeat, the one she'd been missing, had been cut off from for weeks—months?—was singing.

Her eyes tightened and watered. She closed them.

Hard, hard.

A tear welled out, dribbled along her cheek. She wiped it away fast.

The silence, the hum of the world, of the stars close by and the ones very far, at this time of night, it was resplendent. It was tempting. More than she would admit. This was her sugar, her caffeine, her nicotine, her ruby-red strawberry bite.

She savored, her eyes closed, burning, burning with locked-in tears, for three beats.

One.

Two.

Three—

A scream-whistle rippled the velvet.

Berlin came alive, tracking the noise. She shivered from the back of her neck, down, down her spine where the electricity settled in a pulsing ache. Sometimes, during the rut, bull elk wandered into town. But it was the wrong season for that. Probably only a group of men leaving a bar. Men who, for a moment, remembered they, too, were animals.

Across the street, the idling taxi honked its horn. A puny, almost comic beep. Berlin pushed up from the milk crate. A half second later, the convenience store door opened. She gasped, tears salting her cheeks. The hum of the universe intensified, cresting a rise, or maybe it was crashing down, like an avalanche, tearing trees from the earth, moving boulders that had previously seemed unshakeable.

A woman emerged from the store, her winter coat two sizes too big. As if it belonged to a larger body and not a slight . . . girl? It was black, a band of green, or brown, at the waist. The hood was drawn, her face in shadow. She stepped into the exhaust and it marbled her further. It was a painting that no one would ever paint. A lock of hair, night-black with bloody-red tips, flashed under the streetlamps before the woman slipped into the back seat of the taxicab. It was moving before the door closed.

The universe paused—the silence itself screamed—

How had Berlin ever thought the silence to be empty?

—and then the hum resumed. A song of intentional, calming fingers, rolling on a hand drum.

Berlin ripped the staff door open wide, dislodging the insert. "Cameron! Cameron, get out here!"

Saturday, Very Early Morning

CBC Radio One, first week of October: An update today in the case of the missing seventeen-year-old Cree teen Kiki Cheyanne Sound. RCMP have located what family confirms is the girl's schoolbag off the permanently closed Cougar Creek Trail. RCMP say the backpack was emptied of contents. Superintendent Malcolm Andrews states, "We are now very likely looking at a case of retrieval of remains. And with the severe weather forecasted this week, we will hold off on immediate further searches for the safety of my men."

CAM

Berlin hollered his name, a lick of terror inhabiting her voice. He dropped a stack of clean pans, pushing past Jessie, hands up. It was Restaurant 101. Hug the wall. But it was Jessie's first night. She didn't move fast enough, and Cam crashed into her. "Sorry," he exhaled but didn't stop.

Bee was scared.

Bee was never scared.

She was tough like space rock. As Cam passed the Hobart industrial dough mixer, shoes skidding on the floor, he slowed enough to make the turn without flailing.

Berlin leaned out into the night, holding the staff door open with a few fingers. Not wearing her fancy parka. Her cheeks were flushed and, terrifyingly, she was crying. Her very red glasses remained stunning. Completely and utterly.

He hated himself a little for that thought. When he should be thinking more valiant things.

"What's wrong?" he asked, pushing past her. He scanned the parking lot, the street running along one side of the shop as far up as the intersection, for what had upset Bee's unshatterable equilibrium. The night was bitter, freezing the hairs inside his nose. And all throughout his temples, his pulse points, his blood called. It was hard work living in a body fueled by testosterone, Coca-Cola, and other hormones.

Nothing jumped out.

But the worst things often blended into their surroundings, appeared innocuous. Like badgers. So many creatures hid their true nature behind appearances.

Cam's LeBaron was parked tight against the brick wall of the bar next door. A few other vehicles were in the lot, shiny under the streetlamps. Cam pushed his awareness, held himself open to the universe. His temples thundered. Blood rushing, blood calling for blood. It made Cam queasy.

Next to him, Bee was barely breathing. As if she'd frozen solid. He thought to pull her into his arms, share his heat. To snap her out of stasis with a hug—something she'd never expect from him. But he needed to know what was out here, what was hunting a teenage girl in the night.

If it came back—whatever, whoever took Kiki—he didn't know what he'd do. That unknown entity. Not the same thing that had taken his auntie. That man was incarcerated up Edmonton way now.

While Cam searched and worried, Jessie abandoned the warmth of the shop to step out onto the sidewalk too. "What is it?"

Berlin inched his way. Finally cold enough to forget she didn't like him. Had never liked him even when they were toddlers. Thought of him as . . . what? Beneath her?

Then, her fingers released their shaky grip on the door.

The door closed with a click.

"Seriously, someone say something," Jessie stage-whispered. "Like one word. I don't care which you pick. But I need a word."

"Shhh," Berlin offered.

"That's not exactly a word. But I'll accept it, I guess."

Cam didn't have his lacrosse stick handy to bang on the frozen ground. He kicked a milk crate, as if sound would spook whoever—whatever—was out there. The way a noise in the dark could cause rats to scatter. The government claimed that Alberta was rat-free. But Cam knew better than to trust the government.

He'd seen rats of all kinds on this land.

He trusted his senses and the love he had for his family. End of list.

The wind picked up. It didn't exactly howl. More of an eerie whimper. "What was it, Bee?" he asked, noticing nothing out of place, even if the wind was putting on a show.

She was still closer to him than normal. Almost touching, but not. Her hands curled into the kind of fists where nail bit palm.

Behind those red glasses, her eyes were haunted.

A look Cam knew too well.

Sometimes, when his mom was home for the weekend, she'd walk around with this lazy smile on her face—only the gesture didn't make it all the way up to her eyes. Thinking about that, it made him miserable. So he tried not to.

It was a basic fact of his life. Cam avoided things that caused him misery. No one needed that. Better to laugh. Not that he could right now. His throat was tight, his body on red alert.

"Did someone . . . ?" He couldn't finish the sentence. He reached out, closing the gap. Pressed a hand to Berlin's bare forearm, as if to make sure she was whole. She was fucking freezing, her skin raised with little bumps, as she stared across the street. "Berlin," he said. Nothing. No reaction. "Bee."

She tried to form her features into that look she always wore, her perfect-student guise. A little uptight. Completely judgy. But then her face crumpled, folded in on itself. A collapsing star. When she spoke, it was slow, like she was chewing on a spoonful of blackstrap molasses. "I saw . . . Cameron, I think I saw her. I saw Kiki."

At first Cam didn't process.

Then his chest lifted—relief and hope and maybe it was like ice breaking, like falling through into the water, searching for the light, that gap, needing air—needing it so bad. "W-what?"

Berlin's teeth began to chatter.

"I think?" She shook her head from side to side, mixing her signals. "It was only a second. Maybe? I . . . I'm not certain."

And then everything fell. The crash, the knowledge that the cold water would eventually make it too hard to fight for air. Berlin pulled away, rubbing at her arm. The imprint of his hand was on her skin.

Jessie's voice was distant. "Isn't his cousin . . . ?"

She didn't finish her sentence. But she didn't need to.

. . . missing or lost or gone or—

Cam reminded himself he was on solid ground, no frozen lakes in sight.

Across the street, the convenience store's sliding door was closed, its lot glassy with ice. Some other night it would be good fun to slide around on that ice. Another night, another time, Cam would do it. A few voices, like wild animals posturing—the early stages of a fight—called and shrieked and hollered a street over. University students taking the weekend to play in the snow. They might even be in his mom's classes.

Otherwise, no visible rats.

Just Berlin rubbing her arm on autopilot, and Jessie fidgeting with her apron strings, and the echo of his own heartbeat jarring his temples. *Lub dub. Lub dub lub dub. Lub dubbbbb.*

"Okay, so I know I'm new and I'm not in charge. That's not even under dispute. But . . . we should get back to it." Jessie yanked on the handle of the staff door. She yanked again, harder. "Right?"

Cam's stomach rolled. He pushed the acid down. This wasn't the place to forget himself. He wasn't sure he could take Berlin seeing him like that. She didn't like weakness. Even in the days after Kiki disappeared, as if into the ether, Cam had kept it together, at least in front of Berlin. Anyone else, even Cam's dad, even the asshole teachers he had that semester, would have ranked after her in his list of people he'd least like to witness his melting down. "Where's your key, Bee?"

She closed her eyes.

Her apron pocket, the one over her left hip, was flat.

Fuck. They were in the deep. There might not be frozen wide water nearby, but the ice was cracking. After closing, the shop doors auto-locked. It was a safety thing Joe had installed the second time he'd been robbed while the staff were in the back cleaning up. Everyone in town knew Joe did lots of business—that on any given night there was enough cash in the register. And Berlin, always prepared, always on top of Cam's shit, had left her key inside. Probably in the pocket of her perfect parka.

His vision narrowed.

Her teeth chattered. "F-f-fuck."

Curse words out of Bee's mouth were cute. Finally, he wanted to laugh, to dissipate the tension. But if he did, he'd throw up.

"I don't have my phone either. It's . . . in my schoolbag," she added.

She was so damn good, followed that rule of Joe's. *No phones in the kitchen. They stay in your backpacks. Got me?*

"Mine's . . ." Cam gestured. "Plugged in." When Jessie pulled a cell out of her pocket, he almost whooped. "Jessie Hampton, you are a lifesaver."

"Like the candy?" she quipped, even though her legs were shaking. "Wh-who do we call?"

Cam threw his hands up like he'd scored a point, and Berlin caught on. "Maybe. Maybe we don't need to."

"That c-couple?"

39

"I'll check." If their customers were still making lovesick eyes at each other . . . If they were, the night was saved. Cam walked the long brick wall to reach the front window.

But no, they'd gone.

It was laughable. Some trickster was up in Cam's business, always sending things sideways. You'd think after seventeen years, he'd learn to move sideways to start. To enjoy a sideways life. But Cam was stubborn. He kicked at a snowbank and knew as soon as he did that it was the wrong move. His sneakers weren't built for impact. But the crash into ice, the sharp pain, the throbbing in his toes, did something to help him think. To let his blood thunder with purpose. He laughed, finally, tasting acid.

When he returned to the staff door, Jessie still held her phone. And Berlin raised her perfect eyebrows. Both of them. As if one wasn't enough.

Cam shook his head. Felt the reverb. This would turn into a migraine if he couldn't get some painkillers started soon. "I don't have Joe's cell memorized. Do you?"

"He's hours away. At his c-cabin. In J-Jasper." Berlin exhaled hard, like she was frustrated. "Pass me the phone."

But she seemed more like herself too. Always ready to do what needed to be done. It was comforting.

Still, Cam couldn't relax. Wouldn't. Not until they were safe. Back inside the shop, the doors secured behind them. Keeping the world, the cold out. He'd kick another snowbank, but doing it in front of Bee would only make him seem even less capable than she already thought he was. Besides, his littlest toe was throbbing louder, worse than the others. It would be just his sideways luck to break a toe when all he'd wanted to do was find a thread of control.

BERLIN

Other than her parents' landline, she knew only one number by heart. It was the same one Quinta had had since middle school. Berlin's heart thundered with the awkward of it all. This being the first time in weeks that she'd even dialed this number. But not the first time she'd considered it. Another frigid night. Pressing herself against the siding of a neighbor's house, sinking into the banked snow. The pointed voices of the men: *Where'd that little piece go?*

It was too cold to hold the phone to her ear. Berlin hit speaker-phone. The line rang and rang before Quinta's voicemail kicked in: *You can leave a message, but if you know me you know I won't actually listen. Do you hear me, Mom? I don't listen to these.*

Berlin smiled. But it was tainted. She'd messed up somehow. And she didn't know the why or when or what of it. Couldn't figure things out, couldn't speculate. When the beep sounded, she redialed.

She'd never know if Quinta would have picked up last week. Tonight, it was a certainty. She would because it wouldn't be Berlin's name flashing on her screen.

After all, Quintana-Roo wasn't avoiding everyone. Just her best friend.

On the third attempt, a gravelly voice bled into the night. "Who the eff is this? You're messing with my beauty sleep. Do you know exactly how much of the good stuff I need to remain this gorgeous?"

41

There was romance novel beautiful.

There was also surrealist painting beautiful.

And there was teenage girl, sleepless but still stunning. Quinta was always, always the last.

"It's me. Don't hang up." Fumbling with the screen, Berlin turned off the speaker. Her coworkers didn't need to hear this. It would only become fodder for Cameron's laughter, as most things did. "Um, n-no. Not that. I *am* giving you space. It's an emergency."

She sounded so weak.

She didn't want to. It was the cold. Not the way Cameron stared. Like she'd let them all down by following their boss's sensible rule.

"Yes, at the shop," she continued. "We're really locked out. Please? Yes, yes, okay." The line went dead before Berlin could offer thanks. She steeled herself. "She's coming. Said it might be ten or fifteen minutes."

"Anyone else ch-chilled?" Jessie asked. "Like human P-Popsicles?"

The girl was no-meat-on-her-bones skinny. And she was full-on shaking now. This was something different than the quiver from earlier. This was a prelude to hypothermia. The kind of crisis that would land them in Berlin's mom's ER. And that would be epic disaster.

Somehow worse than freezing to death.

If her mom found out they'd needed rescuing in the middle of the night, she'd fast suss things out over the Quinta situation too. Once Bee's mom got started on something, she didn't stop until she knew the root cause. It made her a good doctor, but a stressful parent to have to live with. Berlin was a girl who wanted to tend to her wounds in private. Not exposed in the cold. Not at school. Not with her mother watching.

Cam jutted his chin at the convenience store. "We'll wait across the street."

It would be warm. But Berlin didn't want to walk over there, to stand in the same spot where the exhaust had fogged up the night, muddying her thoughts. Where she'd seen—whatever she'd seen.

A painting.

A living painting.

"Shouldn't somebody stay? To w-wait?" She did and didn't want to be the one to claim that job. She wasn't sure why the universe was forcing this meeting now when she and Quinta deserved privacy and maybe even daylight to have their first real talk in weeks. A full night's sleep would help too. Maybe after sleep, maybe in the morning, Berlin would have some idea what she'd done.

Because she had no answers.

"No, we are, all of us, going to wait across the street." Cameron spoke carefully. "Together. We won't miss her Jeep, Bee. It basically lights up."

Even though Jessie was freezing, she smiled in this really animated way. "Like a fancy Hot Wheels."

But Cameron wasn't laughing. The contrast was too much. His sharp features, his once-broken nose, how his eyes were so brown they butted up against something bottomless.

He was a husk of the boy Berlin knew.

And she feared that any answers she found would reveal she wasn't a good person. At all. Because she was sure now that to set it all straight, to fix whatever was wrong in her most important friendship, she'd cross the sharpest lines.

Maybe Quintana-Roo had seen this. Maybe Quinta knew something about Berlin that she didn't know herself.

Here, tonight, it was obvious she was at fault. She'd gone and ripped off the scab on the kind of wound that never really healed. And while Cameron had been bleeding out, she'd shaken all the salt onto his flesh. It was the cruelest thing, calling him outside, saying Kiki's name, reacting without thought.

Because even though Kiki was missing, she was still present, living among them like a ghost. Speaking her name was an incantation, a call that the people who loved her would follow. It was why no one at FNMISA had said her name at lunch, even if they'd all been thinking of her. Teachers, parents, and students across all grades, they'd loved Kiki.

The past tense hurt because for all they knew, she was somewhere.

It was possible the RCMP had it wrong—to close her file, to label it *Lost/Wandered Off,* as if she were a rabid animal and not a bright, bursting-with-life seventeen-year-old girl. But no, she would be eighteen now. She'd had a birthday, wherever she was. Berlin's parents still celebrated the baby that came before her, her older brother, who'd only lived a few hours. Ice-cream cake every December 6 for Bear Chambers because Berlin's parents liked to think he would have liked ice-cream cake more than anything else.

But her brother had been laid to rest proper.

Kiki hadn't.

Traversing the icy PMP parking lot to the sidewalk, not crossing

44

the street at the stoplight like they should, Berlin wondered if it was possible. Could they lay Kiki to rest without knowing what had happened to her?

Inside the convenience store, under too-bright lights, Cameron stalled out on the wet gray floormat, staring at his running shoes. She'd made a mess of it with her best friend, and now she was messing with Cameron's life. When even if he often irritated her, even if they weren't friends, he didn't deserve this.

Nobody deserved this.

Berlin stepped farther into the store. The clerk nodded and went back to his phone. *Beep, beep, beeeeep.* Happy noises. Some game. The arrival of three teens without winter gear, at night, didn't faze him.

"Do you want anything? Coffee?" Jessie asked, her voice low. "I can cover us, tap with my phone."

"No. But thanks." Berlin glanced back at Cameron, a little sick.

He wandered to the tall tables where tourists could enjoy sandwiches and drinks before heading off on their next adventure. He dropped his head into his hands, thumbs pressing against temples.

At the door, outside the automatic sensor's reach, Berlin lingered. She didn't know how to comfort him. Didn't know what to say to fix this. Even after Kiki's disappearance, Cameron had still laughed. He'd still made bad jokes. He'd been fully himself, even if for weeks he napped in English in the desk behind hers. And Berlin had leaned her chair back as if she could have kept Mr. MacDonald from noticing.

Everyone knew.

The whole class had collectively let him sleep.

But she had felt extra protective. Hadn't trusted Mr. MacDonald to understand. In the end, he hadn't.

Even indoors where the heat pumped, Berlin's hands burned. She wished for her good mittens for a long minute. What must Cameron think of her, after calling for him, after getting them locked out? She wasn't sure what she'd seen. Not really. Not anymore. But underneath all that, a certain dread lingered.

The feeling she got staring at Magritte's *The Son of Man*.

The overcoat. The apple. The mostly hidden face.

That lurking gray.

Her dread wasn't entirely about Cameron. Most of it was over something that should have been less urgent, less life-and-death, but didn't feel that way. Quinta was angry at being woken in the middle of the night when she had to open the shop in the morning. Underneath that understandable anger something heavier loomed.

It could have been as sharp as hate.

Berlin was royally effing it all up. And the very worst part, it wasn't intentional. Whatever she was doing, it was happening on the level of instinct, in the back-brain, terribly out of her control.

Abruptly, she turned, stalked to the bank of fridges. She walked to Jessie, who was buying a tall coffee, and added a Coke to the bill.

"You have pretty hair," the clerk said when he noticed Berlin. And then he turned his head toward Jessie, who was paying at the terminal. "You have pretty hair too," he said. "Real pretty."

The clerk's eyes were glassed over.

Berlin wanted to escape. She hated attempting to reason with anyone under the influence. But she had to try. She couldn't fix

46

Quinta, but maybe she could repair this.

"Did you," Berlin asked, trying to catch the clerk's attention, to know that he heard her, "see a girl? A young woman come in here? Twenty minutes ago? Her hair, it was dyed red at the ends?"

"Hair. You have pretty hair," he said again, and dissolved into laughter.

He wouldn't be able to paint the woman into reality.

To confirm. To deny.

What she'd thought she'd seen.

She approached Cameron's table awkwardly, keeping the road in view. Had Berlin ever done something kind for him? She couldn't recall. That was a no-good, very bad sign. "Here. Drink this."

He looked up, eyes shadowed. "For me?"

"Yes."

Maybe he wasn't sleeping either.

He pressed the can to his right temple and sighed. "Hey, Bee. I've always wanted to know, never asked. You a Coke or a Pepsi Native? Beware," he said, talking slowly. "There is a wrong answer."

"Honestly, neither."

He sighed again. Like he was disappointed with her. "The wrongest answer, that one."

This was going well.

Utterly swimmingly.

"I thought you could use some . . . comfort. That's all."

Cameron's smile was small, but present. The first good thing since Berlin accidentally locked them out.

"This is you trying to comfort me?"

47

"Coke. It makes you happy." She shoved her hands into her apron pockets. "I've noticed."

The pop-top cracked.

"It's not like I'm going to be able to sleep anyhow," Cameron said before taking a long drink.

That stung. Her eyes watered sharply. She couldn't seem to keep her inside things inside tonight. "I didn't mean to harm you. It wasn't . . . intentional."

He was smiling fully now. "Harm me? No one can harm me."

Berlin's whole body tightened like she'd walked into a door someone had opened too fast, too carelessly, and now there was blood everywhere, slicking the ground. She didn't offer up any more of herself, just returned to the entrance. When the purple Jeep tore into PMP's tiny parking lot, Berlin schooled her face. No one could know how much this was truly hurting.

JESSIE

It was a bonkers hour to be drinking a stim. It would fuck up her hands and she needed her hands steady. Jessie's future, it was set. Working hot metal relied on fine motor control. She was lucky-ducked that she hadn't ended up with peripheral neuropathy after treatments. Coffee couldn't do that kind of damage, least she didn't think so. Hitching onto her shoulder the eco-plastic bag the stoned-out-of-his-bucket clerk handed her after she'd convinced him to sell her four packages of cigarettes, she warmed her still-frigid fingers around the insulated cup.

48

Across the street, in the PMP parking lot, a Top 40 hit thumped from the speakers of a purple Jeep Wrangler. Something about sex because every single song these days was about smashing bodies.

Jessie had claimed The Tease as her call sign, but when her friends thought she wasn't listening, they called her worse names. She was good with her body, understood the physicality of lips. She enjoyed a good tussle. And there was nothing wrong with that. She'd take up boxing if the only gym in town wasn't run by one of her father's cronies at the Poseidon Group. As if shrouding themselves in myth classed things up.

Ahead, Berlin stalked toward the Jeep. The music didn't dim. She claimed a key from the manicured hand outstretched into the cold and unlocked the door. Cameron pushed through behind her.

When Quinta spotted Jessie, she hollered over the music: "First night? You surviving?"

Quinta's winged eyeliner was crisp, hair crimped à la nineties mall rat. It was exciting and nerve-inducing at the same time. Her look evoked an actor who played a sex-positive dominatrix on TV.

Laugher bubbled up into the night. Jessie couldn't help it. "Yeah and yeah."

That provoked a half smile and a curt nod. Quinta got it. This shop was special—a place where Joe, the resident adult in charge, trusted them to get it done without his oversight.

That was precious.

Rare.

It was the antithesis of her father's approach to business and life. Quinta was still dressed in the same clothing she'd worn to school. A tight dress over a long-sleeved top patterned with stars. Jessie couldn't see them but knew there would be sun-yellow tights and impractical-in-winter canvas high-tops too.

Maybe the girl hadn't wanted to drive over in her PJs. Maybe she hadn't been to bed yet either.

But even the hardest of the hard-asses took off their eyeliner before sleep. Unless they were soused. A good sousing got in the way of practical things.

The staff door beeped. Berlin returned with her own keys and those eyeliner eyes steeled themselves. Sharp angles, flat. Not full up with hate or love or any other emotion.

This was another sign.

Jessie loved a fucking mystery.

"Thank—" Berlin started.

"Don't."

It was one word. One death cap mushroom of a word.

Jessie knew that tone. She'd heard it between her parents long enough to be a damned expert. Something was totally wronged up in best friendsville. Whatever it was, it was the unforgivable kind.

Berlin's body language shifted, shoulders curling inward, chin lowering.

The scene was frozen. For one, two scorching seconds.

Jessie wanted the confident, no-holds-barred, ride-or-die-for-herself Bee to come back to life. There was something entirely too tempting about Berlin like this, vulnerable.

And then, it happened. Berlin straightened as if she'd zipped all her hurt away into a second-skin catsuit. She dropped the keys into Quinta's outstretched hand. "Okay, then."

The purple Jeep tore out of the parking lot, disappearing from sight.

Holding the door open, Berlin exhaled long and breathy but didn't speak. Jessie dropped her after-midnight shopping into her oversized tote. Thinking through the scene at the Jeep, she scoured flour and other sticky things from kitchen counters. It was clear, even to an outsider, something was major wrong. And it had gone down all quiet at school too. So quiet that Jessie's gossip-minded buds hadn't heard a squeak. But maybe by Monday a fresh story would crop up.

She'd inquire while finishing her homework at the lockers. What she learned might even burn out this mini crush. The very last thing Jessie needed in life was someone she could be vulnerable with. That would end in wreckage. With a person like that in her life, Jessie would have to quit smoking.

CAM

As soon as he tasted the air inside PMP, his stomach rolled. By stacking acid on acid, the Coke hadn't helped any. His kokum had touted it with her wicked grin as an old-timey remedy for upset stomachs. But she was a jokester. Tracking ice through the shop, Cam ran for the little bathroom. Retched into the toilet, the seat down. With an outstretched arm, he closed the door. He'd been numb, concentrating on keeping from tossing his cookies in the convenience store. And Berlin's little kindness, it had wrecked him.

He couldn't remember what he'd said to her—it was a blur. But that moment, her body held by fear, that remained vivid.

He refocused: The girls were inside, moving about, their voices muffled. The rest of the world was held at bay. Now he could let go.

Nobody had seen his cousin for more than five months. Kiki had disappeared. Like she hadn't been sleeping in Sami's room, teasing Tanya and Callie about the ever-loving horror that was preteen crushes, lying in bed with his mom, both of them with their heads where feet should go, topsy-turvy, whispering secrets and eating entire sleeves of Oreos. The only thing found in weeks of searching: her empty neon-orange backpack. The notebook she carried around everywhere was missing too. Like Kiki had been nothing but a shadow all along.

A specter haunting their lives.

Except when she was younger, when her mom lived in town—Before with a capital *B*—Kiki had always been solid. Loud and brash, with big hair to go alongside her large personality. She dimmed a little after her mom's murder. But even that Kiki wouldn't go down without a fight. Without evidence. Without leaving her mark.

And her family had stopped searching.

They'd given in. To her loss.

The empty backpack had crushed them.

Cam fell back on his haunches, and because he was largeish and this room was tiny, he crashed his head against the wall. The space was too tight. He repeated the move, six more times.

Body pain could distract him from other kinds. That was why he played lacrosse. For relief. But he hadn't played since Kiki. Had left lacrosse first, school a handful of weeks later.

Memory was the worst. Cam thought of it the way his kokum had spoken about her nerve pain. The only remedy was laughter. But tonight he couldn't laugh away the hurt. Memory was coming for him with acidic vengeance.

Way Before: His auntie Delphine had gotten in that old rust bucket of a Toyota Corolla to visit a friend for a week or two in Prince Rupert, BC. He still remembered the song playing—Cam's dad kept saying *Turn it up, turn it up*—as she drove away. Willie Nelson, Delphine's favorite.

From the driver's seat, she'd kissed Cam's cheek, and Kiki's, too, and then told her daughter to be good, *not a brat*—and as if that wasn't clear enough, she added, *And don't you cause any trouble while I'm away.* Kiki had laughed, bright like a firecracker against the sky. *Like of course I will. You know I will. You love me exactly like this.* Auntie Delphine had smiled back as wide.

It was a good moment.

It wasn't supposed to be the last good moment.

Whenever he heard that song, Cam got sick. More often than not, he couldn't keep the sick inside. If his sisters hadn't understood, they would have teased him mercilessly for being so out of control. Cam leaned over the toilet again.

Almost a year to the day that the RCMP found Auntie Delphine's remains, when the man who'd murdered her revealed the location for a reduced sentence, Kiki left the house, wearing a neon windbreaker and a pair of bright pink tights—Cam remembered because it clashed with the maroon tips she'd stained half the bathroom and most of their mismatched towels with—and no one saw her again.

It had been the last wild look Kiki had paraded through the kitchen as she grabbed for the toast and honey to make breakfast for herself and whoever else was around. Somewhere between leaving for early-bird curling practice and first period, where they sat next to each other in their History 11/12 split class, his cousin had gone missing.

Now neither Sami or Tanya or Callie would touch the honey. The jar sat on the counter in the exact place Kiki always left it, tucked next to the coffee maker. The girls ate their toast dry. As if honey would no longer taste sweet. Week by week, that honey was turning, crystallizing itself in the jar.

Cam retched until his throat burned.

They'd done everything they could. Reported a missing minor. Filled out the forms. Followed up in person, on the phone. They'd talked to every single RCMP in the building. They'd tried a social media campaign, but Kiki's face had only circulated for a week before someone else, someone with white skin, had gone missing from her suite at the Fairmont Banff Springs hotel. The news cycle gripped on to that story with a fury. That AMBER Alert woke the house, even Sami, who didn't have a cell, and they sat in the living room, the whole family, unable to find sleep again knowing that nobody was searching for their relation any longer. In the end, the last police who came to the front desk to answer their inquiries had said sometimes Natives just run away, the same as sick dogs.

And there was nothing to do about it.

Worse, in the eyes of the public, in the eyes of the law, Kiki was three times cursed. For being Nehiyaw, for being a woman, once more because she was Black too. Three reasons for the RCMP to look the other way. So many reasons for the town not to care that she hadn't made it to school. Fourteen kilometers, door to door. What fucked-up math, how a person disappears in fourteen kilometers.

Time thumped through Cam's veins, his arteries.

He closed his eyes, willing his stomach to settle, willing Berlin to have seen what she thought she had, willing Kiki to be waiting for him at home, sitting on the couch in a pair of her neon knee socks with a hell of a story. If Cam were a character in a movie, this might be possible. If it were a comedy. And not what he suspected: that his life, and the lives of his people, seemed to turn toward tragedy instead. Some real Shakespeare stuff. But who knew? He hadn't been able to read those plays. He struggled with now-times English. Had gotten through Grade 10 by a hair. And when he'd decided to leave school permanently hadn't been passing English or Social Studies or Phys Ed. Mr. MacDonald had stood at his desk backed up by the guidance counselor, telling Cam that it wouldn't be doing him any favors to let him go forward. Later that day, the social studies teacher echoed the same sentiment: *You're a waste of resources, Cameron. Wasting our time and resources.*

Cam's left temple throbbed incessantly. He was in a bad way. Needed to inhale a handful of off-brand ibuprofen. To close the shop and go home.

He'd drive home first, worry about the migraine coming for him later.

When he could lift himself from the floor, he wiped down the toilet seat with the rough eco-paper towels Joe favored, rinsed his mouth out, wishing for a handful of orange Tic Tacs, and reminded himself that the sooner they cleaned this place, the sooner he could open his sisters' bedroom doors and ensure they were safe, asleep, wrapped in those good dreams.

BERLIN

Hovering over the industrial sink, sprayer in one hand, she swiped at her forehead with the other. Under the ball cap, she was sweating. Or it might have been steam. Berlin couldn't tell.

She peered down the hallway for the millionth time. Berlin didn't know what to do. And she hated that troublesome feeling. The girl who needed a solution to each problem.

The used-to-be perfectionist.

Her mind jumped between Quinta's appearance and Kiki's. Or whoever had been in front of the convenience store in the taxi exhaust. Snapshots of what Bee thought she saw—the red-red hair, the figure consumed by a too-large parka—flashed in her mind. They blended, grew, shifted until Berlin wasn't sure if she'd seen something, heard anything at all. Her eyes burned. Closing them for a second made things worse.

Maybe tonight she'd sleep.

A girl could hope.

Out front, Jessie was moving around. Eyes trained on the backsplash behind the sink, as if that would help Berlin rest, she returned to her task. Tonight, it would be a miracle if any of the dishes were truly clean.

She fell into a rhythm, washing, rinsing, stacking inserts. The next thing she knew, the bathroom door was ajar. Cameron had snuck past. She didn't blame him. She was positive now that lack of sleep was driving her to see things. Hallucinate. The foggy exhaust had lulled her into a space where her imagination had taken over. A flight of fancy, as her mom would say. That was it. She'd conjured Kiki from one of the posters she'd helped staple across town all those months ago. Berlin's mind had grasped for an image she knew to fix what she'd seen. That made sense.

It was a rational explanation. Two nights ago, when she should have been sleeping, in the book she'd been reading Magritte described the phenomenon.

Now most of those posters had been torn down or papered over. Even the ones at school near the principal's office had been removed, quietly, one Tuesday morning and replaced with a reminder about winter formal tickets.

After a while, missing became gone.

Berlin exhaled. Her lungs ached. Like lack of sleep meant her cells weren't regenerating. Which was only good science. In this state, it was a welcomed thing she didn't drive. She was starting to worry she was a danger to those around her.

If she could ask her mom for something to help her sleep. If she could manage that, maybe she'd gather relief, hold it close. But some part of Bee, one of the deep, burrowing, vital parts, worried that if she were honest, if she mentioned seeing but not seeing Kiki, Bee's mom would, in one flat second, have her daughter in a closed-door appointment with a psychologist. There, the psychologist would dig and dig. And if Berlin didn't know what was real, what hope would a doctor have of helping her? Of not causing more harm than good?

Maybe she was suffering the same kind of sickness as the surrealists? The warble that opened gaps between this reality and others.

Berlin leaned against the sink, her hands, the front of her apron wet.

Behind her, Jessie interrupted in a quiet voice. "Hey, Cam says we're done up front. It's yachtshape in that kitchen. You know, like shipshape, but with a yacht?"

Berlin tried to smile but couldn't.

"I shouldn't have explained it. That ruined it, didn't it?" Then, getting serious, Jessie asked, "Can I give an assist somehow?"

Berlin gestured to the still-tall stack of dishes in the prep room. "I'll finish. You clock out."

Jessie nodded, all her enthusiasm, her quips, stowed. She zipped herself into her Canada Goose parka. "See you tomorrow."

At school, Jessie was a little bit of a gossip.

It would shatter Berlin for the whole school to know she was losing it.

Shatter her.

She spun there, on that thought. When the dishes were drip-drying on the rack, she checked the clock. It was 3:40 in the morning. Even last callers were likely home from the bar, snoring by now. She had to go up front, had to say something to Cameron, but she didn't know what. She'd tried once already, hadn't succeeded.

I'm sorry I'm seeing things wasn't as competent as she'd like, and there was the distinct chance that whatever she told Cameron, he'd tell his mom, and that would get back to hers flash-flood fast.

Being truthful with this boy was dangerous. But did she owe him? Likely.

In the small customer storefront, he was flipping high-back bar chairs onto the counter to clear way for the mop. The couple from ages ago had left a few toonies on the table. Cameron dropped the change in the tip jar. It seemed another lifetime when Berlin had extinguished the neon sign. Everything was bathed in shadow.

She began sorting the last of the cash, using the light from the drink fridge. Her final duty of the night.

Cameron dragged the mop across the floor.

When he was done, he pushed through the swinging gate between the storefront and the kitchen, the bucket dragging behind him. The water was dirty, likely cold, but Berlin couldn't force herself to care that they were doing a sloppy job tonight. Dirty dishes. Dirty floors.

Her body clung to muscle memory. Even fully exhausted, she faced the bills just as Joe and the bank insisted.

It was a little gift that the boss wouldn't return until Monday. Tomorrow, she'd ensure they left this place looking exactly as she'd left it every other closing shift: perfect. Except Quintana-Roo would be in first. And maybe Quinta was angry enough she'd tattle.

Berlin tried to care. Only a faint headache materialized.

It would depend on exactly how pissed Quinta was. And to figure that out, Berlin would need to know *why*. Tonight, Quintana-Roo had been livid. At the heart of things, it wasn't about the late-night rescue.

Cameron dragged the mop bucket away, his eyes downcast, his forever laughter silent.

Maybe Bee hadn't noticed when she'd hit this point with Quinta, but here, now, she knew. She had to act. If she didn't, she'd ruin this too. Whatever this was. Her acquaintanceship with Cameron Sound.

"I'm sorry." Her hands clawed up. "I shouldn't have said anything. I'm—"

"It's fine, Bee." His voice was raw, pitched low. He stood there. Fixed. Even his floppy hair seemed . . . down. "We're all . . . tired."

She didn't believe him. It wasn't that easy to forgive. "I'm almost done. You should head home."

It was an offering. All she had left to give.

He nodded once, curt. His hair moved now, draping his forehead. It was upsettingly charming.

Hers would be a sweaty mess. The kind dry shampoo couldn't cure. Even when Cameron was a wreck, which was often, he still seemed so eminently himself. When she wasn't put together, she was not.

It was not fair.

But it was fact.

Berlin noted the night's sales on a sticky tab for the boss to tabulate Monday. Cameron sold eighty-five Pupperonis and twenty of his permanent menu specials. A really good take for a fluttery-haired boy who liked puns and wordplay but couldn't be bothered to get the spelling right to save his life. Weeks back, *shark coochie* hadn't gone over well. Joe's unnatural fear of sharks had outlawed it right quick. But it had been . . . witty.

She'd admit that now.

Her own permanent menu specials totaled forty units in sales. When they got paid tomorrow, she'd update her spreadsheet. No, edit that: tomorrow was today.

If Jessie lasted, Joe would give her a go at her first special soon. She hadn't complained at all. A little part of Berlin wished that Jessie were less motivated, that she'd smoked on that milk crate another minute. Because then someone else might have been able to tell Berlin if she saw what she thought she had. If she'd been hallucinating. If, for a millisecond, she'd fallen asleep.

In the dream world where the surrealist thrived, everything was possible.

Even sighting a lost girl.

In the walk-in freezer where she stashed the deposit bag, Berlin realized she could hate Jessie for leaving, if Bee had the energy to hate. Instead of trying for it, she untied her dirty apron and changed back into her mukluks. Then she saw it. "Fuck. The laundry."

It overflowed out the laundry room door.

But she didn't care.

Couldn't care.

Later, when she returned to the shop, she'd correct all her mistakes.

Saturday, Early Morning

Local radio, rebroadcast: The Poseidon Group is sponsoring two-for-one skiing this Sunday at Mount Norquay in honor of Family Day. Grab the kids or a special friend and enjoy fresh powder for half price!

JESSIE

She smashed the radio and then cut the engine.

Abandoning her schoolwork in the Land Rover, Jessie walked around the too-big house, her Canada Goose jacket zipped up mummy-style, her tote bag slung over a shoulder. She'd smudged her mascara artfully, swapped her skin-tight jeans for a miniskirt. Now it looked as if she'd returned from an evening of debauchery.

Not a night of labor.

She unlocked the door, the dead bolt retracting with a mechanical whirl. Kicking off her decoy shoes in the mudroom, Jessie didn't peel out of her parka. She was halfway to the stairs when a light in the living room flickered on.

Her father sat in the shadow, in his overlarge armchair, like he'd been practicing for the role of Evil Parent in a Disney live-action movie. "Where have you been?"

"Out." She bit down too sharply, put too much emphasis on the *t*.

"I told you to quit that job."

Jessie threw palms to the sky, the international sign for *Come on, really?* "Does it seem like I've been working?"

"If I discover you're lying . . ."

"I know, I know, you'll disinherit me or something."

"Or something, Jessica." Her father pushed himself up. He absconded from the room, wandered down the hallway to his master suite without extinguishing the lamp.

Jessie sighed.

Finally, her father found a threat that Jessie's brain could latch on to. *Or something* . . . The possibilities were now entirely endless, like a good nightmare.

CAM

He wanted nothing more than to climb into his shitty little red car and drive. He had a need to be home. Because his dad wasn't there, and someone had to make sure his sisters were okay. Drooling on their pillowcases. To check his mom had made it back from the city safe. But the 1994 LeBaron was a grumpy old man. In the winter, it needed a significant warm-up before it would consider producing heat. Normally, Cam cranked the engine before he clocked out.

Tonight, he hadn't been thinking about the LeBaron's needs.

Berlin had approached him again. While he knew she'd apologized, the actual words were fuzzy. As if he'd been drinking. Which Cam didn't do, wouldn't do to himself and his family. He loathed the fuzziness, the way alcohol took something from him, left him out of control. He sat, holding the steering wheel, waiting for the engine to heat enough that he could drive without his windshield fogging.

The beast was old.

Probably should be retired. But Cam couldn't spend anything on himself until he finished Sami's regalia. And though he wheeled and dealed for as much as he could, sometimes he bought small offerings for the aunties and kokums when they took time to teach him a skill.

A car would be next on the list. The radio in the LeBaron worked fine and so did the tape deck. Tonight, his stomach was already empty. Almost lucky, that was. Because he ached for the music. For a piece of that good memory. He found his dad's tape stuffed under the driver's seat. The speakers came alive with crackles.

Cam closed his eyes.

One song and the LeBaron would be ready to cruise.

One turned into two.

In the pause between songs, Berlin emerged, in her parka, with mittens and beaded earmuffs on. She pushed the shop keys into her pocket, peering across the street at the convenience store as if lost for a moment, then pivoted toward the traffic lights. She'd changed her work shoes for a pair of tall mukluks.

Such a sensible girl.

He knew her parents' vehicles by sight. He buzzed down the passenger-side window. "Berlin, where's your ride?"

She turned back slowly. Like she really didn't want to. "I'm going to walk . . . tonight."

"That's a really bad idea, eh."

"I live ten minutes away," she said louder, surer.

This was the Berlin he knew. Somehow, she'd managed to excise fear from her body. She hadn't let it roost. Inside of Cam, it was brewing. What was that line: *toil and trouble*, doubled? They'd read *Macbeth* in English class last year. And Cam had liked those witches. Why their words were coming for him now, twisted up, not quite right, he didn't know. What he did know: he wouldn't sleep tonight. Instead, he'd run the jar of honey under hot water. Make it new again.

Berlin waited, frozen on the sidewalk. She half waved. "Good night or morning. Whatever this is."

He should let her go.

Even though she'd apologized, she hadn't really made it clear what she was sorry for. *I shouldn't have said anything.*

But he couldn't. Too many nights he'd wondered why someone hadn't helped his auntie on the road to Prince George, hadn't been there for Kiki when she needed it. "Let me give you a lift."

"I'm fine walking."

"Bee," he said, his voice cracking. "I'm going to worry until I see you again if I don't drop you at your door and watch you go inside and lock up."

She laughed.

It wasn't because she thought what he said was hilarious. It was one of those ironic laughs. Somewhere, at some point, Cam had screwed the pooch.

Of course he had.

Tonight, even with Berlin, he would beg. "Please, Bee."

"Fine," she said, exhaling hard. "Can we do a bank deposit? Joe hates leaving that much cash inside. But he told me I can't do deposits alone."

Anxiety climbed along Cam's spine like a spider. He had to get home. Needed to. Still, he owed it to Berlin. "Sure."

His sisters were good. His mom was good. They were warm. They were fed and loved and curled under the covers. Once he'd fixed the honey, he'd make them toast.

He couldn't worry about Kiki right now. He'd fall apart if he did. And then who would keep his family together, Monday morning through Thursday night? Sometimes all the way to Friday. Like this week. An internship thing his mom had to attend.

Bee fished her key from her pocket. "I'll be a minute."

When she emerged again, the fur cuffs of her mittens puffed out of her bag. Sami would adore the gray color, the texture. If she had the chance, she'd swipe the mittens, add them to her collection of pretty, shiny things. He lived with a small criminal, whose bed resembled a dragon's hoard, overflowing with her treasures.

When Berlin slid onto the passenger seat, she made herself small, her arms pulled tight, her body angled toward the window.

Cam shouldn't have forced her.

But tonight, he would have followed her home, no matter how creepy it was, stalking someone in the hours before dawn in his LeBaron. He waited until she fastened her seat belt before shifting into reverse.

Her parka smelled of pomegranates and . . . vanilla. Burnt sugar with pleasant sour notes. Like the kitchen when Kiki had lived with

66

them. Only his cousin avoided sour in favor of another dollop of sweet. She'd always been baking, had hummed off-key to the radio while measuring ingredients. In the morning, maybe he could try his hand at French toast—the honey would sweeten it. They had bread. And no one had touched Kiki's cupboard where the fancy spices were kept, as if it were some kind of fucked-up shrine.

Next to him, Bee gripped her phone but didn't check her messages. He drove to the bank, the streets empty. The tape kept playing. Cam tried to focus.

But he kept imagining that one day the same thing that had happened to Kiki would happen to his sisters. Jesus, to Sami.

Eventually to Berlin too.

It was what happened to Native women and girls. To Two-Spirit people. It wasn't a natural disaster, this. Cam might be hard on his dad, but it wasn't that he didn't understand why he'd given up painting. Eventually, Cam would need to start driving a taxi too. But he'd finish Sami's regalia first. Then he'd quit at PMP, join his dad so there'd be two of them on the road at Sound Taxi, keeping the people safe. In the predawn hours, this was the only future Cam could imagine for himself.

But in the daytime, he imagined other things.

At the bank, Berlin left her overloaded bookbag on the floorboards. "Thank you," she said once she was back in the car. "Joe appreciates it."

Willie was singing in the background. Something about mothers and babies. In his chest, Cam's heart beat fast, too fast. Pressure, like he might throw up again. "Bee?"

"Yeah?"

"I know you probably want to get home and I'll take you right now if you need to sleep or shower or whatever, but I . . ."

She watched him closely, her lips parted. The first time she'd really looked at him in hours. Maybe in the whole time they'd known each other since the kindergarten incident.

"Right now, tonight, I need to get to my house for a minute and check that everyone I love is okay."

She cleared her throat. "I can walk from here."

"I mean, come with me? I'll run inside and be like so fast you won't even register it and then I'll drive you to your doorstep." Cam wouldn't have normally asked this of anyone, let alone of her, but he was so tired, and underneath that there was a panic he couldn't fall into again. He'd barely climbed out of it in the bathroom. "I . . . don't want to be . . . can't be alone right now."

It was a massive risk. She'd only ever shut down every other attempt he'd made toward her their whole lives to this point. The odds were terrible. Cosmic.

If she refused.

If she laughed.

Cam wouldn't be able to hold himself together.

"Oh." The light of the bank's sign threw blue across her face, across her pretty glasses, her lips. "I can manage that. Sure."

BERLIN

Cameron drove in silence with only the old-school country music for company. His car had a tape deck. An actual working tape deck.

It was absurd. But it fit, weirdly.

She owed him another apology. She'd really effed him up, and she owed it to see him through this. But now didn't seem like the proper moment for more apologies. When he brought it up again, she'd be sure he knew that she was certain she was seeing things and so sorry. She'd fallen asleep, dreamed a ghost into existence. The girl's hair was redder than what Kiki preferred, a deep maroon. And Berlin would take what may come, even if it was her mom escorting her to a psychologist's office.

Soon they were on the highway, traveling away from the mountains. The night was clear and the road was fine. Nothing glassy, nothing icy. The heater in his car wasn't powerful, but it would be rude to put her mittens back on. Instead, she tucked her fingers under her arms. Fifteen minutes later, they swept into the Sounds' driveway.

He shut the ignition off with a full-body sigh, sank into his seat, letting his floppy hair loll against the headrest. "Come in for a sec. It's snappy out. You'll freeze into a solid block."

"I'm fine."

"Don't be a keener when it comes to winter weather, Berlin."

"I'm not being a keener. See, parka? Mittens? Contained wind-breaking shelter-like thing around me," she huffed. "I am fine."

"Bee."

His tone said she was being unreasonable. But she was too guilt-ridden to tell him that at the moment he was the one being a bit unreasonable. She popped her seat belt, following him up to the rambling split-level house. The front door wasn't locked.

In the open-concept living room, Cameron's mom looked up from her laptop screen, her hair tied in a messy bun. "Hey, baby," she said. She raised her eyebrows when she spotted Berlin standing behind her son but smiled, pushing her reading glasses into her hair. She scrambled up, heavy textbooks sliding from her lap to the floor with a thud. "Oof. Come here, you two. Give me a hug."

Her son went first, holding his mom tight. His voice went deep and low. "Welcome home, Mom."

"I should be saying that to you."

Cameron smiled but didn't laugh. "I—I need to check on them. I'll be a minute. Then I'm driving Bee home."

He climbed carpet-covered stairs, taking two at a time. Berlin stared. Even after he'd turned the corner and stepped out of view. Like she, too, needed to know he would be okay.

"You don't get away that easy," Cameron's mom said, calling Berlin back to the moment.

She schooled her face, sank into the hug. "Sorry, Auntie Mel. It's been a really long, no-good, entirely exhausting night."

The hug tightened. "I didn't think you and my Cam were friends . . ."

"We're not." Berlin shrugged, stepping back. "He wouldn't let me walk home."

"Oh."

Gathering fallen textbooks, Berlin placed them on the coffee table before sitting on the worn leather couch. She crossed her ankles, perched at the very edge.

"He's still struggling. He can't . . ." Auntie Mel's voice broke. She closed her laptop with an audible click. "I don't blame him. Thanks for indulging my kid."

"It's nothing."

"Now, that's untrue."

Berlin used to crave this. Gentle reprimand.

What she believed it signified: a mark to remind her to never make the same mistake twice. A kind of confirmation.

Even now that she was warm, Berlin's body refused to settle. The ache was low, angry. "Can I use the washroom?"

"Down the hall. Same place it's always been."

Berlin rarely came to this house. Last time, it had been with Quinta, to pick up Callie and Tanya for that self-defense workshop. As she stood, her abdomen pinched, and Bee half knew what was wrong. But her bookbag and supplies were out in Cameron's car. "Do you have a tampon?"

Her body had timing.

Offering up another thing she had to carry.

Auntie Mel's face offered sympathy. "They're under the vanity in there. Want ibuprofen too? We have the good off-brand stuff."

"No, thank you. I'm fine." Berlin wondered if she kept saying it, if it would eventually come out true.

After all, the pipe that wasn't a pipe didn't exist in a static state.

It wouldn't always be, in all times and places, a *not* pipe.

Just like *fine* wouldn't always be a word divorced from meaning.

CAM

His baby sister slept, blankets tangled up in her legs, snoring loudly. Sami's collection of stolen things was scattered in the bed with her. A silver spoon from their kokum's collection. Assorted rocks found in parks, some painted. Hair ties. Pennies, cleaned. And three of six fancy pens that used to be Kiki's prized possessions. Her poet's pens.

Tonight, the trundle bed was tucked away. As it had been since . . . what seemed like forever ago. And also not. A time paradox in Treaty 7 territory. Wait until Cam told his buddies at the next intertribal. He began to laugh, imagining their eyes, the way they wouldn't brush him off, the way they'd debate the issue in all seriousness, but Cam swallowed it so as not to disturb his sister.

Tonight, he wanted to pull out the trundle bed to see if the covers had been washed, if they still smelled like Kiki. That mix of vanilla and rising dough and coconut oil hair products. The only thing stopping him from indulging: he'd basically forced Berlin to come to his house in the middle of the night and he promised he'd be quick. Already, he'd dragged her far enough into his bullshit.

He left the door cracked. That way, the ambient light in the hallway would ensure his baby sister was never alone in the dark. Maybe, too, it would protect Sami while he was gone. Down the hall, Tanya and Callie were curled up tight, each in their own bed. Some nights, Cam would find them huddled together as if to stay warm. He knew it was about a kind of unsayable comfort.

Cam wanted that.

Someone to hold. Someone to hold on to him.

But he had his mom and his sisters. And at work, he had Joe.

The deep-down fear in Cam's body wasn't gone, but it was at

least settled. It would wake again. While he had a break, he had to drive Berlin back into town. It wasn't the most efficient trip known to humankind, but it had quelled his anxiety and kept Bee from walking the streets alone. Out there, anything could have happened to her. He was too tired to imagine the possibilities. The other timelines.

In the living room, his mom and Berlin talked quietly.

"You set to go?" Cam asked.

"Yeah." Berlin pushed herself up, wobbled.

He reached out. It was instinct.

She flinched, brushed it off by saying goodbye to his mom, who used her best mothering tone. The no-BS one. "Drive safe. And text! The minute you get to Berlin's."

"Will do." Cam noticed how tired his mom looked, how absolutely late it was to be up studying. "Why don't you go to bed? I won't be long."

"I'm waiting for your dad," she said. "He texted. He's on his way."

Cam's jaw got tight. His dad should be here. With his family. But he wasn't.

Berlin stepped outside into the cold first. On the porch, Cam tensed as his dad's taxi pulled into the driveway. Now at least his mom could go to sleep.

It's not that Cam's dad had been okay after what happened to his own sister, Kiki's mom. But since his niece had gone missing, he'd sunk into himself. He stooped, didn't smile as often or as fast. And maybe the saddest thing, he hadn't been in his basement-level studio since. It used to smell of oils, turpentine. Now it was a little

73

damp like any other basement. He was too busy working, too busy grieving, to paint.

"Morning." Berlin smiled with teeth. Her cheeks pushed her glasses up.

Slowly, his dad returned the gesture, as if he were genuinely pleased to see her. On their porch. In the dead of night. But Bee had always been skilled at charming adults and Elders. She was well-liked. Had style, yeah, but she made time to greet everyone. To make each person, even at a crowded community event, feel seen.

Except Cam.

Maybe that was changing. It was the optimist's perspective. But the whole bit, it hinged on how in the living room, when she'd stumbled, when he'd tried to help, she flinched away.

When his dad spoke, it came out worn. "Shouldn't you be in your beds?"

"Shouldn't you?" Cam volleyed back. "Old man."

That used to be a joke. These days it came out different.

"Cameron," Berlin chided.

Cam's dad didn't react. "I was getting the last of the people home safe, son."

"It's a good thing you do, Uncle Stephen," Berlin said.

His smile sharpened, and for a blip Cam wondered why that smile seemed to be reserved for clients. Why it was withheld in the family home. Like they didn't need their dad as much as the rest of the world did.

Cam gestured at the LeBaron. "Let's go."

But his dad wasn't done. "If you ever need a ride, Berlin, you call. I don't like you working late at that pizza place without a car to get you home safe."

Her mouth tightened, like she was remembering something unpleasant. "I don't usually walk. Only sometimes. And it's ten minutes, on sidewalks, under streetlights. It's really fine."

"It's got to be one of the reasons your ma has all those gray hairs."

"Those are work-related, thank you very much."

Cam's dad pinned her with a look. "Let's call it sixty-forty."

"I'll settle at forty-sixty."

His dad laughed. "Forty percent isn't *that* low, you know?"

Her mouth tightened again. "True story."

How many other nights had Cam driven away, leaving Bee to walk home alone? How long had she been walking? She used to ride with Quintana-Roo. When those two started, they'd only worked shifts together—but that had changed too. Cam pushed his hair back from his forehead.

"Did you do what I asked, Cameron?" His dad's hands were in his pockets, but his eyebrows were raised.

"It's not there. Like I said last time."

"Check again."

"It won't change anything. This isn't the Twilight Zone, where missing things appear because you want them to. If you care so much, why don't you ask the girls to look too? Why is this only on my plate?" With that parting shot, Cam moved toward the LeBaron and Berlin followed, waving goodbye. Kiki's notebook wasn't anywhere. Cam had searched. The school claimed they'd returned all her belongings, and Cam's dad was twisted if he thought her notebook was at PMP. Kiki had quit long before the second week in September. It made no sense for her notebook to be in the shop. Besides, Joe would have returned it—he'd cared about Kiki too.

As they walked away, Cam's dad hollered: "The highway is in good shape. Still, take your time on the roads, son. Better safe than sorry."

Climbing into his red car, Cam silently vowed that Bee wouldn't walk home alone at night ever again. He didn't know how he'd make it so. But he would. He hadn't been vigilant enough with his cousin. The week after Labor Day, he'd been running late. Kiki needed to be at school early. Curling practice, the only time they could get extra ice time. Eventually she'd tired of waiting. Or that was the story he'd been telling himself: that she left in her own vehicle while Cam had been brushing his teeth in the shower.

In his worst imaginings, it wasn't mankind who took Kiki, but aliens. It was laughable. Cam's family had Auntie Delphine's bones—they'd held Ceremony for her. But what if it wasn't so laughable? What if Kiki would never be found? Would never be able to rest? Because: aliens? Because she was alive, with the aliens?

Exhaustion was a real trip.

If Cam had a therapist, his therapist would tell him he was spinning this tale because at least in this version his cousin was alive. Cam got that. He understood why that narrative seemed to be both the worst and also the best.

In his chest, his anxiety turned over, restless. Cam steered the LeBaron onto the highway and finally asked the question he needed to: "Do you think it was her? Out there?"

As if at the mention of his cousin, in an instant the roads went from tacky to slippery. Cam slowed before the LeBaron had a chance to really get up to running speed. Winter tires helped. Still the beast wasn't a match for extreme weather.

Berlin cleared her throat. "I don't know. Not any longer."

"But you thought it enough in the moment to call for me."

The tape reached its end. It ejected. The first handful of flurries came from the sky, caught themselves in the headlights' reflection, illuminated so that, for a second, Cam thought he could see each crystal of ice. Segment by segment.

It was beautiful.

Precise.

Mathematical even.

He shook his head as if to clear it. His hair flopped around his ears.

"How old is this car?" she asked.

Cam laughed, maybe at her tone, maybe at the fact that he was driving Berlin Chambers around somewhere right before dawn, on the night when she maybe might have seen his missing cousin. "Don't change the subject, Bee."

"Sorry," she said, as if she'd been chastised.

"It's not like you need to apologize here."

The snow continued its descent.

"What if I do?" She sounded so earnest. "What if I only think I saw her? If for a tiny moment, I maybe fell asleep?"

The snow intensified. The air inside the car, around them on the road, it tightened. An electric crackle boomed. And then a flash of light broke from the sky.

Thundersnow.

Cam's luck was garbage.

He focused on the road. "Do you dream about . . . her . . . often?"

Berlin cocked her head, thinking. "No. Actually, I haven't dreamed in months. Longer, maybe? When I sleep, it's all nothing."

Smart as she was, some days she didn't make a lick of sense. "Then why go there? Why torture yourself?"

"Point to Cameron," she said with a little huff.

It killed her that he was right. But for once, she was a good sport about it. He could get used to this version of Berlin. Could even like this version.

He hated that she wasn't sleeping well. That she wasn't dreaming.

The road got worse. Cam turned the wipers on high to keep flurries from clouding his vision.

They drove into the storm.

"I wasn't sure . . ." Berlin leaned forward, pressing hands against the dash, and, as if they were hunting together, she trained her eyes sharply on the road too. "I'm still not. Sure, that is. But something told me it was her or it could have been her. Something . . . I can't explain."

Cam digested that. For uptight Bee to admit that the inexplicable took over, showed her a vision of a long-lost girl, even if it wasn't Kiki, there, in the flesh, it was a sign, somewhere, that Kiki was alive. Of this, Cam was certain. "Good enough for me."

Snow blew across the highway when only a short while ago things had been clear. The wind howled. Clouds dampened the moonlight, drawing a heaviness over the land. Moments like these, the world was speaking. And it was saying, loudly and clearly, *Pay attention! Listen! Be present!*

Bee felt it too. It was in her posture. In the way, when Cam dared look from the road, that her face seemed relaxed. At peace or as close as she could get. Like the way she'd look soaking in the bathtub.

Cam mentally berated himself for that one.

He meant the way she'd look when she let go. Not the way she'd look naked.

Breath fogged the passenger-side window. He reached for the heat dial. When he couldn't find it by touch, he turned away from the road for a second, nothing more—

Berlin grabbed his searching hand, yelled: "Stop, stop! Pull over!"

He listened, reacted, trusting her. Even before he saw the wreck. An SUV, thrown onto its side, half in the ditch. Cam stopped the LeBaron carefully, the way his dad had taught him when he was fourteen, not slamming on the brakes but pumping them. Old-car stuff. Throwing his four-ways on, Cam pulled up behind the accident.

Before the car fully stopped, Berlin unbuckled her seat belt, opened the passenger door. She ran toward the SUV, leaving boot prints in the snow. On the vehicle's rear glass, two side-by-side decals glowed a toxic green, a bikini-clad babe and, next to her, a large, stylized trident. Like from *The Little Mermaid*. Cam ignored the wrongness of the decals, joined Berlin.

"It's empty," she said, standing next to the driver's door.

The windshield was smashed, the front end ruined, stained with blood.

For a minute, the quiet of the night and the ticking of Cam's emergency flashers was all there was. Then, a cry rose up. High-pitched whistling, shrieking. Something not human, but Cam's body understood: pain.

Berlin spun. A few meters ahead of the SUV, off in the ditch, lay an injured wapiti.

"Oh no." Bee spoke low, almost too low for Cam to hear. She wandered toward it, like a sleepwalker, unaware of the dangers around her.

Cam gripped a handful of her parka. She slipped, collided with his body. Her vanilla-pomegranate perfume was the best thing he'd never known he needed. No part of Cam wanted to let go. Ever.

He softened his voice. "Careful, Bee. She's badly injured. She could lash out." He released his hold. It didn't matter how good she smelled, how much he was finding he enjoyed touching her—Berlin fucking Chambers—when she hadn't been an enthusiastic participant.

It wasn't all *ice ice baby*. They weren't even friends.

Bee stepped away, leaving him cold. "She won't hurt me."

The wapiti's eyes were open, glassy.

Even Cam, on high alert, was momentarily seduced. Poor, sweet kin. Her front legs were broken. And she had, finally, given up trying to drag herself into the bush.

Bee stepped close to him again, reached out and placed her hand against his shoulder. "Can we do something for her?"

Through his winter jacket he could barely feel her touch. At the same time, all he could feel was her touch. It muddled his thinking something fierce.

"Cameron?"

"Yeah. I have a good knife, some medicine. You understand, that's what's left."

Berlin nodded.

With one more look at the wapiti, who had quieted with their approach, they turned to make their way back to the car. There, Cam pulled out from under the driver's seat his hunting knife, the one his dad gifted him when he was twelve.

"Reach under your seat for me? I think that's where I left my kit. If not, it's in the trunk."

She fished around. Pulled out a leather satchel, passed it to him. Then, she leaned against the LeBaron and exhaled a ragged stream of breath.

Every minute they spent together, Bee was becoming more human.

"You can come with me if you want?" he said. "I'd . . . appreciate having you. You don't have to do anything. Just, you know, support."

Berlin shook her head, her blunt bangs, flattened from wearing the PMP ball cap all night, swaying against her forehead. "I shouldn't."

"Please." He didn't want to do this alone.

Bee's voice sharpened. "I mean I *can't*."

She was shaking. Her teeth chattering, big and out of control. It wasn't from the windchill. He stepped closer, brushed snow from her bangs. "Bee, it's okay. Sit here, would you? No arguments, eh?"

Once she'd closed the door, Cam exhaled. His breath escaped like smoke. But he knew better. His breath, something that was inside him, part of him, was becoming ice. Crystals formed in the air. Returning to be part of the universe again.

He approached the suffering wapiti with his heart open.

BERLIN

The night ran onward seemingly endlessly. When Cameron returned, he stored his knife and leather medicine kit under the driver's seat with care. He climbed inside, rubbing his hands briskly. Even in the pitch dark, Berlin noticed he'd gotten blood on himself. The leg of his sweatpants, his parka.

"It's done?"

Cameron nodded. "She's at rest."

"Should we call somebody? So they can harvest the meat? Some good should come of this."

Morning was near, though no one would know it in this storm. The engine fired up, the windshield wipers engaged, fighting snow. Trying to lift their burden.

"Her body was emaciated. She wouldn't have lived much longer. Even without the SUV. I think she was infected." Cameron made a noise in the back of his throat. "I'm not certain. Fish and Wildlife will have to test to be sure."

"It's such . . . a waste." Berlin meant the loss of life as much as she meant the loss of sustenance for hungry families.

Cameron didn't say anything. He stepped back outside to clear snow from his car, not with the brush in the back seat but with his bare hands. When he finished, he navigated onto the road carefully. The storm carried on around them. He turned off his flashers. A

82

minute later, a little farther down the road, the weather cleared too.

The moon returned, offering her light.

The road wasn't slick anymore.

What flurries that remained were gracious, floating perfection. The kind of snowflakes in movies, not in real life. And yet—

Borders between what seemed real and what seemed more than real were porous. It was not so much comforting as terrifying.

Ahead, the town of Canmore was fast coming into view.

Finally, Berlin warmed enough. There in the background, behind the terror, the worry, the forehead-creasing anxiety, the same call she'd listened to sitting outside Pink Mountain Pizza, only hours ago, while she stared at the convenience store.

No, no, it wasn't in the background.

It was all around her.

She shivered with it.

Next to her, Cameron seemed oblivious. He caught her looking.

"I just can't . . . ," he said, hesitating. "I can't imagine Kiki out there, somewhere, needing me, hurt or scared. It's worse, I think, than if she's already left this world to be with the ancestors." He swallowed hard. "Is that . . . twisted?"

Berlin's abdomen pulsed in response. Not exactly cramps. Her whole body wanted to bathe in the song of the universe. To close herself to anything but those resplendent notes. She pushed words out. "No, Cam. No, it's not. There's nothing wrong with wanting closure, even relief."

She'd shortened his name. Said it for the first time. And it settled right.

83

"I have to find her," he said.

He hadn't noticed the shift. How in its own way it was earth-changing, geological.

"I know," she offered back.

That was all they owed each other. Even if things were changing, they weren't changing radically. It was enough and not enough at the very same time. He was hurting. Not like the first few weeks after his cousin went missing, when he'd been withdrawn and cold. When his grief was anticipatory. Before he'd returned to cracking jokes and acting the fool in the classes they'd shared. Acting that stereotype, the usually-but-not-always-drunk Native, laughing when settlers mocked them, not understanding that his laughter wasn't fighting back but giving in, giving up.

For the past few hours, Cam had been almost serious. And last year, when his nose got broken, he never did tell anyone what happened. Even though it would have gotten him a ton of laughs, he kept her secret. Maybe to him it was but a small thing. Holding confidence.

Berlin paused, her pulse thrumming in her ears, her whole body singing with that alive-alive feeling. Like the kind that followed an excellent wipeout on the mountain, snowboard skidding under feet, the cresting wave of snow flying at her, peppering her goggles, her face, this rush was overwhelming.

Too much.

And yet, her body wanted more.

Craved it, *needed* it.

She couldn't make conversation like this was any other night, like she was absolutely fine, not drowning under the assault of the thrum of the world inside her very own body. It seemed wild, untamed, utterly miraculous that before, she'd lived with this feeling inside of her, connected to her, every day, every minute, each blessed second. Before, before it stopped.

Somehow, she'd been cut off.

No, there was a reason they could talk about Kiki tonight. The world had undone herself, had stopped Berlin and Cam with a storm to care for the dying elk. A storm that weathered around them, to create space for two people who'd never really gotten along to have a moment of utterly terrifying connection. Even after she'd smashed his nose with that door at school, they hadn't connected.

But this feeling, it would pass. It was as much a part of this night as the elk, as calling Cameron *Cam*. She wasn't cured. Didn't believe in miraculous solutions. She needed to treasure it now while she held the song of the universe in her body, while it inhabited her cells.

Hold on. Hold hard.

When they pulled into her driveway, the porch light was on. The front door immediately swung open. Her dad, wearing his bathrobe and a pair of indoor mocs his sister had made him for his last birthday, leaned out into the night. "Is that Cameron?" he asked, his voice muffled by the engine.

Berlin stared at the clock. Five fifteen a.m. "Ignore him. You do not have to come inside."

"Of course I do." Cam smiled his old smile, the goofy one, as if the spell they'd been under had broken. "Does he normally wait for you?"

"If he's home, he's usually in bed. I don't know what's going on."

Cam nodded. "My mom's a worrier. She can't sleep until all her kids are safe."

Berlin wondered if that had always been the way.

No, the something strange still locked them together. Cam read her mind. "It's her normal. It's not new, you know."

They both exited the car into the crisp early morning, walking along the salted sidewalk to the doorway.

"Dad, is everything okay? Is Mom okay? Auntie Jamie? Snap? My bats?" she asked, waiting for something to come crashing down. Tonight it was possible that she and Cam hadn't been caught in the universe's only freak storm.

"Everyone's fine," Berlin's dad said, dismissing her worry, stepping back, making room. "Thank you for driving my daughter home. I keep telling Berlin to get her Class 7, start the process, at the least."

"It was nothing," Cam said, stepping inside.

No, it wasn't.

Her parents had been pressuring her. They didn't understand that before what happened with Quinta happened, Berlin hadn't needed to drive. They didn't understand she didn't want to either. It's not that they didn't know she walked—in the daytime—and it's not like she was hiding that she was walking at night. Not exactly. But if they knew she'd been walking since the start of Christmas break, they'd absolutely force her to get her driver's license.

"Now, Cameron, don't make your kindness into something small when kindness is unmeasurable." It was a dad-ism. Her father was full of them.

The house smelled good. The wood fire was banked. She closed the door. Some of the rescue animals were bolters. But this early in the morning, even the nocturnal ones were, if not asleep, then at least resting. Too tired to trek into the basement, she'd tend to her bats, the ones being rehabilitated for release, when she woke. They didn't mind her schedule. And the less contact they had with humans, the better.

Berlin had attended a program in Calgary, one weekend last summer, to be certified for at-home rehabilitation. Quinta drove. They made a whole day of it even though Quinta cared more for bees than bats.

Dropping her schoolbag in the entryway with a thud, Bee said, "Dad, let Cam go. It's really late. I'm sure he's as tired as I am."

Her dad offered an indulgent look. "That's an excellent point. Joe's going to hate that you were clocked in until . . ." He checked his watch. "Well past five in the morning. Busy night, was it?"

That storm, if it was still raging, Cam would have to face it alone. She wondered if they should set him up in a guest bedroom. But she ignored the idea. It was too, too strange. "What are you even doing awake?"

"You might be getting ready to sleep, but I'm up for the day. I thought to get a run in on the old treadmill and check on yesterday's surgery patients before clinic. And, you know, I don't sleep well when your mom's on call."

The smell of coffee registered. The kitchen appliance that got the most use in their household was a toss-up between the French press and the fancy dual-boiler espresso machine.

"So, it *was* busy, then?" her dad asked again.

She tried to tell Cam without speaking that they didn't need to air the whole story. If they started, they'd never get to sleep. And for once, the lull that would drag her under was lurking. Her limbs were heavy, ready. "Super busy, Dad. Let Cameron go home, would you?"

Her dad laughed. "I forget sometimes while I'm used to next to no sleep, you're teenagers—you basically do nothing but sleep."

Cameron laughed, too, the sound eerie and wrong after what they'd seen on the road.

How could he flip so fast? So easily?

Berlin opened the front door, shooing the boy out. "Thank you for the ride," she said formally.

"Text Berlin when you reach home, please."

Her dad's words were a small reminder of what she owed Cam's mother, who would be worried, their drive taking longer than usual. Bee pulled out her phone before she forgot. But she lingered at the living room window, watching Cam's red car back out of the drive. Even if they weren't friends, she didn't want anything to happen to him. That stretch of road between his house and town, it had been as if an invisible bubble kept the rules of the universe from being put into order.

Keep him safe. Until he crosses the threshold, until he falls into the arms of sleep, until the morning light comes.

This was prayer.

Her dad lingered behind her, his blue Métis-flag coffee cup in hand. "You've put the kindergarten incident to bed, then? After all these years actively avoiding each other you've decided to become friends?"

"We work at the exact same place. We don't avoid each other."

"Oh, consider me corrected. His mom is your mom's best friend. Mel was at your birth. Come to think of it, Cameron was at your birth too. And yet . . ."

Something flash-boiled inside of her.

Something uncontrollable.

Something red.

"Dad, to that boy everything's a joke. He doesn't have any goals. Has no plans for his future. He'll be happy working at Pink Mountain Pizza for the rest of his life." It might have been cruel to say these things about the Cam from tonight. The one who had medicine in his car. The one who knew the wasting disease from sight. Who'd insisted on caring for Berlin—even as his need for his sisters, his mom, had pulled at him.

Still, she let the unkind words stand.

Her dad settled his coffee on a coaster and then pulled her into his arms. "I guess your mom and I raised you to care about those things."

Her cheek pressed against the too-worn fabric of his bathrobe. Berlin's mom was a terrible gift giver, but her dad claimed that his wife had a way with bathrobes. Once a decade or so.

"A side effect of the double-doctor-parent thing, possibly," she said.

He released her, and Berlin missed the warmth almost immediately. She hadn't sunk into a hug, not in her heart, in too long.

How long, exactly?

Longer than she'd thought. Months and months, season after season. Since she saw Kiki-not-Kiki, in the taxi's exhaust fog, it was as if Berlin's sleeping self had woken. Now everything was too alive. The colors of the universe too sharp. Clothing chafed against skin. Skin against the rest of her.

If she could paint like the surrealists, she'd paint ants traveling along veins, arteries, burrowing inside a body.

After some sleep, maybe all this sensation, all this confusion, would wash out clear. Correlation, she knew, didn't necessarily mean causation. Kiki of the exhaust, the snow squall, the elk, and the universe's song did not have to be connected. Did not have to make meaning. She stumbled toward the stairs. Her bedroom was in the finished attic, a space all her own. She craved it. Wanted to strip her clothes away, go to bed nude, hope her bamboo sheets would soothe.

But Berlin's dad wasn't done yet.

"Plans are good, eh, daughter. Goals are nice. But it doesn't mean that someone like Cameron is doing it wrong if he's living in the moment, you know? Not if he's happy. We all contribute in our own way. We can all take care of our relations, our own hearts, differently. It doesn't have to be with a university degree."

Another gentle rebuke. She'd been raised on them. Yet, after the night she'd had, its impact wasn't gentle at all. It railed like a slap.

Berlin had big plans: She was saving money to attend a Michif language institute in Winnipeg this summer. There, she'd immerse herself in the language, to ensure she was helping in the efforts to keep it healthy. Neither of her parents spoke Michif. Her mom had some Plains Cree. Her dad only English and French. The year after the institute, after graduating from high school with at least a 95 overall average, she'd take her BA in Indigenous Liberal Studies at the Institute of American Indian Arts. Bee's future was planned out like a chemistry experiment, measurements exact.

In Grade 8, Quinta had helped her rank all the Indigenous studies programs in North America—location, cost, number of Native faculty, depth and breadth of the program, and Quinta had insisted they add adventure as a qualifier, too—and the IAIA had come out with the top score. There, Berlin would blend the natural sciences, traditional and not-so-traditional arts, social studies, and the humanities, all with an Indigenous understanding of the world. It was perfection. Exactly right. As a graduate, she'd do something important. Something lasting.

Right before everything between them soured, Quinta had been helping her figure out what that something was.

"Berlin?"

"Good night, Dad."

He folded his arms. "You know, you can always phone me or your mom for a ride. Always. Even in the predawn hours."

He said it like he knew she'd been walking. Like he was worried for her. But still, an asterisk lived at the end of his statement. *Except when we're at the hospital.*

All she said was "I know."

"Sleep well. I love you."

"Love you back," Berlin offered because she did. Even if her parents were busy almost all the time, taking care of other people's children—she did love them. It was indisputable fact. These days, even that feeling had numbed. Tonight, tonight, it was present.

Love was integral, a fundamental part of the song.

She climbed to the second floor of the house. At the far end of the hallway was her parents' massive bedroom with their walk-in closets and en suite bathroom. Bee's room from when she'd been small was next door, with its own en suite. The two bedrooms on the other side of the house shared a bathroom. When her parents bought this place, they'd planned for a large family. But they'd not had any other babies.

Plans didn't always work out. This was something Bee hadn't thought might apply to her as much as it applied to everyone else.

She should shower, wash away the flour tacking up her hair. But she only brushed her teeth, staring into the mirror.

Bone weary, she climbed higher. The narrow stairs let out into her room, the door always open, tied to the window casing with a piece of red string. The taxicab surfaced, painted in her mind's eye. She collapsed onto her bed, peering through the skylight her mom had installed years back while on one of her home improvement kicks. The scampering of nails on the wood floors echoed through the room. Snapdragon, Bee's favorite rescue cat, missing one of her back legs, scaled the bed. And for the first time, warmed by Snap's body, surrounded by her gentle purr, Berlin was certain that it had been Kiki. Sure in the marrow of her bones where passed-down memories from the ancestors lived. Right before Berlin was claimed by sleep, she reminded herself to tell this to that impossible boy, who, like it was just that easy, laughed at all things, even pain.

Almost Three Years Ago

Anger.

Mornings, I dress this body, careful
not to wake my baby cousin,
who lets me sleep on her trundle bed,
who lets me cry at night
& doesn't call out
for a mother. She climbs next to me,
little fire with sweetgrass breath,
pressing her button nose against my shoulder
& hums.

Nothing songs, songs without words.
The kind we don't remember
our mothers humming to their taut bellies
before we join
this furious world.

Songs before breath,
warm like campfire in winter,

lasting like banked coals all through the night,
bright & living, the oranges & reds, of sacred fire.

My anger cannot come out in hums,
or tears, or by endless talk, or in burning medicines—no,
this anger is unspeakable.

Do you get me, Mr. X?

This is a farce.

But we agreed & I was taught by my mother not to break
promises, to hold myself to my word. Even if my words aren't
angry in the way you want them, they're here & in existing
on this page, I'm not breaking our bond.

Bargaining.

Where I try to get my grades up, in exchange for poems.

As in, Mr. X finds me by my locker in my bumblebee
yellow jacket, begs me to visit his classroom
after school & there, leaning hip
into desk, he offers up a bargain.

(Is this classroom a crossroads?
Is this teacher wearing devil's horns?)

If I write poems that delve
into this pain. If I bare myself to him,
all this grief, all the weighty & open
wounds, like I'm his own personal CBC
news anchor. If I spill this loss, my
whole self
on display,
he'll forget the assignments
I blew off during the months after—

(Is the teacher perched on this desk standing in as priest?
Is this classroom a confessional?)

If I make myself spectacle,
if I show him what shapes me,

if I open up Nehiyaw & carve out
missing, assumed dead, mother
& travel to the otherside, to seek my father,
to crown myself Makeda, Queen of Sheba,
to imagine the other half of me,
what I know,
what I don't,
if I show Mr. X exactly how I'm busted, broken, he'll pass me.

(Is this classroom a prison?
Is this teacher holding me against my will?)

This is a safe space, *he says, like safe*
spaces exist, like words become real
things, like safety isn't relative.
What he means is: our bargain ties us,
knots us together with leather cord.
Which is to say, we'll keep it a secret so that even the therapist
Auntie pays to see me, once a week since the RCMP stopped
looking for my mother, in that little office off the main road,
even she doesn't need to know.

Denial & Isolation.

When the hurt burrows, when the tears
dry like a forgotten creek, when
my breath calms, but sleep
refuses to take me under, I lull
myself with stories:

ONE.

She had enough of mothering,
of the messy bathroom—hair clogging
the drain—bedroom a flood of clothes,
all the living spaces, the kitchen
sticky with honey—

surfacing into her dreams.
When dreams became only

of her daughter's future
(of me-me-me),
she lost sight of herself.

& so she left (me-me-me).

TWO.

She'll call—
one day, when she's settled,
when she doesn't sleep
on someone else's couch—
to invite me back into her.

Every time the landline
rings in my auntie's home,
I stop, I hope.

THREE.

When she drove away, she
planned to come back. But
we can't always do what we plan.
Sometimes, we are swept up
by a hungry wind—no, no, not wind—
sometimes we are consumed by the tides
& the waters take what they want,
throwing us under, pulling us, wave
by wave, into the deep.

Forgetting—
not caring—
that we have wants too.

FOUR.

She's searching
for my father. Looking under
boulders & across their old haunts, the ones she loved
before she loved me.

She's searching. She's searching still—

With stories a million paths curve
away from the last minute I spent
in her presence. Within stories, she's alive
& not alive, here & not here, ready
to be called up & threaded through
this: my life without her.

These stories, a place to escape, to travel
& seek her, until she's found.

Depression.

Six photos.

One. I'm newly born, wrinkly & brownish
with warm undertones & I have more hair than any other baby
I've ever seen. Mama is curled inward, staring at me
like I've changed the world already, like I change it
breath by breath.

Two. A weed-strewn yard. It might be my uncle's
house, my cousin playing outside the frame.
I stand in a plastic bin filled to the brim, naked,
swimming in the only pool I need, my smile
radiant.

Three. Kindergarten school photo. Polka-dot top,
natural hair, because I won't suffer
the pain of braids. Missing-tooth
grin. Looking off into the middle distance
as if waiting for something to arrive.

Four. Instant. Edged with thick white borders.
Mama when she was only seventeen. Smoking,
green eyes smile as if she holds a secret & I've always
imagined: off frame, my father is seventeen too & he's

looking at her with the same smile. Would his eyes
be brown like mine? Did he refuse
to sit, to be wound up in scalp-tight braids too?

Five. Mama & me at powwow. My hair oiled, two
long snakes down my back. Beaded earrings
from a vendor's table, bought & installed
in newly pierced ears. What can't be captured:
the smell of the rodeo grounds, the way I can call
back the moment, but I can't bring my mama home
to me.

Six is infinite. A folder, on Auntie's laptop,
every single upload to my mama's
social media pages. I download
the last photos I'll ever see her in,
not trusting that the internet is forever,
not trusting they'll comfort me when I'm
old, unless I gather them in one place.
I told myself to print them at the Walmart,
make them into paper, paper to hold in hands.
I told myself that wouldn't be a sad moment
but a good one. Told myself I'd do it next
week or the week after that. But I still haven't
brought my mother's last pictures
into the world, worry I never
will, that it's easier to let go

102

than to hold on, easier to accept nothing lasts
forever.

Mr. X, is this the lesson? Nothing lasts. Nothing is forever.

Except poetry.

Bargaining.

We drove to a patch of bramble. Some place our relations knew. Some-one's uncle. Someone's kokum. They had stories about berries, where to find them. Fuzzy & sour. Fuzzy & sweet. Remember your bear bell, *my mama would say, strapping one onto her backpack.* They're hungry this time of year. Waking from a long sleep. We only take some. Remember always to leave the sweetest ones, the fattest ones, on the branch. Bears crave sweetness too. *Juice stains my fingers, my sharp chin, the collar of my Land Back tee. Lips swollen from too much of a good thing. I tongue the fattest berries, gorge myself, knowing later, when the berries are almost gone, I'll regret this. Want to have gifted each of them to my mama. For she loved them as much as I did. The best of dreams, it's how I can buy her back: trading rubies for love. I tell myself this, no word of a lie, that day, the day I gorged on the berries, I entered into an agreement without knowing what I'd bargained when I was small, trading hunger for love.*

Anger.

This is just to say

I have written
The poems
That you were
Expecting

& which
You were probably
Missing
To tabulate my final grade

Forgive me
If they are not
The poems you dreamed of,
Not the conclusions you desired I settle on.

Saturday Afternoon

Alberta Ministry of Transportation blog post: The province has completed the clearing of record amounts of snow from the Bow Valley Trail between the towns of Canmore and Exshaw. No accidents have been reported and Highway 1A is again running at normal speeds.

BERLIN

Sitting on the edge of her tidy bed, she stretched her neck but couldn't release the tightness. It didn't matter; she didn't have the time. The sun was already beginning its descent into the mountains. Berlin slipped into her parka, hurrying downstairs. She wasn't late. But she wouldn't arrive early enough to fix things at the shop. Not after sleeping the day away like she didn't have stacks of reading to get ahead on for ELA and World Religions.

"You're awake!" her mom said from the couch, curled under her prized Pendleton blanket, the fireplace lit. "I was starting to worry."

"I have to run."

"That's not very accurate, eh? We both know you don't run."

It was fact. In middle school, Berlin had refused to do more than speed-walk during that awful timed 5K her school insisted on calling the benchmark of health. And while she always beat her previous fundraising goal for the Terry Fox Foundation, she didn't run the race. "It's a saying, Mom. People say that."

"Sounds like an excuse. Almost like you don't want to talk with me."

Berlin huffed. "I have to walk at a normal pace so I'm on time for my job. Is that more accurate?"

"Wait. Come here. Are you getting sick?"

"I'm going to be late," Berlin said, but she marched over to the couch.

"You feel warm."

"I'm fine, Mom."

"But what do I know? I'm freezing so you always feel warm to me. Maybe I should get the thermometer from the first aid kit?"

"Don't you dare." Berlin laughed, because her mom wasn't serious. She was only teasing. "Like I said, I'm fine."

Her mom softened. "Want a ride? I could be convinced to go out into the cold."

"Nobody seems to believe me, but I do enjoy walking. I'll keep repeating it until it sinks in."

Her parents couldn't understand why someone would prefer to walk. Like they didn't think about the damage that cars and trucks did to the land. How her bats were losing habitat, had fewer places without vehicle noise, couldn't survive a collision.

Though much larger, neither could elk.

The only reason the bison reintroduced into the park were safe was because they were deep in the backcountry where motorized vehicles couldn't access.

"I'll ask your dad to back off the Class 7 licensing talk, how about that?"

"You might be able to reach him. Because I cannot."

"I love you, Berlin."

Bee made the hurry-up motion in the air. "Yeah, me too."

"Oof, they warn you about the teenage phase," her mom said. "And I thought we had it hard when you were biting and stabbing Cam like you were a little vampire, craving his blood."

This was what her mom had been working up to.

"What exactly did Dad tell you?"

"Nothing," she said and laughed. "He told me nothing much. But he's been texting increasingly worrisome fears that the kindergarten incident might be heading toward a resurgence."

"Never," Berlin said, and she marched to the door. "Can I go now?"

"Walk safe, baby."

"I always do," she said, knowing it was a lie. That she couldn't control what happened, not when the sun went down.

In the brisk cold, last night's failure ached. She ought to have tried harder, worked until it was done right. Screwing up should have kept Berlin awake. But the deep pull of the otherworld had grabbed firm, dragging her under.

Strange dreams plagued her rest. A taxi outside the convenience store—its paint flashing too-yellow, almost neon. The tips of Kiki's hair, deep as old blood. The exhaust melding with fog, the fog imbued with ammonia. In Berlin's dream, her bedroom window had blown open. Snow piled onto her window seat unreasonably fast. Sound from outside traveled in: Cam's laughter, that laughter devolving into frenzied sobs.

Berlin tried to scream, her body refusing. Wished for Snap to bite her. Anything to wake. To draw the lines firm again between awake and asleep.

The next dream, it was relief. Until it wasn't. Quinta, her lips kiss-bitten, her eyes vacant, twisting a long piece of red yarn around her forearm, tightening, tightening.

Jessie's nervous hand shaking.

And Cam's laugh, again, this time as sharp as his hunting knife.

It went on throughout the afternoon.

When she woke covered in sweat, the quilt tangled up in her legs, the bedroom door was closed. Pushing herself out of bed, Berlin searched. But the red yarn was nowhere to be found—

As if it had been left behind in the dream.

Exhausted, truly, yet standing naked in her bedroom searching for missing string, Berlin felt more alive than she had in months. The alive feeling had carried with her out of the house and through town on her walk. It wasn't fading.

And that made this worse. Turning around the corner, she found Joe's shiny truck parked in his normal spot. Berlin hesitated. "Creator help us all. This is disaster."

The universe didn't answer her.

It wasn't that Joe would be furious, because he didn't do furious, not with his teenage staff. Worse, he'd be *disappointed* in how badly she'd closed last night.

Berlin had only heard of Joe furious once, and that was a sec-ondhand story: in the days after Kiki had disappeared, when the

RCMP came to the shop and questioned him like he was a suspect. After the uniformed officers left, Joe punched one of the brick walls. He'd fallen to the floor, cradling his broken hand, and he cried.

She'd heard this story from Nico Vasquez, who'd graduated a year and a half ago, at a Halloween party last fall when Nico had been the kind of drunk you don't remember in the morning. He'd recited the scene from memory, holding Berlin's hands in his own, staring into her eyes, saying: *He was so fucking angry and so was Emilie. They were so fucking angry.*

But Joe's wife had been angry at Joe. For getting himself messed up with the police. For being too close to his employees, to Kiki. So said Nico, in his story.

Berlin could only imagine how it would have hurt to watch that happen to Joe, to witness his pain.

In the parking lot, the wind lifted, blowing an empty pop can across the pavement. It was too cold to stand around outside, and it was cowardly too.

She'd messed up.

Perfection, this thing she'd been pushing for, it could be possible that it wasn't as warm, as inviting, as she'd always assumed. Her dad's words came back to her: *It doesn't mean that someone like Cameron is doing it wrong if he's living in the moment . . . Not if he's happy . . .*

The wind whipped through the parking lot again with a big exclamatory gust. Berlin shivered.

She passed Joe's open office fast and pushed into the washroom hallway where she could peel herself out of her parka. Up front,

110

in the kitchen, Sasha and Ira, fraternal twins who moved to town following their famous restauranteur mother from Dubrovnik, Croatia, at the start of Grade 9, gently ribbed each other. A third voice joined in: Cameron saying something, followed by a rough laugh.

Berlin tied a very clean apron around her waist.

Ira was talking about buying a new gaming system. Sasha would rather be on the actual mountain. The siblings couldn't be more different. But everyone in Canmore loved them, wanted them at every party, at each excursion into the backcountry. Wanted their likes on social media.

While Ira wore his hair shoulder-length, sort of greasy like a musician even though he didn't have a musical bone in his body, his twin wore theirs short, with soft curls. Ira was a dirty blond. Sasha a sun-kissed mahogany brown. They both had the same nose, too big for their faces, but that, to Berlin, was charming AF. Sasha wore thick plugs in their ears, always black metal. Ira no jewelry at all. Sasha was genderqueer, using they/them pronouns exclusively—*at this time*, as Sasha often said.

Berlin enjoyed working with the two of them. But she especially liked working with Sasha. They were an artist, a thinker. They always challenged her.

Rounding the corner into the kitchen, her keys clicking against each other in her pocket, she was shocked to realize she was smiling. Then, Berlin spotted Quinta, her back to the group.

"Have you heard, Bee?" This was Ira, pivoting to cock an eyebrow.

At the mention of Berlin's name, her best friend's shoulders tightened. Every interaction lately between them was worse than

111

recovering from wisdom tooth extraction. Only with this hurt, the swelling wasn't visible. Berlin's smile faded.

"Have I heard what?" She was ready for anything. After last night's storm, she was unshakable.

Sasha smiled their pretty, welcoming smile. And then wilted, like this was bad news.

Cam stared, lips tight.

"Are we in it deep over the close? I expected that. I got us locked out. I'll take the blame."

Cam shook his head. "No, Joe understood. I told him the story."

Berlin's fingertips burned, the way they did after she'd been carding and felting wool for hours. But she hadn't touched her felting kit for over a year, when for a while, it had been her go-to stress relief. Those hard-won calluses had softened. She pressed her thumb against her fingers, to stay the burn. "Then what is it? Seriously, you're making my head hurt."

Quinta issued a rude sound. She might not be speaking to Berlin, but she was listening very carefully. That, more than anything, told Bee that her best friend wasn't as done with their friendship as it seemed. If it would help to simply ask what was wrong, Bee would do it. But under direct confrontation, Quinta's habit was to bare her teeth, to fight back.

She needed more time.

Sasha cleared their throat. "We just found out. Joe's selling the shop. To a group who will franchise PMP."

Berlin clung to the nearest metal counter. "Excuse me?"

This was the worst possible thing. Another Canmore business

112

going under, another place that made this town, if not unique, then at the very least quirky, human, livable—soon to be gone. Bee seethed. A deep-down rumble—the kind that the perfect student, the perfect employee, would never have—took over. She didn't think. She abandoned the front of the store, marching toward the boss's office.

Joe sat at his desk, hunched over his laptop, gray running through his close-cropped hair. He wore outdoor clothing, Joe's favorite: anything technical, anything from Mountain Equipment Co-op. The collared shirts he owned all had gripper snaps instead of buttons. He could blend in at events where he was expected to dress up but know he was doing it his way.

"Tell me it's not true," she said, her words coming out pointed.

He knew exactly what she meant, didn't require a lick of context. "Sorry, Bee. It's time."

The fine lines around Joe's eyes were deeper than they had been when she started work two-plus months ago. She stepped into the office. "You can't."

Joe turned his chair so that his back faced the row of pictures tacked along the wall—years of Pink Mountain history. The good employees. The rotten ones. Snapshots from when they'd disastrously tried running a mobile pizza oven to cook up the same quality eats at the base of the mountain. Joe loved telling those stories, loved his shop's history.

He smiled carefully. "As the sole owner and proprietor of this establishment, I most certainly can. And I'm doing it. We'll be ready to sign the papers this upcoming week."

Berlin sighed. Her eyes felt watery.

She hadn't cried properly in . . . months.

Joe glanced at the box of facial tissues on his desk and they stared each other down.

When Berlin spoke, she slowed, like she would if she were trying to get an A on a speech: "Franchising will destroy what makes this place special. Look what happened to the Green Bean or to Bowls, Bowls, Bowls. Now both those places are nothing but corporate trash. They've dropped wages to the provincial minimum and the food isn't quality. It doesn't taste right. And the people who work there are miserable. They can't pay their rent so half of them have a second job at the Walmart these days. Is that what you want for your legacy?"

Joe pointed to the other end of his desk, where she usually sat when they talked. Sometimes about schoolwork or FNMISA projects and people—SarahLynn's tendency to get movie-star dramatic or Vincent's excellent business sense—or sometimes about Berlin's growing pack of rescue animals. Joe told stories about the shop, the hard years making it as a Black restauranteur in a tourist town on the prairies, or about his life when he was young, before he wrecked his back, when he lived in South Portage, Winnipeg. Even back in Joe's day, it was a neighborhood where crime was high, where Black, Indigenous, and people of color lived, where they were blamed for poverty as if it were their fault.

Joe's dad had owned property in the national park, even then. But Joe said he'd gone off to try to make it on his own—to try his hand at music.

"Legacy," he said. "Who are you to talk about legacy? There's still a lot you don't know. Things to learn in this life."

And all the stories, all these conversations, were coming to an end.

She settled onto the desk stiffly. She stared at the wall of photos as if to memorize them. Now that Joe was betraying everything Pink Mountain stood for, she didn't want to engage in their ritual. But she couldn't blow him off. He was an adult, older than her parents by a bit, and she'd been raised to respect Elders and people with more life experience than her. Even worse, Joe was her friend.

Or so she'd thought.

As much of a friend as he could be.

"I've been doing this for eighteen years—longer than you've been alive. My shop is finally worth something. And more important than money, I'm ready for change. You know my dogs would love to live at the cabin full-time. Surrounded by pines and peace, the only traffic on the road caused by the occasional mountain goat. That's where I want to live out the rest of my life."

Joe's great-grandfather, who made his career as a fur trader in the 1870s, had leased the land in Jasper. It had been in the family for well over a hundred years. There was no Wi-Fi at the property. It was remote, sounded nice. But she wasn't telling him that.

"Will Emilie be happy there full-time?"

Joe cleared his throat at the mention of his much younger, white wife. "Happy enough, I suppose."

Three weeks ago, they'd had a massive argument in front of the staff. Well, Emilie had hollered and Joe had taken it. She'd called him a bully. It didn't fit. But she'd said it so full of fury that Berlin knew Emilie believed it. Their fight at work should have been a sign something was changing for the worse.

"You don't have to sell in order to retire from the day-to-day."

"I don't," he agreed. "But I want to. That's the rub."

A want, not a need. Berlin could work with that. "It's not final yet, right?"

"No," Joe said slowly, raising an eyebrow. "Not yet."

"How much time do I have before you make everything official? Exactly? I'm going to change your mind."

He leaned back into his chair, lines deepening on his forehead. "I don't think you can. It's not like this is a spur-of-the-moment decision. I've been thinking about this seriously . . . going on five months now."

"How much time do I have?"

"We sign on Thursday. At my lawyer's office." He sighed. "Berlin, you need to know that your odds of success are so slight they don't register on the bar graph."

"I have to try, Joe." Her voice was unusually warbly. "I have to."

Joe nodded. It wasn't unfettered consent. But it wasn't a no.

"Is this the best use of your time? Only last week you were saying how much maintaining your grade point average matters for your future, how Tashie has been asking you to do more and more for the Native student organization. I promise PMP will still exist and you'll have a job at the flagship store as long as you want it. You're a great employee, Berlin." He waited a beat. "Even considering the sloppy close last night."

She hung her head.

"Here now, none of that. I'm only pulling your leg. Cam explained things."

"I'm not worried for me, Joe. I'm worried for everyone who works here and the whole community, the people who love this place just as it is."

She had a selfish thought, not community-oriented at all. If she and Quinta didn't have this Pink Mountain, not whatever Pink Mountain could become, but exactly like this, they'd never make up.

And Joe, he was abandoning them. Leaving Berlin, and everyone else, out in the cold.

Like he didn't care at all.

"My on-the-book employees as of the moment of signing will have a job, protected as best as the law can do, until they're ready to move on. I've had it written into the contract. You'll get your hourly and your bonuses. Even if the new owners make changes to the business, you're grandfathered in."

He didn't get it. Before, Berlin had been sad when another of Canmore's legends went corporate. Hadn't done much but sign petitions and grumble about the unfairness of it all—and that changed exactly nothing. She should have known Pink Mountain would be the very last straw. This place had been part of Bee's childhood. In the Chambers house, the phone number to order was tacked on the fridge next to all other important numbers: poison control, her parents' offices, her parents' and her aunties' cells, and both the in-town vet and the local wildlife rescue.

This wasn't only about Berlin or Quinta or the others in the kitchen. It was about stopping capitalism's endless march to ruin everything too.

She stared at the wall over Joe's head, at all the memories that wouldn't have a home once this place became yet another overpriced pizza joint. What would happen to the local Native hunters? What would they do, losing the premium Joe paid, the one that nobody else would? Joe paid more than the ritziest chophouses in Banff because Joe's politics were good.

He believed in Black Lives Matter and in human rights for all. Indigenous rights over settler wants.

In paying high wages for work. Even if his employees were teenagers.

In Land Back, full stop, no asterisk, no marginalia. When he died, the Jasper property was deeded to a coalition of Indigenous Nations whose traditional and ancestral territory ran through the park.

The photo collage on the wall was mesmerizing. Before Tashie got a gig working for her Nation's band office, she had worked alongside Kiki and Nico Vasquez. Not that Berlin could find Nico's photo up here. In Tashie's, she was smiling, red sauce on her nose.

It wasn't that Bee was searching, but in the way of things since last night, Kiki was on Berlin's mind. Her photo was different from the others. She wasn't wearing a uniform ball cap. She was maybe sixteen. Her hair was big, natural. Her earrings were beaded hoops in vibrant neons. In front of her sat a huge plate of half-eaten fries, an empty milkshake glass, and what remained of the main course: a discarded pickle.

It felt loving.

Like whoever took this photo had loved Kiki.

Joe wasn't in the frame, but for some reason Berlin knew that he was the one who'd treated her to lunch. The universe's song focused in here, the drums repeating their pattern.

She'd been silent too long. Joe watched her carefully.

Turning away from the photograph, she had an unpleasant thought. It tasted of ammonia, the way ice rinks did. But it was impossible, this thing. Joe couldn't have hurt Kiki. He'd been heartbroken when she went missing. Inconsolable, according to Nico Vasquez, who had witnessed Joe's distress at being treated like a suspect, in the prep room, right outside this office.

None of the other staff had photos off the premises, none out of their ball caps and aprons. Joe didn't hang with his staff after work. Personal chats happened on the property, usually while prepping vegetables or cutting dough.

But what if?

What if Joe's love had been toxic?

A shiver ran down Bee's spine. Suddenly, she wanted to throw up the nothing she had in her stomach. The safest thing would be to get herself out of this tiny room, until she could think it all through properly. "I should get back to work," she said.

"That would be wise." Joe sighed again. "Let this thing you're obsessing on go, would you?"

Why his words fit for both conversations, the one between them and the one in her head, she didn't know. Small outrage fueled her then and outrage quelled sadness. Outrage she could work with. She pushed off the desk and walked to the staff washroom, ignoring Ira, who was at the prep counter slicing rounds of fresh mozzarella, likely eavesdropping.

She needed a minute. And then she'd do her job. If not perfectly, then at least as close as humanly possible. To figure out if Joe, a person who had always, always supported her, had anything to do with Kiki's disappearance, Berlin would need to be perfection itself.

The lights gave the room a sickly glow. She smoothed out her bangs, pulled her hair back into a low ponytail. Her cheeks were pale, her eyes shadowed. But she could do this. She'd been coloring inside the lines since she was three. Her parents had been so ecstatically proud of that. It was a sharp memory, still.

Kiki had trusted Joe. It was the way she and Tashie talked about their jobs during FNMISA meetings, how often they volunteered Pink Mountain to donate lunches for the Elders' program, how clear it was that both Tashie and Kiki regretted quitting.

But Kiki's extracurriculars and her dismal grades needed attention more than she needed a job. By then, her mom's life insurance had come through. A small unwanted mercy.

Washing her hands with cold water because the washroom water warmed slow, Berlin worried and wondered when this good job, this good place, had gone wrong too. She opened the door and stepped into the tight hallway, moving with purpose like she always did, only to collide with Jessie like they were playing one of those full-contact sports.

JESSIE

Oof.

Impact.

Berlin's hand smashed into Jessie's stomach. Jessie's chest into Berlin's shoulder. Walking with determination might be hot, but it stung. Only the hurt didn't last. And the sheer thrill of getting this up-close was worth it.

Ye gods.

Jessie took it all in. Even after a jolt, Bee's glasses stayed in place. The jaunty angle of her chin as she tried to pretend nothing had happened. Her bangs. Straight cut. Full under the brim of the baseball cap.

It was all hot. So hot.

"I'm sorry." Berlin stepped back into the washroom to create space between them, all prim and proper. With parkas lining the other wall, they were still awful close.

"It's not even a thing. No need to do an apology," Jessie said, practically beaming down at Berlin.

Ye gods, ye gods.

This one, she was put together like a flight attendant. No flyaway hairs. Her clothing clean, maybe even ironed. Yet, her lips were constantly reddened, a little too plump. No, Berlin was like Snow White—if Snow White were Métis. Paired with her new glasses, those lips were the one and only feature that suggested she wasn't fully zipped up, that she could go wild, if she wanted to snap that way. They were the perfect kissable lips.

Jessie felt a pang in her chest. An actual, honest-to-JC pang. Snow fucking White. That was a dangerous reference. To be awakened by a kiss.

If Berlin woke up . . . if she let her hair get mussed on occasion . . . Jessie's body tingled.

Action, action.

Do it.

Yes.

And so Jessie did what she wanted. Like she did almost all the time when it came to kissing. And she'd been holding this back for an age: since last year, when she first noticed Berlin walking that serious walk one Monday afternoon, in the hallway, smack in the middle of fifth period. Jessie had cut out of Social as if to use the washroom, but instead she'd smoked a half dart, and when she stepped back into the building, she'd been blown over by Berlin, walking into the midafternoon sunlight, her hips swaying a titch.

In the tight, dead-end hallway, it was like they were the only girls left in the world. Jessie stepped close and this time Berlin didn't move away. In retrospect, Jessie would think: the girl didn't really have an escape path. But in the absolute present, Jessie leaned in, tilted Bee's ball cap up, and pressed her lips against Berlin's red ones. She moved gently.

This was a wake-up kiss. A let-your-hair-down kiss.

Berlin froze. She let a little breath escape.

It mingled with Jessie's.

Just right. That was the wrong fairy tale, her back-brain offered.

She smiled against Bee's lips, then kissed her again, harder. Come on. Wake up, wake up. And still Berlin didn't move. At all. A tiny disappointment announced itself. A sleeping princess maybe needed a prince to wake her. Those were the breaks in patriarchal fairy stories. Jessie pulled away, forcing space between their bodies when for a small time there had been basically none.

Then, Berlin's hand jetted up, fingers thrumming along her lips as if to check that they still belonged to her.

Jessie's cheeks flared with heat. In the best way. Maybe she'd misread the inaction. Berlin was suffering from kiss shock. That delicious lag between body and brain.

And as soon as Berlin spoke, the heat turned bitter.

"Why did you do that?" She said it like she'd been hurt. And then the most devastating sentence emerged, in a too-quiet voice. "That was my first kiss."

Jessie was struck. Not awestruck, only struck. With a two-by-four. "Oh JC. Oh fuck. I'm sorry. I . . . I couldn't help myself. Like my body hijacked my higher being. My thinking self. This happens . . . t-to me," Jessie stammered, taking two steps into the prep room to give Berlin real space. "More often than sometimes, to be real honest."

Still, Berlin's fingers pressed into her lips, shaking, like Jessie's did when she needed a smoke more than she needed oxygen. Even if it tempted fucking fate to strike her with the big C all over again.

Berlin had frozen.

This was bad. Very bad.

Noise echoed from the front of the house. They weren't alone.

At all. Anyone could walk back here to fetch something from their bag, to use the washroom.

And then it hit Jessie, hard like a sock with a bar of soap weighing down the toe box, like the very last time she'd roughhoused with her brothers before her father outlawed it as unseemly: Jessie's kiss was basically workplace sexual assault. And Joe's office door was open.

He could hear all this. If he were listening while the fairy tale got rewritten: Jessie as the Wicked Witch. Certifiable impulse-control issues mixed with a tendency toward self-destruction.

"I'm so sorry," she said again, more quietly, meaning every word. Her mind had caught up with her body and it was horrified. Jessie's mind usually was. But this was next level. "I'll leave and I won't come back, and you never need to see my sorry face again."

Berlin laughed under her breath. "No, it's fine. I'm . . . just exhausted." She slumped then. Leaned against the doorframe like it was the only dang thing holding her up. "I'm having a really bad, no-good day all of a sudden and I honestly cannot tell if this made it the smallest bit better or a lot worse."

Jessie exhaled. "Better, I'm going to hope. When you get a chance to reflect."

She hadn't fully fucked it. Like her parents were sure she would if they stopped exerting their influence on their only female child. That word: *female*. The way her parents said it made her hate it more. Because the narrative for women was so limiting, especially if your father was a card-carrying member of the United Conservative Party. Besides, Jessie couldn't be that storybook person, the one her father wanted her to be. It was physically impossible. "Ye gods, I really messed up the consent thing."

This time Berlin laughed louder. Her smile was less shaky. Her ball cap, tilted rakishly upward. And Jessie hated to think it, but this Berlin, a little off-kilter, was even more of a stunner.

"Yeah, you did," she agreed.

A person could become addicted to Bee when she broke out of her mold. It would be the kind of rush you'd never be able to stop yourself from wanting. Jessie checked her phone. She'd been exactly on time when she'd rolled in. Now they were late. Still, she knew she owed Berlin more than fevered thoughts. The ones rolling through after that kiss: more, please, and yes, that's what I want.

She owed a reciprocal moment of vulnerability. "I've . . . Okay, I'm going to just say it, like rip the *Bob's Burgers* Band-Aid off fast." Jessie slowed. "I've never kissed a girl before."

Berlin's head cocked to the side, like she was thinking. She fixed her hat. When she spoke, she'd found her composure again. And she served a devastating set-down. "Can we forget this happened? Entirely? It's not that I don't . . . It's that I can't. Not tonight. Or this week. Actually, I'm going to say I'm booked until spring. Can we table this until the spring?"

Jessie nodded.

What had she expected? A moment of something real between them? This wasn't a Disney flick; it was real life. Gathering her ball cap, Jessie forced it on top of her curls. A second after Bee left, a new brewing anxiety inhabited Jessie's body.

She could use a smoke, but turned out that only made her nerves worse. It was a terrible, horrible cycle.

She'd vibed hard with kissing a girl. As much as she thought she would. Next time, she'd do the pretty and ask first. It wasn't NASA science. Consent was common courtesy. But somewhere, behind the anxiety that made her hands and legs unsteady, it was nice knowing that suddenly the world was open a little wider than it had been before.

Girls, what a revelation.

As she tied her apron, Jessie smiled. Her father would hate this. And that made things all the sweeter.

CAM

The neon lights inside PMP pulsed. Cam blinked. He'd been staring into space. Whipping up breakfast for his sisters, even having his mom and dad at home, cuddled up on the couch together, both of them recovering from late nights, hadn't shaken the storm from his heart. Family, normally, was the cure for everything foul. But he'd dreamed of the wapiti, her flesh filled out, her heart beating, her eyes living pools. As if she could peer into the secret center of him, where he huddled, in a bid to stay warm, safe, loved.

The wapiti, she'd been overlarge instead of emaciated. He'd tasted her musk, a little like cattle, but fuller, like he could sense in her very smell her desire to run.

The wapiti hadn't spoken. It wasn't one of those dreams. This was serious shit. No cartoon spirit guide, hamming it up for laughs.

Underneath the wapiti's hot breath, Cam had sensed his cousin. Not her body or her voice or even her scent, but a presence, like her name, in all caps, the way she used to sign everything in a hurried, proud flourish: KIKI CHEYANNE SOUND.

He slammed a piece of dough onto the flour-covered counter to soften it, pushing away the weird feeling the dream had left in his head. Cam liked to take the dough out a half hour earlier. To let it relax naturally. But he hadn't been on days today. He'd arrived a bit early to offer up their story, so Berlin wouldn't have to. Last night, she'd done him a solid.

At the build counter, Ira was arguing with his sibling. "How'd you do it? Again? I outsell you on the permanent menu."

"But I create things that the people want to try. You're . . . basic."

"No, you didn't."

"I did."

"That's the third unforgivable thing you've spoken to me today."

Not that Cam was taking sides, but Sasha had a winner with the Every Day Is Taco Tuesday pizza.

Saltwater crust with cornmeal bottom, house-made chunky salsa featuring heirloom tomatoes and Peppadew peppers, organic ground beef. Topped with shredded lettuce, more tomatoes, sharp cheddar, scallions, and gentle dollops of avocado crema. Optional: fresh jalapeños and other in-house pickled hot peppers. 37

To make it wild, swap out beef for the daily ethically harvested local game. +8

Gentle dollops! That was the good stuff. Even the description was art.

127

Sasha had put it on the board, since Cam hadn't trusted he'd manage all of that without screwing it up. Even now it was hard to read when the letters wouldn't remain a finished picture in his head long enough to decode.

To each person their own strengths.

Sasha and Ira continued one-upping each other while they moved around the kitchen stocking stations for the dinner rush.

"Do not."

"Ira, I live with you. I know this to be true."

Cam worked the dough. His strengths were something like: holding his family together, working that lane stitch on Sami's regalia, being able to laugh about almost anything. It was the most predictable thing in his life—laughter—other than the fact that the day would break, the rivers would run, and that good sun would set, letting the moon have a turn in the sky.

But today, something was rotten.

At home, Sami had called him out. Her teachers always said she was incredibly emotionally literate. "What is wrong?" she signed.

The whole family had learned to sign, even Kiki, long before Kiki had been forced to move in.

"Nothing," Cam signed back. Signs worked in his brain as easy as speech. But if Sami had decided she communicated best by writing things down, Cam would have been right next to her. He would have been slow like a turtle. But he'd have rocked a good shell.

His baby sister had frowned. But she'd let it go, biting into her French toast, ending the conversation.

He threw the dough against the counter again. There was a

sweet spot. Too cold and it was stiff. Too warm and you'd put holes through it with your fingers as it stretched out to fit the pan. But you could overwork the dough, too—make it stiff, without tenderness.

That was a life lesson.

One Bee could maybe work on. If she was a tad more elastic, she'd be happier. It was like yoga for the personality.

That brought forth a smile.

In the kitchen the siblings still bickered, but now about whether Ira should leave the vehicle they shared for Sasha or if Ira would swing by at closing. "That way the truck will be warm, Sash."

"You'll fall asleep. Strand me here."

"That was once!"

Cam laughed. "I'll give you a ride if you want, Sasha."

That was when Berlin stepped back into the kitchen. The whole vibe shifted. Cam hadn't meant to do it, but he pulled his chest up. Even slouching around Bee felt like breaking some unspoken rule.

Today, she was back to her no-nonsense self, as if she harnessed control over her feelings that quick. As if they hadn't spoken to each other like people yesterday—

Berlin would correct him, remind him that had been only this morning.

As scary, as intense, as it had been, Cam had liked having Bee with him. He hadn't wished for someone else to step into her mukluks. Not his buddies. Not his mom or his sisters. Certainly not his dad. Berlin had felt right. On that instinct level. Like she cared. Maybe even understood beyond thinking, right into feeling, how close to losing control he had been.

He'd tried to stick to the script. He remembered now. Asking her if she was a Coke or Pepsi Native and her no-nonsense response: *Honestly, neither.*

Soon, he'd tease her over that.

Stretching a new piece of dough, Cam realized it, all fast and sudden—what his favorite former teacher, Ms. Ducharme, called an epiphany—that, probably, all this assuming Bee hadn't warmed to him was in his own head.

In all likelihood, she didn't look down her nose at him. That Bee's stuff, what she said and did, it was about her. He threw his head back and laughed, loud and long. The heartsickness retreated. And miracle upon miracles, Berlin glanced his way, one side of her mouth curving up into a pert half smile. It wrinkled her nose.

"Jessie, you're on cash tonight," Berlin said. "You had a whole day practicing on the phones and it's more of the same."

Not waiting for a reply, Bee examined her cut table, shifting the knife to the right-hand side, where she liked it. She hauled a stack of now-cool pizza pans to his station. There was color high up in her cheeks. A blush or muddled anger.

She wasn't fully under control.

Worse, she was upset.

"What's got you all flustered?" Cam asked with the kind of smile he'd use with Sami. It wasn't the wicked grin his school buddies were used to. Not that they'd had much to do with him since he left. His out-of-town friends lived in the Calgary suburbs and on Blood and Piikani Nation lands. A long way to travel when Cam was working full-time. And taking care of his sisters. That, without

130

factoring in the LeBaron's relative unreliability.

"I'm fine," Berlin said a beat or two later. But she didn't storm away. The red stayed in her cheeks. "It's nothing."

She stood next to Cam, her back ramrod straight, staring across the road at the convenience store. With floor-to-ceiling windows, PMP had prime visibility and a decent view of the street. If Cam had been paying attention last night, he might have glimpsed Kiki too. But he'd been dicking around, joking with that couple.

Berlin sighed. She was mouthy today.

"Joe selling, it's really throwing you into a tangle, eh?"

Like always, Cam had been off base. He'd been so sure of Joe, of this place staying as it was, he'd started to assume he had a future here. Maybe it would have become one of those stories where a longtime employee eventually bought the place.

"It's a terrible idea," Bee said in her haughtiest tone.

"Did the boss ask what you thought?"

Softening, she glanced his way. "No, but that doesn't mean I don't have strong opinions."

"Bee . . ." Cam laughed. "You have strong opinions about everything. If you were a Cylon, it would be your default programming. I'd be worried about the state of the universe itself if you didn't have a strong opinion to offer up on all things."

"I shouldn't ask . . . ," she hedged. "But what is a Cylon?"

"The robot antagonists on my mom's—and, well, mine, too—our favorite TV show, *Battlestar Galactica.*"

She frowned, her eyebrows drawing close. "Is that how you see me? Like a machine?"

There was true curiosity in her voice. Also, maybe, a little hurt.

"It's not a burn." He wanted to tell her the Cylons were hot. And brilliant. But Cam's better self stepped in. "You're just firmly that type. You know the one? Don't you?"

He wasn't playing. It was on the tip of his tongue.

"And you're type I'll-laugh-about-it-and-it'll-shake-out-in-the-wash. Type it'll-all-be-all-right, eh?"

He laughed, nodding. She'd pegged him and managed to correct him, too, in the same sentence. Cam knew he was mixing fandoms and did not give an owl's hoot: she was sharp like a lightsaber. It was work, but he schooled his face, his mood. "Neither of those are bad things. It's just another way of looking at the world."

Now she smiled at him. "You know, my dad said the same thing last night—I mean, early this morning."

"See, I'd have let 'last night' stand. You and I both know what you meant."

"But it wasn't—"

"—accurate," he said, right as she did.

Berlin spit out a small laugh. And Cam wanted to revel. Only yesterday, she'd been so straitlaced that sometimes he worried she really was a Cylon. Though the show was old, at his house they had all the DVDs. Including the spinoff, which Kiki had—

Cam's cousin wasn't far from his mind today. When he'd returned along the highway, the weather had calmed. The SUV had been cleared away. Those snowdrifts were intense, challenging for the LeBaron. A part of him worried the SUV—with its toxic green glowing decals—had never been there at all.

Yet whatever had happened, or hadn't, Kiki's presence was sharper now. The unyielding grief coming back not in waves but in electric jolts along the crest of every memory.

Berlin reached out, laid a hand on his forearm for a second, before the printer next to his station started to run out tape—the dinner rush was starting.

"I should get to work." She retracted her warmth, threw a tentative glance at Jessie, pushed those librarian glasses up so that they were perched high on her nose, and stalked across the kitchen to her big knife.

It was the second real conversation they'd ever had. Her touching his arm. That was . . . a mystery. The universe, she was a beautiful quagmire of weird and wondrous, inexplicable things. Cam tore orders from the printer and started shaping dough in earnest, thinking, yeah, he could be happy doing this, with these great people, for the rest of his life. But that wasn't in the cards for Cam.

Maybe an hour passed. Joe peered into the kitchen. "I'm off for the night. Do you all have what you need?" he asked the room, stepping around the oven, making his way past Berlin toward the drink fridge. He grabbed a to-go root beer from behind the register.

Bee's voice was icier than the windchill in bitterest January. "Why do you care? You're selling, aren't you?"

Joe tsked against his teeth. If he engaged, he'd be arguing all night. Berlin was good at arguments, at having follow-up statements for everything. Cam couldn't even put together bullet points yet. How he felt about Joe selling, about Jessie's rumor being truth, about Cam's own future becoming cemented before he'd had a chance to think it through.

On the other side of the oven, still carefully building pizzas, Sasha, who wasn't afraid of Berlin at all, said, "That wasn't kind, Bee."

Their creation, the Every Day Is Taco Tuesday pizza, was selling like hotcakes.

It was a twisted metaphor, but it gave Cam an idea. He pulled out his phone, and since he couldn't use voice memo without the others hearing him, he typed: *hotcake pizza*. As he shoved his phone into his apron pocket, Berlin spoke again: "Well, he can't care that much if he's walking away."

Cam stepped around the oven. Pizzas were backing up on the upper track. Bee tightly held the tongs she used to lift hot pans from the oven.

"Berlin." Joe didn't drop his voice, was speaking to all of them, in a way. "I get that you're angry. That this came as a shock. Even that you're hurting. But you have to know this wasn't an easy decision. I care about you. I do. You know I never had kids of my own. I've loved being here for you all. Still, it's time."

She exhaled through her nose. It flared the littlest bit. And Cam realized how that idiosyncrasy—no way in heaven, hell, or the Catholics' in-between place that Cam could spell that word right—was completely, totally, fully adorable. He stepped back to his station, ripped orders from the printer.

Soon the sound of metal on metal returned as Berlin extracted pizzas from the track, laying them on the counter while she caught up on cutting and boxing.

Joe took his root beer and left. For his big house in town, where his smoking-hot wife, Emilie, was likely running one of her Peloton classes. For a while, even Cam's mom had been on that kick. So had Kiki. In fact, his cousin had started it. On the advice of her coach.

Everything today returned to his cousin.

Well, not everything. Bee's nostrils flaring. There was another tiny epiphany. She'd sat comfortably in a box, labeled with that chalkboard paint Sami loved, as his mom's best friend's inflexible daughter for so long. He didn't want her to hate him, but he didn't need to add her to the list of people he cared about either.

The very last thing Cam needed was to find Berlin's nose or anything else about her person cute enough that he gave it a second thought. Or a third. Those were reserved for the most important things: thinking up hilarious riddles for Sami or new ways to tease Tanya and Callie. And here he was, still on about Berlin Chambers's nose, throwing dough up in the air in showy moves the boss didn't like but Cam practiced because they thrilled him, because sometimes the world called for bold moves, and because, for a moment, Cam had needed to throw something.

Across the kitchen, Berlin had simmered down. But a pot could simmer so long that all the water evaporated. And the scorched pot would always smell a little like burning even after you'd soaked it, cleaned it with a scratchy S.O.S. pad, the weird blue ink leaking out but never fully wiping away the unseen stain.

Twice in a matter of weeks after Kiki went missing, he'd gone to boil water for Kraft Dinner, to feed his sisters and himself, and had somehow gotten distracted. It was the second time that sealed it as laughable. Because had Cam fucked up the same pot? No. He'd wrecked another piece of his mom's fancy cookware.

The way her face had remained blank, how she'd said: *Really, Cameron? Might as well do the whole set now. So they match.*

How they'd both laughed until they fell to the kitchen floor.

Even so. Berlin simmering, without anyone keeping a close eye on the pot, was bad news. She didn't know she needed Cam, the high school dropout, but she did. Somehow Berlin had slipped into that gray zone, where she had people around her but maybe not enough were paying attention. Her parents worked a lot. She'd been on opposite schedules from Quintana-Roo almost since they started. The girl had attempted to walk home in the middle of the night—okay, in the very early morning.

If someone had been watching closer, the morning Kiki left for her early-bird curling practice, maybe, maybe she'd be safe.

He could watch Berlin, he could help her out, he could give her lifts home, he could do all this and that didn't mean he needed to start caring for her or her cute nose.

BERLIN

The line out the door evaporated just before ten p.m. Berlin cleaned her station. She was parched. But the rhythm of pulling pizzas, the practiced wrist fling used to box them up, and the precise addition of final touches had focused her thoughts.

"I'll put together dinner?" Sasha offered. "Not the taco pizza. I'm already sick of it. Someone gather the sodas."

From her place at the cash register, Jessie smiled. "Joe's really okay with that?"

Everyone nodded and saved Berlin from answering. "Water for me, please."

"Sure thing, Bee."

Jessie was fitting in great. If a person ignored the incident earlier.

Tonight, half the pies coming through the oven were Sasha's inspired-by-tacos pizza, and the extra work to finish each one with fresh add-ons—well, someone other than Bee might have balked.

It was exactly, perfectly, what she needed. Her hands had moved; her mind had worked over the problem.

A plan came together all at once.

Almost like it was obvious.

They needed to demonstrate. To protest. To get the rest of Canmore upset enough to leave their homes and stand outside Pink Mountain in the cold. That would show Joe what really mattered. She wasn't the only person who believed selling to corporate people from Toronto or Vancouver so they could put a neon sign in towns across the country was a disastrous idea. Everyone else just didn't know they agreed with her yet.

Big opinions. Yes, that tracked. But robot? It stung. Even if only because it might ring a little, a very tiny bit, true.

As she waited for whatever Sasha created to emerge from the oven, Berlin brushed flour from her apron and it hit her. Things could worsen. The buyers might be Americans. The way Tim

Hortons had been sold to Burger King, which was owned by Kraft Heinz. She thanked her Grade 9 Business class for that knowledge, remembered how Quinta had been right beside her, shocked at how insidious it all was. Unknowingly, Mr. Prasad had done the exact opposite thing that he and the Alberta curriculum had intended. Rather than ensnare them into the boring cult of capitalism, that class had radicalized them.

Everything was international these days. Or aspired to be. But some things should stay local. Were better that way.

Joe leaving them was deeply wrong.

Sasha wandered over to the cut station. "I'll finish these."

"I don't mind."

"Don't you want to read ahead in your English homework or something?" they teased.

Actually, she did. "But I don't have to. I finished next week's reading on Thursday, during lunch."

"I eat my lunch at lunch."

She flicked the first pizza off the pan and onto the cutting board. "Some of us can multitask, Sash."

"Isn't that what I'm doing?" they asked, grabbing the insert of arugula from the mini fridge. "Cooking and having a conversation simultaneously?"

"Some would argue sprinkling spicy greens on pizza isn't quite cooking."

Sasha laughed. "Well, this is a conversation, right, bella ragazza?"

"Italian," she said, and kept cutting.

"You win again."

"Romance languages are too easy. Try harder, would you?" Even if tonight was heartbreaking, now that she had a plan, she could smile.

At first, the entire crew ate. But once several slices of Sasha's newest recipes-in-progress were chowed down, Cam started up conversation: "The arugula is good with pepperoni."

Jessie offered a big smile. "Controversial food opinion incoming. I'm more into the pineapple, apple, and fig. It's brilz. My tongue is very much happy."

A wave of heat rushed over Berlin. Her arms, neck, cheeks. She thought she'd buried that unexpected kiss way deep in her subconscious. But Jessie mentioned her tongue and Bee's whole body reacted.

She'd done a garbage job compartmentalizing.

Something to work on. Even if Berlin didn't want to be robotic, she couldn't *feel* everything, all the time. In this life, a person needed to distance themself. Needed to be a little numb to survive it all.

There would be time to fix things later, to consider that kiss, her snobbery over Cam's life choices, and the inexplicable forever-upsetting Quinta situation. The only way Berlin would succeed was by leaning into her tendencies, even if, maybe, for the first time in her life she was thinking they could be problematic.

"Pineapple does not belong on pizza," Cam volleyed back. "It's a minor crime."

"I believe it's a scam to buy salad dressing." Sasha shrugged, joining in. The gesture was very European, so refined it seemed practiced. "I know, I know, you're shocked."

"Even ranch?" Cam asked, mock-worried.

"Isn't ranch like tang-ified cow's milk? And aren't most Indigenous people lactose intolerant? Or is that a microaggression?"

"That's low, Jessie." Cam held a straight face. "To go for my body's one weakness."

Berlin couldn't help herself. "Only one?"

"Not you, too, Bee? Don't tell me you rep for team pineapple."

"One, yes, I totally do. And two, I saw you take a Lactaid. But I've also heard rumors that you"—Berlin smiled wickedly—"once broke your nose by running smack into a door. That fact suggests you probably have other weaknesses. You know, like for example, you cannot spell to save your life."

Cam's jaw dropped. "You're right, I have at least three fatal flaws."

"So do I," Jessie said. "Maybe even four."

"Topic change, friends." Sasha cleaned their fingers with a napkin. "I'm thinking I'll pitch the savory-and-sweet dish next time. What do you all think? The arugula-and-cured-meat combo has been done before. It's not . . ."

Cam smiled big, not at all upset he lost. "Sasha enough?"

They curled their lip, mimicking a self-conscious expression before nodding. "I'm building a brand, my flawed friend."

Cam laughed, throwing his floppy-haired head back, far enough he dislodged his ball cap. He twisted awkwardly, caught it.

Jessie cheered. Sasha slow clapped.

It wasn't that Berlin didn't know that as a team they needed to decompress. Everyone other than Cam was juggling school and work—and sometimes at least another major life thing. Like

140

a best friend cutting a friendship off without explanation. While this chitchat was fun, none of Berlin's coworkers were seeing the long-term effects of what had been dropped on them. What would happen in a month or a year if Joe was allowed to sell Pink Mountain, allowed to leave them.

She cleared her throat. "Do you all realize that once Joe sells, the pizza of the day might not be a thing anymore? Or we won't have carte blanche on ingredients? That the new owners will care for money above all else?"

Sasha shrugged again. A small, sad gesture. Next to them, Jessie fidgeted, her leg bumping against the bottom shelf of the prep counter.

"Even if Joe protects us in the contract, the new owners will simply find a reason to fire us. And then—ta-da!—they won't have any grandfathered-in employees." Berlin wiped her hands on the rough eco-paper towels Cam had torn from the roll, the one that always sat on the shelf next to his phone charger. "It will be as easy as dinging that one for not doing the wash one afternoon even though the shift had been real busy. Or deciding that you, Jessie, are taking too many smoke breaks. Or, Sasha, if the wrong person buys PMP, they'll find a way to get you out. They'll make up a reason. Fall back on the easiest thing: thinly veiled prejudice positioned as the moral right."

"That's how this all works, Bee," Cameron said, helping himself to another slice. "It's that late-stage capitalism at its best, eh?"

Sasha cracked a smile. A real one. "Cam's right. What's there to do? And, honest to God, Bee, I would be signing up to sell my restaurant, too, for the right price. This is the dream for a restauranteur."

"But you love the food, Sash," she said. "You can't deny it."

They offered their most pointed look. "One can love food and still desire to be financially successful."

Berlin didn't fault anyone who needed to put a meal on the table or even those who wanted to be comfortable enough not to worry about bills. Her parents were doctors. They'd pushed through the schooling knowing that once they graduated, they'd be okay for the rest of their lives. Berlin didn't fault people; she faulted the system.

And maybe those who refused to see they were ensconced in a system. Certainly, folks who thought there was only one way, one system. If that was too close to home after her dad's speech this morning, well, so what.

She tamped down the uncomfortable feeling.

Sasha leaned against the counter, anticipating her rebuttal. Like go ahead and say it, so I can shut you down, little Bee. Even though they were ethically opposed to her in this, Berlin found Sasha appealing.

They were her first crush. When she'd told Quinta how she felt, Quintana-Roo had agreed that Sasha was gorgeous, eminently crushable. A perfect choice.

It wouldn't serve to offer Sasha the same speech she'd given the boss. She pushed her glasses up on her nose even though they were already in place. "Maybe the real problem is nobody really cares about anyone other than themselves these days. Sure, go get your money and don't worry about who you screw over in the process.

142

About what you destroy on the way to the bank."

Berlin grabbed her water. She tightened and untightened the blue plastic cap. Quinta, Joe, and now Sasha. It was too much.

But Cameron met her eye and for a moment they were both thinking about Kiki. How for almost a week the town had rallied. Half the high school had ditched to come to the first public call for justice in front of the cop shop. Joe had closed Pink Mountain to be there. People over profits—that had been Joe's policy.

He hadn't wavered.

Until now.

By the end of that week only Cam's family, Berlin's, and two of Kiki's curling friends had still been stapling up posters. If the RCMP ever cared, it was that first week in September. If they had found Kiki, alive and well, they'd have earned a spot on national news. They could have claimed they had a handle on the Missing and Murdered Indigenous Women, Girls, and Two-Spirit human rights crisis. See, they'd found one. They would have emphasized Native over Black, of course. As if it was possible to parse a person in that way. The police would have styled themselves heroes in the story, even if in this imagined universe, Kiki had saved herself.

"Oh, Bee." Sasha moved closer.

One night, when it was only the two of them in the shop and no one in town was ordering pizza, Sasha had told her all about their father's family. Every one of them, murdered at Srebrenica by paramilitary Bosnian Serbs.

They'd told her their family's story, and now Bee carried it alongside her own. Bee's uncle, her mom's older brother, had died as a

143

teenager after an OxyContin overdose on the streets of Edmonton. Then there was Kiki, and Kiki's mom, and all the other Native women, girls, and Two-Spirit people whose stories Berlin carried.

"I'm fine," she said to the group. "Stop looking at me like that."

Sasha nodded. Cam and Jessie stared a second longer, then, paradoxically, looked at each other as if they knew a secret.

It wasn't the same thing. Pink Mountain wasn't a person. But even in Berlin's numb state, this place was important to her. "It's not the same thing as when we stop caring about people," she said aloud to her coworkers.

Not exactly friends.

"But it's a symptom of the same disease. When we can let the things that bring us together fall apart, become places without souls, it's another way we learn not to care about each other. Or about the land. Capitalism eats and eats and never satiates its hunger. It eats without thought. And that's not eating anymore. That's consumption." She didn't look at Cam, who was finishing off the last of the pepperoni pizza. "Am I making sense? Or is what I believe absolute garbage?"

Cameron pushed himself up to sit on the prep counter. He was the first to speak. "No. It's not that."

Sasha's green eyes didn't break away from Bee's when they said, "You are right. There has to be more."

Before last night, or maybe before the brain fog, the sleepless nights, the feeling that she'd been a ghost walking through her own life, those were words Berlin craved.

Tonight, it didn't hit like it used to.

144

Tonight, a new feeling. Not rightness for the sake of rightness, for the sake of perfection. But instead this verved because this was heart-right.

Jessie smiled at Bee in a dreamy way. It was warm, comforting. Confusing AF too. Somehow, only hours ago Jessie had totally, completely kissed Berlin. Whenever she sort of thought of it, her lips tingled.

But there were more important things than first kisses.

First kisses didn't matter in the same way. They couldn't or the whole universe would fall to pieces.

"So, what's your plan?" Jessie asked, her eyes softening.

"We have to help Joe see how this place matters to the community, that it's more valuable—and I don't mean financially—it's more valuable in the way that matters most, as it is, having Joe here with us."

"A strike?" Sasha asked. "We are very good at those in Europe."

Berlin's stomach rolled. She didn't want to hurt Joe's business. She wanted to stop him from hurting *his* business. "No. But maybe if people were to start writing letters? About what PMP means to the community? Of their memories and how this place is more than pizza? Joe's been here, in town, for like more than eighteen years. That's forever."

Berlin fell silent. She didn't know what else to say. If she hadn't convinced them now, she might never get them on her side.

Normally, she'd at least have Quinta around to pitch in. A project this big, tackled alone—really, truly alone—would be something only Perfect Berlin firing on all cylinders could manage. And somehow, over the course of uncountable months, Bee had misplaced that girl.

Maybe she'd always been a shimmery mirage.

An ideal.

The pipe that looked like a pipe but wasn't one.

"I'm in. Can't write a letter to save my life . . ." Cam laughed self-consciously. "But I can recruit. My sisters' soccer and curling teams have always been sponsored by PMP. And Joe gave me this job even though I struggle with some of the basic tasks. You know, my learning disability. Writing, reading, and such."

He didn't say spelling.

He wasn't that cruel. To call her out.

Even when she deserved it.

Instead, he'd said it like it was just another thing. Hot shame inhabited Berlin's body. Her fingertips ached with it as if she'd burned herself on the oven. She'd always known that for Cameron it wasn't only laziness; some of it might have been not enough drive or even a lack of interest. But over the years, throughout the classes they'd shared together, she hadn't ever considered that he had a disability.

He'd never said it before.

Or she hadn't been listening.

For the first time in her life, Berlin hated herself.

"I'll join this crusade too. Least we can do is let Joe know how many people will miss him if he's gone. My brother will be a harder sell." Sasha rolled their eyes. "But what my brother needs to see is that there's maybe an alternative way to make Joe happy, to help Joe do what he wants, while keeping this place whole."

"That'll be a trick." Cam played with the pop-top on his can. "It's not often that everyone gets what they want. Without compromise."

"Just tell me what to do." This offered last, from Jessie.

"Okay. I'll get something written up and text it to you all? Then we can start collecting letters." And because Berlin had to do something, she gathered empty pop cans to rinse in the dish sink. All the empties except Cam's because he was still holding it. Not because she was a coward. Who couldn't look at him without hating herself.

The doorbell, the one that had been quiet for too long, rang.

Jessie slipped her phone into her apron. "And I'm up."

The recycling station was another thing that Joe did for the community: he paid extra to divert this stuff from the landfill. Other businesses in town and across the province couldn't see the money in that. Joe was different. He was a conscious businessperson. A true member of the community.

Maybe he'd lost his way too.

When had it happened?

And why did Bee worry that it had something to do with Kiki?

Maybe now that Berlin was completely awake, maybe she could help Joe wake up too. If he was sleeping and not running away. She needed to know which was which. To know if selling Pink Mountain was a choice fueled by guilt.

Sunday

CBC Radio One: Alberta Fish and Wildlife note an increasing number of hit-and-runs on provincial highways. Incidents are up 45 percent from last year, with deer, followed by elk, topping the chart. Remember to slow down at night and watch for wildlife.

CAM

This time, when Cam said he wasn't leaving Berlin to walk home alone, she didn't argue. Or throw him one of her glares. It was unlike her. Cam worried she was coming down with something. One of those brain fevers. He'd joke it was possibly fatal. But considering the context, that wasn't remotely funny.

He'd spent the last half of the shift devising rebuttals to her inevitable rejection. Then, just like that, they weren't needed. But it had kept him from dwelling over Kiki.

Except now, in the LeBaron, sitting next to Berlin, he was thinking of his cousin again. Yesterday, adrenaline buzzing in his bloodstream, he'd been primed to do something. He'd paced the kitchen. Let the jar of honey soak in hot water. But once he'd fed his family, he had fallen back into his regular habits. Even dreaming of the wapiti hadn't shaken him to action. And now it was the early hours of the morning again. When everything seemed possible, but nothing was open. Except for the cop shop. And Cam would never go there for help. Ever again.

His nose hairs were frozen. The LeBaron was barely producing heat. "Sorry," he said, gesturing at the dash. "This piece . . . is a real piece."

Berlin tilted her head toward him, staring out the windshield. "It is what it is."

"Well, it's a piece. But it gets me home most days. Two weeks ago, it refused to start. For forty very chilly minutes after close."

"What did you do?"

"I waited the LeBaron out. And I won."

Her voice got small. "I'm glad that method works sometimes." She fidgeted with her mittens. "At least you can drive," she added quickly.

"You can't?"

She huffed. "I don't want to. There is a difference."

"That's what your dad was on about last night—I mean, this morning?"

She looked at him then. "It's become a biweekly thing."

"I could teach you, if you wanted?"

"Don't you think my dad's tried that tactic already?"

Cam laughed. "Yeah, but since I'm not your dad, Bee, it could be fun."

She didn't say anything for a long minute. And he knew she was going to shut him down. But knowing didn't stop it from hurting. A little more than Cam thought it should.

"I'll pass. But thanks."

Cam navigated through her neighborhood. It had been a long, trying night. Across the board. Joe was selling. And he hadn't said a thing to his one and only full-time employee. Slowly, Cam had started believing that Joe trusted him. The things he said about his youth, about his family's history—his great-grandfather who had fallen in love at first sight in Junkins, Alberta, with a newly immigrated Black American woman who'd come up from Oklahoma Territory after statehood—and Joe talked about nameless women from his rock-star days. Joe even talked about his wife. It had seemed like trust, to offer up stories like that. A person could have built a future on trust like that.

But no. It was that sideways shit again. That unfunny sideways shit. Cam wanted to rub at the ache beneath his sternum. But the ache wouldn't ease that way. Feelings weren't like that.

The residential streets were empty, snowbanks rising high on both sides. In ways, it made the drive . . . intimate. In the passenger seat, Bee sat, her eyebrows drawn, creasing her forehead. Her nose—

Stop. Focus on what was at the forefront.

Joe's news had unsettled them all.

Whenever Cam did drift toward imagining his future, it was fuzzy. Unclear. Yet, even if it wasn't easy to read, he'd assumed it would be him and Joe working together. Eventually, Cam training the new employees, as a kind of manager. And when Joe was old enough to retire, Cam would be the one to take over. He'd have a share in the company, too, maybe.

Something to protect him and Sami when they were older. Tanya and Callie if they needed it. But those two wouldn't—they made high Bs and As in everything. He sighed. It was a future a high school dropout could pull off. It was feasible. But more than that, it was one that Cam would have liked.

He pulled into Berlin's driveway and shifted into park.

"Do you want to come inside?" she asked, and Cam was floored. "I might not want to learn to drive. But I'd appreciate help with putting together something to share around. For the public library community board and school."

His whole body warmed. And it wasn't the LeBaron finally doing its job. She actually wanted his help. Still, he had to remind her: "You know I'm garbage at that kind of stuff, Bee."

Disappointing his teachers, he'd handled that. On the daily. Dropping out solved the problem lickety-splits. He wasn't the kind to disappoint his parents, his sisters. Not in ways that counted. Sure, Cam's dad hadn't been a fan of his son leaving school, but he hadn't been disappointed. He'd shrugged, gathered a glass of apple juice, and returned to bed. But if Cam disappointed Berlin, he wouldn't like himself very much.

And he had a need to like himself. It was the prime directive. Whatever his choices or his failures, he had to like himself.

"I'll throw in hot chocolate." Her lips framed perfect teeth. Cam thought her new glasses were something special. All sparkle and drama. But Bee's smile. He'd never been under its full force before. It was breathtaking. That or it was much colder than Cam thought in his crappy car.

A smile couldn't be that powerful.

Maybe he had the brain fever. That under-the-weather winter

flu Joe's wife had been complaining about. That would explain it.

"If you're sure . . ." He watched her for signs that this was all a kindness, rather than true want. With his mom home all weekend, he didn't feel the same deep-down worry he normally carried. It might look like his mom wasn't focused on her family, heading off to the city four nights a week, but she did everything for her family.

She was Cam's role model. In most things.

"All right, all right, you win. Unlimited marshmallows too," Berlin said, deadpan.

Cam laughed.

And *whoosh*, all the air in the LeBaron sparked when, a second later, Bee joined in. It was sweet, and Cam worried he liked her laugh more than her smile. More than hot chocolate. That maybe Berlin's laugh could even ruin marshmallows for a guy, if he wasn't on guard, if he wasn't vigilant. As he turned off the ignition and climbed out into the cold in front of Bee's bougie house, he caught himself thinking about her nose again. Fuck. He was already there, stranded in an entire universe of trouble.

BERLIN

It was morning. The sun was bright in her room.

Berlin scowled, rolling over in bed, hoping to fall back asleep. To be sucked into the dream world. To be comforted. It had been too much to wish that for a second night in a row, she would sleep hard. Instead, she'd woken as if in time for her weekday alarm, a boy's laughter echoing inside her head.

Because expectations, promises, and other important things mattered more than rest. Her parents could count on one of their collective hands the number of times their child had wasted away her day in bed. Seasonal flus and once, that hell week, the one she didn't remember, with the bronchitis.

Snap slept in the puddle of sunlight on the padded window bench, where Berlin did her homework, where she read her books on the surrealists and their impossible art, where she used to trade stories with Quinta.

But getting out of bed would mean showering. Brushing her teeth. Finding breakfast—likely eggs from the chickens in the snowy yard. Lately, Berlin had dragged herself through the motions without realizing that's what she was doing. Now, conscious of that fact, it was tempting not to have to do any of it. And it was Cam's fault she could see so clearly. The way he'd broken down her systems in the living room the night before with that always-infuriating laugh and other times by making rock-solid arguments.

But it was something she knew the way she knew her parents loved her: Once the numbness had Berlin fully in its grasp, she'd never recover. She'd be stuck in the mire. And nothing in this universe would ever spark again.

Every good time. All the bright stars. Every breath of cold pine air.

Remaining in bed would betray everything she cared for. There was too much to do. Things to save, broken systems to outsmart, a missing girl to find. But collecting her own eggs was still a step too far.

She'd eat cereal.

Thirty seconds passed. Berlin rolled over again. She needed to check her calendar, see what time she had to be into work.

The phone light was too much. But before she closed her eyes in recoil, she caught the notification number on her Instagram account. It was unusually high. Her other socials were too.

Then she remembered: after Cam had left, she'd decided to post the text of the posters they'd argued over, hot chocolate mugs in hand, to her social media accounts. It was faster, more efficient.

And in a few short hours those posts had been liked and reposted and commented on over and over again:

jamiepacton If Joe sells, who will sponsor the junior curling teams? I'll write a letter, Bee.

heylauragao Is it okay if I share this with the teen writing group I mentor? We usually buy from PMP, but will take our monies elsewhere if the place sells.

jusmunkaur I'll drop mine at your house today. Mailbox okay?

presidentsarah I hate this. So much. We do not need another franchise in town!

It was the same on her other accounts and on the neighborhood app Berlin's mom liked to spy on and then laugh about. Stress relief, she called it. Petty neighborhood feuds, mostly. The color someone

154

painted their door, their fence. How Canada Post parked the truck in front of a house—blocking the view. It was the last place she'd uploaded the post before bed. Berlin wasn't above wrangling those kinds of people into this one, though she'd not call it petty.

Downstairs in the kitchen, coffee was brewing.

"You're awake." Berlin's mom smiled. "But you had a late night. Least that's what your dad said before he took off for that cross-country club of his. And you've managed to get the neighborhood app all worked up."

Berlin poured herself a black coffee in a FNMISA mug they'd designed last year for a fundraiser and joined her mom on the couch.

"It's not even eight a.m. yet. You closed, right?"

"I slept enough. Plus, there's way too much to do." When Berlin realized yesterday she had to act, she hadn't thought any of this would be easy. It was never easy. "I worked on a poster after close."

"Alone?"

"If you know the answer, why do you ask?"

Berlin's mom laughed. "Because it's in the good-parent handbook?"

"When did you have time to read a handbook?"

"Okay, it was one of those pop-psychology talk radio hosts the nurses in the ER listen to. You caught me."

Maybe convincing Joe not to sell his shop to the franchisers wouldn't be such an uphill battle. Even floppy-haired Cam had been shockingly helpful—sprawled on the leather love seat like Snap would, as if he didn't have bones to hold him upright, rewording Berlin's prose out loud until her words didn't feel so stiff. He'd argued successfully against adding in a mini rant on the evils of

155

capitalism. And Cam had been 100 percent right. It was a backup argument best used with people in real life, not on a poster.

Or a social media post.

"Your dad may have also said that Cameron was here again. You haven't maimed that boy recently, have you? I don't have to remove a foreign object from his body?"

Berlin choked on her coffee. "That was once."

But *that* was a lie.

"You're right. Kindergarteners are bloodthirsty little things. It's in their nature. Most of them grow out of it."

"You get bit again?"

"Not this week." Her mom laughed. "Want some eggs? Maybe we have that excellent bacon too?"

"Bacon's gone."

"I need to text Mel, see who can fill our freezer. That or go grocery shopping at the Safeway."

"If Joe has his way, a lot of hunters will be out of work soon."

"That's my daughter, always looking on the upside."

"Mom. That wasn't a joke."

"I know, Bee. Just wanted to see you smile."

"Want me to make the eggs?"

"I fought the chickens already. And I promise if you let me cook, the eggs will come with a nice layer of burnt stuff."

Berlin did smile then. It was true. Her parents were both terrible cooks. As she cracked and scrambled eggs, she had this feeling: Joe wouldn't cave for anything less than an overwhelming show of support. It would have to be a force of nature. An avalanche.

Only then would this turn out okay.

"What's Quinta been up to?" Berlin's mom asked, taking a seat at the kitchen island. "She hasn't slept over or tried to get your dad and me on whatever new weird vegan health food her parents are peddling for weeks. She okay?"

Berlin raised her hands, like not guilty. "She's busy. You know, winter sports season is prep for spring, and she's got curling too."

"That girl does not slow down."

"It's the vegan health food."

Berlin's mom laughed again, refilled her coffee, and thankfully dropped that line of inquisition.

Later, stomach full of a good breakfast, her blood fueled by caffeine and one of those rare unhurried chats with her mom, Berlin decided she deserved to do something for herself. Usually, she didn't have the time to spend a whole day on the hill. Today, she was claiming it. And while she rode the chairlift, she could spread the word about the campaign to save Pink Mountain. As a single, to get more people up the mountain in the most efficient way, she'd be paired up with strangers. It was almost perfect. A day off with purpose. Once she took care of the bats, cleaned litter boxes, and fed all the creatures currently residing in the Chamberses' house, Berlin would indulge in her favorite pastime. The one she'd never be perfect at but still enjoyed.

Quinta, ever the levelheaded best friend until whatever happened had happened, believed everyone should have one hobby they sucked at. Snowboarding was Berlin's. She spent more time on her behind than on her feet.

Toothbrush in hand, Berlin googled the bus schedule with the other, thinking of how two nights ago, on the shoulder of the highway, her first thought in that freak storm was how she'd rehabilitate the elk. In the end, it hadn't mattered. So now Berlin was trying to let the elk go. To let her have peace.

When she reached the bus stop, she was breathing heavy. It was less work loading this gear into Quinta's Jeep. Bee could be as patient as the next person, but this was getting way out of hand. How could someone apologize if they never found out what they'd done wrong? It seemed . . . cruel. Quinta sometimes drew a little blood. But she was never cruel.

The bus pulled up with a screech. She didn't need a best friend. Not to drive her around places. She could have these little things for herself. By herself.

Berlin hefted her snowboard up, the strap digging into her shoulder. She liked the front where she could see out the windshield, see what was coming. But today, the bus was filled with sprawling families, couples, groups of friends. Near the back, she spotted Sasha, sitting alone.

Berlin's face broke into a smile.

They called out. "Bee, come join me."

She stored her snowboard in the spot reserved for gear as the vehicle accelerated. Sasha was dressed in a vivid green sports parka. They were good on the slopes but didn't snowboard—they skied. *It is*, Sasha said, *the European thing*. As if snowboarding were too new world.

They'd had that fight before. Over the terminology. It was only the new world from the colonizers' perspective. The term was harmful.

Sasha refused to capitulate.

So had Berlin.

And yet she continued to genuinely like them.

"You're awake early, considering," Sasha said.

Berlin slid onto the seat. "You too."

"But I do this every morning I can manage. Who needs sleep when you have the mountains?"

"Ha," she said. "You're like an expert."

Sasha cradled a mega-sized coffee in their hands. "She caters to my ego and pulls off those red glasses too. Wunderschön!"

A crest of dizzying warmth flooded Berlin. Swooning was something women did in books, not in real life. She tempered her voice: "German. Are you even trying?"

"You're five for five. Suppose I'll have to work harder."

"You didn't say anything yesterday—last night." She tried to sound as if she didn't care. "You really like my glasses?"

In fact, nobody had. She'd noticed.

Sasha sipped their coffee before speaking. "Things were tense. It seemed not of the moment to comment on your excellent fashion choices."

Berlin settled into the seat, leaning into Sasha's shoulder. For a while, she'd thought that maybe they would have been her first kiss. Even when the two of them argued, they got along, and Sasha flirted like they breathed, involuntarily.

"I worried they didn't suit me. Or that people think I'm too . . . cold for compliments."

Sasha rolled their eyes. "Did Quinta assist in selecting them?"

The bus turned and the sun coming through the window blinded Berlin. That was all it was, a tight feeling on account of the sudden light. It wasn't heartbreak threatening to roll from her eyes onto her cheeks. "Um, no. She wasn't there."

Sasha shifted the conversation. "So, I noticed, we've sort of gone viral. Or, at least, we've gone locally viral. Ira was not happy with us."

"I knew the community would get involved. What's happening is wrong."

Sasha made a noise in their throat. "But did we agree we'd take this to social media? It didn't seem to be the plan, not the one you outlined last night."

The pleasant heat from earlier shifted into something else. "It's more efficient."

"But is it fair to our boss? To try him in the court of public opinion like this? That's Ira's piece."

"Is what Joe's doing fair to us? To the community? He's leaving. Like we don't even matter. Like it never mattered."

An awkward silence settled between them.

"Things are off with you," Sasha said a minute later. "I've noticed."

First her mom and now Sash. "Can we talk about anything else? Maybe instead you describe one of those indie horror films you love? Frame by gore-laden frame?"

"Message received." They offered their coffee to Bee, but she shook her head.

160

The bus was approaching the national park gate. Opening her snowboard jacket, she searched for the interior pocket where she kept her phone, her money, and her Discovery Pass. Parks Canada officials would sell day passes to anyone without.

Inside the park boundary, trees passed at a faster and faster rate as the bus picked up speed. Sasha cleared their throat: "I'm not speaking about it. But . . . are you well? You've seemed . . . somewhat less . . . yourself lately?"

Something tightened inside her. "Have I slighted you somehow?"

"No, Bee," they answered quickly, too quickly. "You're allowed to be off at times." Sasha pushed a hand into their hair, mussing it. "It's that you've been less vibrant. Since, I don't know, since the Christmas holiday."

She could feed Sasha all the excuses she wanted. Could pull away, close down. The option was available. Instead, she made herself act braver than she felt. "I don't know. I think it's been longer than that. In truth. I don't feel . . ." Her airway tried to close. She fought back. "I—I don't feel anything."

Sasha reacted immediately, sitting up straighter, staring into her eyes. "Berlin."

"I know," she said. "I know."

"Have you talked to someone?"

"Does this count?"

Sasha threw one of their arms around her, pulling her close. She inhaled and thought two things at once: one, that Sasha smelled really great, like superior to others, and two, that even in talking about it, Berlin felt nothing. The way Sash was acting, it would seem that she should be hurting.

The numbness was back in force.

The dying elk's power, her gift only lasted so long.

Berlin brushed wetness from her eyes, still pulled against Sasha, still held in their arms. "It's okay. I'm fine. You can let me go."

"No. You're not," Sasha said argumentatively. "You only just said you were depressed."

"Actually, I didn't."

She had *not* used that word.

She had a 95 overall average. Always finished her homework. Was the VP of the FNMISA, and acting treasurer too. On top of it all, she held a job, and she freaking excelled at it. Depressed people were not like that.

Right?

She waited for an answer to a question she hadn't asked aloud.

When Sasha spoke again, they were gentle. "When you feel nothing, no motivation or drive to eat or shower or get out of bed, when you feel empty, blank, hopeless, that's depression, Bee." Sasha didn't let her go. Against her hair, they whispered, "I should know."

"You?" she whispered back.

The world became small. Nothing else registered but the way Sasha held her, spoke into her ear.

"Yeah, me. I'm an excellent human specimen, but I am not infallible. No one is. And the world is fucking hard. Fucking heavy. All the fucking time." They shifted but didn't let go. "I'm better now. My antidepressants help."

"I didn't know."

162

"Things haven't been truly bad. Not for a while."

It wasn't enough. But it was all Bee had to offer: "I'm glad."

She didn't feel glad.

But she could say that she was.

The bus drove through some of the most beautiful country on the continent, but Berlin was hyper-focused on Sasha. Eventually, she pulled away. To ask what she needed to, she had to be holding herself up on her own.

"Okay, what if? Then what?"

Sasha's practiced European shoulder shrug emerged. "Come on, Bee. You're too smart not to know."

"Talk to my mom."

"Ding, ding," they said without fanfare. "And lucky you, she's both parent and doctor. I had to tell my mother, then my father and Ira, and after that, our family physician. Four times the labor."

At that, Bee laughed. They didn't talk about feelings or about anything at all for the rest of the ride. They peered out the windows, Sasha resting a hand against her shoulder. At the top of the first chairlift, they parted ways. Sash was all about the black diamond and double black diamond runs, whereas Bee challenged herself enough on the beginner hills.

She'd do damage on the other runs. To herself. To others. And probably to the trees. And the trees were entirely innocent.

Everyone was here today. On her second go up the crowded mountain, she rode with a few seniors she knew by sight but didn't speak to. Their personalities were leashed to snowboards in the winter and climbing gear in the summer. They offered her a wave and returned to the conversation they'd been having before boarding the lift.

SNOWBOARD ENTHUSIAST #1: Yeah, it was totaled. Like wrecked, man. Nico says it's serendipity. That he deserves whatever shitstorm fate wants to serve up.

SNOWBOARD ENTHUSIAST #2: That's the devil's luck. Real bummer, man. Even if he did deserve it. No one likes taking the bus.

SNOWBOARD ENTHUSIAST #1: It's not that bad. The bus. Plus, Nico says he has insurance.

SNOWBOARD ENTHUSIAST #2: The fuck it is, man. Don't play me. That bus is too corporate. Like, don't come to the mountains without your soul, brah.

SNOWBOARD ENTHUSIAST #1: And the worst part, he didn't get to keep the meat. I would have hauled that carcass right into the garage and gotten to butchering.

SNOWBOARD ENTHUSIAST #2: You and roadkill, man. It's fucked up. Go to the store like everyone else.

SNOWBOARD ENTHUSIAST #1: Lol, man, lol. Hey, get your shot out, let's do that one TikTok for my fans.

They filmed their video, downing their alcohol, tapping the chairlift supports like they were in church. At the top of the mountain, the boarders went left. Berlin strapped her loose foot in and aimed for the right. There were thousands of SUVs in town, probably a million-plus in the province. If you didn't drive a truck in Alberta, you drove an SUV. It could have been coincidence, but it could have been luck too. She wished she'd interrupted, asked them who they'd been talking about.

Quinta would have done it.

Instead, Berlin found herself seduced by the cold and the quiet, which even the snowboarders respected.

Pushing herself up, Bee forced thoughts of Quinta away. This day was for listening for the hum of the universe. For being open to it. Flying down the mountain, falling down the mountain, it was exactly what Berlin needed. She lucked in a few times, riding the chairlift with harmless kids from the snow school, who were only threats on the dismount but whose ski instructor listened enthusiastically to Bee's "save Pink Mountain" speech. So far, everyone she'd spoken to agreed to write a letter.

"Not Joe," one of the ski instructors said. "He's an institution. It won't be the same without him in Canmore."

Things were looking up.

And then Berlin had gotten screwed: standing in the singles line, a few feet behind Quintana-Roo and her cross-country friends. A mix of snowboarders and ski devotees, dressed in tempered colors, they laughed loudly, ignoring Berlin like it was an Olympic sport. But they taunted her too.

PINK PARKA: What's she doing with herself? Like does she think anyone actually cares?

SALMON PARKA: They make the best pizza in town. Own that, at least.

QUINTA: We do. That's fact.

PERIWINKLE PARKA: Are *you* pissed about it, QR?

QUINTA: It's only a job.

PINK PARKA: Someone tell that to Little Miss Perfect. Like she could use her energy to save starving children or something. Even work on her boarding skills. She's a complete wrecking ball on the hill.

Halfway down the green square run, Berlin wiped out, knocking her head against a patch of ice-glazed snow. They had laughed. They hadn't looked, but they'd known she was there. Quinta had known, right?

Bee's hip hurt. Lying there in the snow, she considered quitting. Selling her gear. She didn't have the time for hobbies. Even now she should be working on that World History project—and, ugh, dealing with the donation of baking supplies. Tashie had texted a reminder: **Yo, it's urgent-like we get this accomplished before Monday!**

But Berlin was terrible at quitting.

She promised herself three more runs was enough not to make this an utter failure. After, she could go home, settle into her attic window seat with Snap and a book—not her Dalí biography but a novel with a happy ending in order to forget about the rest of the world. The whole universe.

It would be self-care. Not giving in.

Once, last year, during lunch—Berlin with leftovers from the Japanese place her parents loved, Quintana-Roo with her classic brown rice, tofu, and veggie bowl—Quinta had claimed that self-care must be fundamentally selfish to count.

166

Today, she hadn't defended Bee or Pink Mountain at all. It stung. Maybe, just maybe, she hadn't noticed her used-to-be best friend standing there?

Hope was a thing with flimsy wings.

Berlin transitioned to her heel and picked up speed, caught in the thrill of a good run. So much so that when she boarded the chairlift, almost breathless, she hadn't noticed she was one seat away from her English teacher. There was another man to his right.

"Berlin," Mr. MacDonald said, nodding. "Good afternoon."

"Mr. MacDonald, hi."

He tsked, flicking his blond hair back from his forehead. He wasn't wearing a helmet, just ski goggles. "I've told you to call me Alex how many times now?"

She hated when he insisted—truly, madly, deeply. But she didn't say that. Only smiled. Let him think her too shy to use his first name.

"You've finished *The Tempest*, I'm going to assume."

"Last week, actually."

Fresh bruises crowned her teacher's eye. His lip was split, along the bottom.

He caught her staring and grinned. "Sparring. This one has a killer right hook." He jutted his head toward his friend. "Berlin is one of my ELA 20 students. Always so . . . efficient. She's Native, yeah? Her parents are doctors."

The friend pressed himself against the restraining bar to peer at her.

She didn't like his smile.

"My great-great-grandmother was Cherokee," the friend said. He had to be twenty-five. Or older. His face was messed up too. "Their kind of royalty. Full-blooded, you know? Not like how it's all diluted now."

Berlin wanted to find the energy to scream. But this wasn't the place to set her English teacher's friend straight. To debunk the Cherokee Princess myth. To explicate how the Indian Act was used in Canada to force First Nations women who married non-Natives off status, seemingly making them disappear. Instead, she nodded the way you did when you needed to escape a conversation with an adult you didn't trust.

"Berlin's a top student," Mr. MacDonald said to his buddy. "Always checking off the boxes. Highest marks. She might lack some elemental passion, some of that thing nobody can fake, no one can practice, but she always exceeds the provincial standards."

It was a backhanded compliment.

No, a slap.

His friend muttered something under his breath, something she couldn't hear.

"Yeah." Her teacher laughed self-consciously. "I do love my Native students. It's one of the best parts of working here. Other than the skiing."

This chairlift ride could not last forever. Nothing did. Mr. MacDonald and his friend exchanged a few more words but left her alone. After all, what did you say after *lacks some elemental passion*? At the top of the hill, Berlin tracked to the right again. She wished she could get angry. That she could rage.

But Mr. MacDonald was correct in his assessment.

She was lacking. The universe was too quiet. The silence surrounded her. Even here, in nature. She wiped at her nose on the soft part of her gloves. It was the cold. Everyone's nose ran in the cold.

And then, it got worse. Mr. MacDonald had followed her. "Berlin, wait a moment."

Off to the left, his friend checked his phone for messages.

"I meant what I said."

Her English teacher didn't blink. A frontal view revealed his bruising was bad. Worse than she'd thought on the lift. He'd allowed his friend to pummel him. For sport.

"You are technically perfect. And you know it," he said, ignoring the rush of families with small children heading for the green run. "But you'd do better with an extracurricular or two. Show us you have soul. You can be stoic. But so are a lot of the more studious Natives."

She didn't react. Didn't tell him she was the VP of the FNMISA, would probably be president after Tashie graduated. Because he knew that. He mentioned FNMISA to their class every other week, said each word aloud, rather than reciting the acronym. Mentioned it even when it wasn't tangentially related to the topic at hand.

"You should join curling. It's not a traditional sport for your people, but I coach them, you know?"

That and cross-country and swim. Mr. MacDonald had been one of Quinta's favorite teachers when they started at the high school. He was funny, so down to earth. She'd joined as many of his teams as she could. Then in the middle of Grade 10, she dropped swim.

It's too hard on my hair, she said. *I'm a little vain, I've discovered.*

Mr. MacDonald waited for a response. Staring, smiling at Berlin. "My schedule is pretty tight."

"Quit your job at that pizza place," he said, like it was the easiest thing. "In high school, nobody needs to work."

Another thing she didn't have time to remedy today. Some did. Need to work. Some worked for other reasons. She'd been still too long. The cold was seeping into her. "I'll think on it. I need to go. To meet a friend."

One of those things was true.

Mr. MacDonald inclined his head, the way he did when the answer offered wasn't the one he wanted. It might have been right technically. But not right in his books.

As she took off, he hollered at her. "You'll end up just like Mr. Vasquez at this rate. He was exactly like you. An ethnic student, technically perfect but empty where it counts. And now he's . . . a lifty." Her teacher paused. "Or worse, you'll end up like Cameron Sound. Your community deserves better from you."

Mr. MacDonald, it turned out, was an asshole.

How could Quintana-Roo have missed this fundamental fact? When she'd been exposed to him so often, in class and out?

The wind whipped Berlin's braid against her shoulder. She tucked it into her parka and escaped down the hill. Even if she couldn't feel much, she'd noticed something, the start of a pattern. For the second time today, someone had mentioned Nico Vasquez. The elk called to her, told her in the way of the universe to talk to Nico.

And maybe it didn't matter. But Berlin wanted to know whose

SUV had been wrecked on the side of the highway, and she wanted to make sure they were okay, and if they were, she wanted to them to know they'd left a living creature to suffer. She needed to know if they cared. What she'd do with the answers, that was pure mystery. But suddenly, she needed this more than most other things.

JESSIE

"Get gone. And don't cause mischief," she said as her brothers pulled their gear out of storage in the owner's suite.

"It's our fucking mountain, Jessica. So, like, who gets to tell us what trouble we get to make? Not you," Junior, the oldest, said.

Spence followed him with a smirk.

They'd kissed sweet boyhood goodbye over the last couple years. Now all they wanted was their father's approval. His attention at the dinner table. His words of praise.

Cutting Jessie as often as they could. That was one path to success.

Chad, the youngest, was last to leave. "Thanks for the ride, Jess."

For now, he still carried a thin layer of kindness that living in the family home hadn't quite managed to sand off. If the older boys weren't watching.

Since lying to her father about quitting her job, it had been too cinch for her parents to order her to drive the boys to the mountain. Like Jessie was one of the revolving-door nannies who had done the hard labor of raising the Hampton kids up, by ferrying them to and from a barrage of approved activities. Mount Norquay wasn't the most profitable of her family's businesses—that was a toss-up between the chophouse in the town of Banff where literal bloody princes dined or the container-shipping biz importing goods from China.

Yet, the mountain was the showiest jewel in her family's empire.

It was a fucking mountain. Junior had that right.

When she was younger, she loved it the way other girl-children coveted ponies. Fun on skis with her baby brothers. That birthday party when she was eight. Later, those good, good times, unsupervised Saturdays with school friends. Until she sprouted boobs. Then it was fun on chairlifts with the dudebro of the week.

Jessie settled into the suite to wait. Her brothers knew they needed to be back by 3:15 p.m. or she'd leave them to fend for themselves. They didn't know why. But they knew she was dead-as-a-doorknob serious. If they were late, she was jetting. They could take the bus home. Not that they'd know how to take the bus.

How to pay.

She pulled her heavy-knit sweater off, igniting her hair into a static poof. If she could smoke a dart in here, this place would be perfect. The view of the mountain, of the trees, the snow, was exquisite like a postcard, which a friend had once told her was basically time travel. She yanked a very annotated copy of *The Tempest* from her oversized tote. She had to finish it before Monday morning or Teach would flip. Last week, he threatened to call her father.

Normally, teachers stuck with the mother.

Truly, Jessie didn't care one lick about *The Tempest* or ELA. A passing grade would suit. And Jessie was trying. Or she was trying to look as if she was trying.

It was all a bluff.

A long fucking con.

Her parents could not be clued in until after graduation. Another year and a quarter. Or until she turned eighteen. Which was only a few months shy of graduation anyhow.

She'd make it.

For now, she even flubbed it a little in Metal Works so her grades there wouldn't stand out compared to the rest. Opening the heavy book, throwing her socked feet over the armrest of a leather chair, she got comfy. Against her will, she'd like the record to show, the play drew her in. When she closed the pages, hours later, her neck was tight. She needed a dart.

And she'd earned it.

She was stashing her book away when the door to the owner's suite opened. "You're early, you degens! Congratulations, you win a free ride home!"

"Language, Jessica," a voice she recognized, but never expected to hear in this room, said.

She pivoted, stood tall. Slinging her tote over a shoulder, she tried hard not to let the shakes reach her legs.

Dustin Patrick Granville filled the entryway of the suite. His face was messed up. But he smiled, with teeth. Behind him, sporting his own messed-up face, was none other than Mr. Mac, purveyor of fine English literature.

"That's my line," her teacher said, pouting the way he did when he wanted to get his audience's sympathy. "I'm the authority figure here. You're a—"

"Business owner, bro," Dustin interrupted. "But, yeah, I was only kidding. I like her mouth. So many good uses for a saucy mouth."

Jessie couldn't show weakness. "What are you doing in here? This is family only. Get out. Now."

Dustin Patrick Granville made a sound in his throat, a half purr, and when it hit Jessie's back-brain her stomach rolled. He liked this, her pushback. He wanted it.

"We're just taking a look-see." The man stepped farther into the room. He turned a full 360, brushed his fingers across the leather sectional set in front of the fireplace and that obnoxious TV. "After all, I'm gonna be family or something one day very soon."

Jessie did not like the sound of that one iota. "Out," she ordered.

Dustin Patrick Granville laughed. But he threw his arms up in the air, a mocking surrender. "I'll see you at dinner tomorrow, Jessica."

She didn't let her knees lock.

"But I'll be seeing ya first," Mr. MacD said, an undercurrent in his voice. "Why is it that you always sit at the back of the class, eh, little missy? Like, that's far from the front. Too far."

She realized it fast, but also way slow. Both men were a step beyond buzzed. It was dangerous to drink on the mountain. Accidents happened, and they multiplied in horrible ways with alcohol. Jessie had a few disasters with drink and skis under her belt.

But it was especially unsettling to see one of her teachers in a shit-faced state. Almost as bad as running into one of them in their street clothes. At the mall or a restaurant.

"What are you waiting for? Do you need me to call up a taxi?"

The men laughed at her. Alcohol fumes invading the air, they left.

Now Jessie needed that dart like her bloodstream needed O_2. Now she would have to stop by the security office to request the door lock be recoded. It wouldn't stop things if it was her father handing out the code to men like Dustin Patrick Granville, as if it was some kind of incentive in their business dealings. But it would be something she could do. To take back some of the power she'd lost here, in the owner's rooms. On her family's fucking mountain.

Outdoors, things were crisp, but the sunshine kept it pleasant. Jessie leaned against the lodge playing with her unlit cigarette, weaving it finger to finger and back again. She had the shakes bad. But her body hadn't failed in the moment. Now it was letting go. Even though caffeine wouldn't help with her current symptoms, she'd need it to close the shop.

Before she could light the dart, she heard her name.

"Hi," Berlin said, a bit breathlessly.

The universe could sometimes send a balm after it had screwed you up the backside.

"You should have told me you skied here." Jessie smiled. "I would have hooked you up with a complimentary pass."

She would've ditched her reading to chairlift with Berlin Chambers. But Jessie didn't say anything like that. Not after that failure of a kiss between them. Something they hadn't talked about. Still weren't talking about. Because it wasn't spring yet.

But Berlin laughed at Jessie's words, all bright and free. Then this determined look crossed her face. She started to speak. Then, as if changing her mind, shook her head. She tried again. "Did you know that my dad's mother was a Norquay?"

"For realsies?"

"Completely. The man who this place is named for, he's one of my ancestors. Like my ancestor was John Norquay's brother."

"The Métis guy who tried to climb this thing and failed but still got them to name the mountain after him is your granduncle. That's green bananas. Maybe you should have a lifetime complimentary pass?"

Berlin noisily blew air between her lips. "Or . . . you know, you could give the mountain back. To the people who have taken care of it since forever. Before John Norquay showed up and got accolades just because he was government."

"My father would never." Jessie laughed low. "I have zero, zip, nada influence on him and his business partners. If I did, we'd have better coffee up in this place."

They walked into the café together.

"Want one?" Jessie asked. "On me. Or on the Poseidon Group's account, which is better because it's like putting the screws to my father one overpriced, unsatisfying hot bean drink at a time. We can find a seat and . . . do the talk?"

Berlin pulled her helmet off. Her bangs were sweaty, compressed.

Jessie wanted it to be regret on Bee's face, but she couldn't be certain.

"Actually, I'm looking for someone. Nico Vasquez? One of the lifties mentioned he's on break."

Nico.

Of course Berlin was into him. Vasquez was older. Super shy but

176

once you warmed him up, he was a trip. His brand of humor was bone dry. He was into politicking too. Real change-the-world stuff. And art—he claimed all art was political. Even Taylor Swift, BTS, Britney Spears. Dude was also a gossip, traded in some good stories.

Jessie tamped down her ugly feelings. She'd not make herself a nuisance, chasing after Berlin. She had self-respect. Plus, she'd already assaulted this girl once. She owed it to both of them not to do it a second time. "I'll show you to the break room. He's probably in there, warming up."

Berlin beamed like a My Little Pony. All shine and good energies. "Thank you. I realized today . . . well . . . I need to talk with him."

Jessie checked her phone. She didn't have the minutes for a sit-down anyhow. She had to drop by the security office, corral her brothers to the Land Rover, and get her undercaffeinated behind to work. And queen of the damned, her body, it was still revved up, still completely ready to fall into the shakes.

Fucking men, Jessie thought. And she looped Vasquez in with creeps and drunk teachers even though most rotations around the sun, Jessie supposed Nico was a good duck. But today, today, he was only another bird, feathering with the rest of his flock, in the dumpster out back. It wasn't fair. But Jessie didn't feel like being fair today.

BERLIN

Already, bruises blossomed under her skin. Tomorrow they'd show. She followed Jessie, weaving through a back hall next to the café kitchen and then down another hallway deeper into the lodge. Not speaking. As if Jessie had disconnected. Or remembered what had happened between them only yesterday.

"This way," Jessie said, opening another door.

One of Bee's elbows was throbbing. But it was good pain. A reminder of her body. Of a connection to something larger. Within herself but also beyond.

She'd mentioned Pink Mountain a dozen and a half times today and the locals were fired up. Now she needed to talk to Nico. To avenge the elk. To thank her for the gift, a reminder of what it felt like to be connected to the universe. Because of that offering, Berlin could sense the numbness. Because of that gift, she'd let Sasha in. She'd let Sasha put a word to what was blandly, slowly, terribly suffocating her.

Even if Sash had seemed upset that she'd made an executive decision on the Pink Mountain front.

"Here you be." Jessie unlocked the break room door with a keypad. "I have to rile up my brothers like rodeo and get. Work this afternoon, you see."

"Good luck," Bee said, trying to smile.

She had no idea how she felt about this girl with curly hair and an elastic approach to language.

But it was something other than numbness.

Inside, the lifties were stripped down to T-shirts, their parkas discarded. The room smelled a little like sweat and a lot like patchouli. There were no windows, no natural light.

She spotted Nico in a corner, eating a green apple and scrolling through his phone. While the other lifties in the room watched her enter their space, they didn't say anything. This was theirs—one of the only places on the mountain where they could relax—and she'd invaded.

She'd apologize when she was done. "Nico?"

"Heeeey?" he said before looking up. His face had been animated, but when he spotted her, he went flat. "It's Berlin, right?"

She nodded.

They'd only spoken twice. Both times, Nico had been sloppy drunk. Once at a Halloween party Quinta had insisted they attend. On the walk back to Quinta's family's apartment, Berlin had emptied her stomach into someone's bushes. And she'd spoken to him during one of the early search parties, when they'd used a grid approach to trek through the nearby woods, back when the whole town still cared about finding Kiki, while Nico had been sipping something hard from a flask.

"I remember you," he said, but his body language was closed off. He bit into his apple again. A great big bite. "Is this about saving PMP?"

He chewed slowly. Carefully. But there was something else, something Berlin recognized from her rescue animals. Nico was fearful.

"I'd love to talk to you about that." She claimed a chair across from him so she wouldn't hover. Animals didn't like that either.

They didn't like that at all.

"But also, I have a question," she said.

His left eyebrow, the one with the piercing and the double slash through the hair, all alt-gorgeous, peaked.

She met his eyes. They were green, tight. "It's a weird one."

"Well, ask it," he said.

He was trying to take control.

"Do you know who owns the SUV? The one that got into the wreck Friday night? Just outside of town?"

Nico nodded, finally relaxing. "It's not that weird of a question. Everyone is talking about it. I've been telling this story all day. He's the owner of that new boxing gym. The one next to the climbing place. He's youngish. Maybe twenty-six? Twenty-eight? Moved here late last year and he's . . ." Nico's voice dropped. "Sketch."

Berlin raised a brow this time. "What do you mean?"

Asking questions was one way to keep a person talking.

"This guy's got a fascination with everything . . . messed up." Nico settled back into the chair, his body opening. "He encourages people to fight without gear. Like bare hands, no rules. He's into teeth and that old-school Tyson garbage. Laughs in the face of concussions. Rumor has it he's running, you know, that kind of outfit? Recruiting people who don't know any better to partake in underground pseudo fight-club shit. Who don't have other choices."

Now that the sweat on her body had cooled, it itched. "Is he on the mountain today?"

"Yeah, with—"

"Mr. MacDonald's friend."

Nico's voice dripped with vitriol, but he nodded. "I fucking hate that man."

Later, Berlin would want to have asked which man. But half a dozen lifties started getting geared up and Nico stood, pulling his snow pants straps over his shoulders. He gestured to the door. "I've got to get back out there."

"Thanks. For talking with me."

"No problem." Nico shrugged into his parka, pulled his sunglasses out of a pocket, and put them on. His voice rose so that they weren't having a private conversation anymore. Now he was inviting the rest of the room in. "I'll sign your petition or whatever too. Pink Mountain makes the best pizza, eh, guys, gals, and nonbinary pals?"

The rest of the room echoed their agreement.

"Would you send your coworkers my social posts?" Berlin asked. "You can friend me? Help spread the word?"

Even if Sasha wasn't on board or hadn't come to terms with the plan changing, social media was the fastest way to get done what they needed to get done, when they had only four days left.

"Of course." Nico nodded. "I used to have a hookup there. Made the best pizzas."

Berlin shivered. She wasn't cold, but her body was reacting like it was. "I thought you used to work at PMP?"

"No. Never." He laughed and it opened up his face. "Just a pizza fan. Showed up often enough, I started getting frequent-flier discounts. I went to a staff party once, after hours, in the prep room."

That story drunk Nico had spun about Joe, the day the RCMP had come to Pink Mountain to grill him, it wasn't firsthand, like how in the telling Nico had made it seem. Because a Nico who didn't work at the shop would never have been in the back of the house that day, would never have witnessed Joe's breakdown.

She leveled her voice, like they were just gabbing, like lying wasn't serious, dangerous even. "Oh yeah? Who was your hookup?"

Bee knew.

She *knew*.

But she needed to hear it.

"Ah, Kiki Cheyanne." Nico's skin lost its warmth, went grayish. "We were . . . friends."

The hurt was alive. In the room. Radiating from Nico. Beating like a heart.

"I'm sorry," Bee said.

"Sorry back," Nico offered. He held the door, guiding her toward the public part of the lodge. He waved goodbye as he pushed through the afternoon crowd, heading to his lift.

Even if he hurt, he'd lied. And people only lied when they had something they were trying to keep hidden. Was Nico's secret dangerous or only painful? Berlin wondered, standing in the café. The place smelled of fried foods. Against a bank of windows, Quinta was holding court, enjoying her après-ski. Late-afternoon sunshine flooded her table.

Of course this week would not stop.

A teacher gone off script, a smashed SUV, an elk dying roadside, the bite of a best friend's cold shoulder, an unasked-for first kiss, and Joe abandoning his business, his employees, all the people who needed him.

That conversation on the bus.

That word.

Depression.

It was a black hole.

"No, nope. I don't believe you," Quinta said, loud, threw her head back, her coppery hair wavy and loose, as if she'd walked out of the salon minutes ago. On the table were baskets of French fries and greasy burgers. Quintana-Roo, of course, had a salad with tofu. But she stole a fry from the boy sitting next to her.

She finished it in two bites. Snatched another.

It was out of character.

Quinta hated anything deep-fried with a passion, even cinnamon sugar bannock.

Berlin's body wanted its own grease, its own fat. Fries would be perfect, fresh bannock better than that. But she couldn't order, eat alone here while Quinta and her friends laughed.

She could not do it.

It was impossible to live life in proximity to a black hole.

Monday was coming with a vengeance and there was nothing left for Berlin on the mountain. At school, she'd have to sit in ELA and pretend she didn't know Mr. MacDonald had said those things. The man was in control of her grade, could tank her if he decided she wasn't scare-quotes passionate enough. And on Thursday Joe would sign the papers. Pink Mountain would cease to exist as it had before. So there just wasn't time left to understand the shifts in Quinta's behavior, to figure out what made her heart tick, what had torn them asunder.

Two Years Ago

In the change room

I peel   off   clothing
like I'm   shedding
skin   & around me

the others   giggle
drinking   last sips of   morning
coffee   slipping into blue
& black   & red   swimsuits

All high necks   full coverage
racing bottoms   &

      like this

I'm exposed   uncovered   opened
as if on display.   When we invite
friends & family   others' mothers
others' fathers to watch
they see us   in school   colors,

our wins   & losses,
our goldenrod   swim caps,
but they cannot   see
the way   I sink   myself

to the bottom   of the pool
when   everyone   has   left

&

    I

    practice

            breathing

                    underwater.

I believe

in the power of arms
shoulders & legs—muscles contracting
pushing bodies through
water, across the ice.

& I believe in secrets

in seeing what you shouldn't
& choosing to swallow it
down, let those secrets roost amongst
your own.

& I believe if you wait long enough
with a secret not your own, one day
it will blossom like algae does—
fast, spreading,
growing, multiplying
in the manner of malignant cells.

The secret I'm holding belongs to [scratched out]:
The way she was caught unaware
on the deck, long after everyone had left—
(me, above,
forehead pressed to the viewing glass

staring at movement
in the water, at his shoulders
breeching with each stroke)
& how he leapt
from the pool
a starving animal, cornering her.

It was only a kiss. Taken, not offered.
When she pushed him aside, when he tried
to apologize, when she ran, when I watched,
when I swallowed this secret, I didn't think
it would become something I craved
like milk chocolate, like any other
sweet thing, like my mother's
deep & powerful love. As if I could
fill myself up with someone else, as if
I could be sated.

Not his daughter

I should wear a sign across my neck, hung on neon plastic lacing, keep it right-side out to stop them asking if I'm his daughter. He says, They do the same to my wife, *turning it back on himself, like it's only a thing to laugh at & I can't help but wonder why he's this kind to me, this careful with me. It can't be that we share skin—colored with shades sitting side by side in the crayon box. After we'd laid my mother to rest. After the ceremony. After the flowers died off, after the weather turned cold, he wrote me a letter:* She was bright like no one I've ever met, your mom. Laughed like she was never going to stop. When she walked, she danced. She loved you more than anything. I want you to know these things. *Weeks later, I quit. He doesn't question my decision. He takes me out for a fancy-like-that lunch. Asks permission, snaps my picture with his phone & breaking now, fractured now, I never ask how he knew her, why he felt he could say these things to me, these things that used to be true, things that I cherish as if they were* mine.

Breakfast

Spin sugar into love
& love into breakfast foods.

& when the meal is over
you'll crave muffins, the oven at 350,
the butter yellow & salty. You'll
wonder why this isn't magic,

why magic is outlawed,
why you can't bake your love
into a pie crust.

Your love language is feeding
& being fed. Is that why
when he asked you to join him
for a meal, when he opened
a bottle of red wine, when he
offered you beignets from his fingers,
that you went willingly
to his bed?

In the morning
you found the empty cardboard
box & a sleeve of powdered

sugar on the kitchen island. You
wanted to clean up, to hide
the evidence of intent—
but you were already late
for school.

Crushed

> When possibility is present, when the air
> sparkles with flour, when it grits under
> my sneakers, when the dinner rush ends
>
> & he comes into the storefront
> still wearing his winter gear
> & when he sits on that bar stool
> for hours, we talk.
>
> When the printer spits out orders
> he reads from a book, a slim volume
> this boy stores in his pocket
> like that's where books belong.
>
> This boy writes in the margins
> in tiny spider script he never lets me see.
>
> I deliver him tiny pizzas
> with flourish, these experiments
> tempered to his taste.

What held him apart, what made him shine like crystallized honey?
That he never asked. Never assumed. That he didn't use me. That
he returned & returned. That he stayed until closing. Listened &
listened. That he spun safety like sugar crystals.

What made him like all the others, sticky & unwelcome? That two weeks before I quit, he stopped showing up, stopped texting, just stopped as if he'd woken & realized he'd been crushed in slow increments by the tenacity of my grief.

Well, you did it, love. You broke the tiny perfect thing we were creating.

Monday

Local talk-radio station DJ: Did you see this social media action supposedly trying to halt the legal sale of a local business? Yeah, yeah, I know I'm not supposed to say anything against the kids—but what are these kids thinking? They aren't. That's the answer. They're idealizing. They forget socialism failed or haven't learned it in school yet. This sale is only progress, only the way of the world, and the kids, they'd better sit down.

BERLIN

Joe's truck wasn't in the parking lot, but he was always in the shop on Monday afternoons. Sometimes during the week, Emilie did come by and borrow the truck—especially in winter. As Berlin pulled on the handle of the staff door, the aroma of yeasty dough escaped into the cold. The office was notched open.

"Hello?" she called.

No answer.

Even though Berlin had to talk to Quinta for FNMISA, she'd ditched out of gym class fifteen minutes early. Again. Walking away from school, she had checked her phone. Her notifications were out of control. Nico Vasquez—even if he'd told a lie, or misrepresented how he'd come across the story about Joe—had sent another volley of support through. Most of it centered around the mountains. And Jessie and Cam kept reposting and dragging their friends and foes into the fold.

Even Sasha had shared a few posts.

#KeepPMPLocal was trending provincially.

Berlin peeled off her gloves, her earmuffs. She couldn't confront her boss if she was sweating. She hung everything in the crowded hallway next to the washroom.

Light flitted from under the door. A sickly yellow.

Not all of the online comments were supportive. Since local news media had picked up the story, dissenting voices were going for cheap shots—saying that capitalism was the only choice. One person had said something especially cruel: *This is our chance to take politics out of pizza and eliminate a Black-owned business.*

But there'd been no dogpiling. Instead, the replies were full of statements saying how hate speech wasn't welcome and examples of all the great things Joe and other Black business owners did for surrounding communities.

Still, things could get uglier. *Eliminate* was a scary verb. It lived adjacent to *genocide*. On the internet, it was always possible a hate group would jump in and turn this into something it was not. Even against that possibility, Berlin fueled herself with the knowledge that what she was doing was right.

Joe couldn't leave them.

Admitting to herself that it was weird and stalkerish to wait outside the washroom, she was exiting the hallway when laughter came from behind the door. Not one person. But two. A higher-pitched voice. A lower register.

"That's good," the higher-pitched voice said.

More indiscriminate noises followed.

Berlin blushed, stumbled, caught herself on the wall with a thud. Her elbow, again. Her whole body hurt the way things hurt the day after being on the mountain, and tomorrow would be worse.

She retreated carefully into the prep room, and on a whim pushed herself up to sit on the metal counter. This was the most casual pose she could imagine. It was 100 percent Cam. He always appeared so chill, so very not engaged with whatever was happening outside his sphere, and that was what she wanted to be like when Joe and his wife emerged from the washroom.

They had been arguing.

They made up.

That was nice.

When the door opened and Emilie giggled the way she did, low and sultry, it wasn't Joe following her, walking out of the tight hallway, fixing his jeans.

It wasn't Joe.

The moment Cam caught Berlin sitting in the prep room, he had the good grace to first meet her gaze. Then he closed his eyes and muttered a rather enthusiastic "Fuck."

She should have laughed and then it would have all worked itself out. A release of tension. How in Shakespeare's tragedies the audience was always offered a moment of relief. She didn't laugh.

Couldn't.

"Fuck," Cam repeated.

Emilie's lips were swollen, her posture ramrod straight. She went on the offensive. "What are you even doing here? You're not on the schedule. And Ira isn't in until five."

"I, um, needed to talk with Joe."

"As you can see, he's not here." Emilie brushed invisible lint from her expensive sweaterdress.

"Oh."

In high heels better suited to a fancy event than a pizza shop in the middle of winter, Emilie retreated toward the office. She hung around often enough and did something in that room but never socialized or helped like Joe did. It seemed to Berlin that Emilie didn't actually like any of the people her husband employed.

Correction. She liked Cam.

At least as much as a person needed to do . . . that.

"And, Berlin," Emilie said, pivoting, "please take this the right way, sweetheart. You're young so you think that you can have everything. You think that what you want is what you need. Well, I'm older. And I'm telling you that you can't have it." She set her gaze across the prep room at the brick wall separating the front of house from the back. "None of this social media stunting will change what Joe does. Your impassioned speeches won't either. Begging doesn't work on the man. You can't win him over to your side if he's decided he'd rather not be there."

What did you say to that? *Don't call me* sweetheart? *Who hurt you?*

But Emilie wasn't done. "And it's none of your business. At all. But, sweetheart, I don't want you thinking anything other than

196

what is exactly happening here. Joe and I are for all intents and purposes finished."

Across the prep room, Emilie shut the office door with a sharp click.

Cam lingered near the dough mixer, hands deep in his pockets. But he'd stopped swearing. All of a sudden, he seemed awfully young. He might work full-time, but Cam wouldn't turn eighteen until next year. Emilie was over thirty. That was not right. Even if the legal age of consent was sixteen, it didn't work when one partner was way older. Or when someone was in a position of power. All of that made what Emilie had done wrong.

And yet, Berlin wasn't angry at Emilie.

That was the problem.

Because, yes, Bee burned with anger. And her ire was directed at floppy-haired, always-laughing Cam. As if she'd expected better of him. Or something.

He stepped closer. Offered her a hand, helped her dismount from the table. "Come up front, would you? So we can . . . um . . . discuss? Oh, that's . . . I sound like my mom," he finished self-consciously.

When had Berlin started expecting things from Cameron, of all people? This was the elk's fault. That freak storm's fault.

Berlin followed, his hand still holding hers. His was warm. His hand that had recently been who knows where. On Emilie's body. Berlin disengaged. In retribution or to protect herself, she tucked her fingers under her arms.

She didn't miss his warmth, could provide her own body heat, thank you very much.

As if unaffected, Cam attended to the order printer, where a few dangling pieces of heat-transfer paper waited. He added them to the line one by one. He washed his hands at the little sink at the back of the kitchen and began prepping dough. "Give me a minute. To sort these."

It wasn't until all three orders were in the oven, until they both heard Emilie exit the shop, until they saw her silly sports car come from around the far side of the building where it must have been parked, struggling with the icy pavement, that Cam broached the silence.

"That was . . . I . . . um . . . I'm sorry?" he said, completely unsure, completely unlike himself.

If she was adrift, he was holding on to flotsam, hoping it would keep his head above the flossy water, that it would hold his weight, help him fight against the current.

Berlin should let it go. Accept his apology and walk home. On Mondays, her mom was done with clinic by seven. They could have dinner together. Order anything but pizza. Maybe even try what Sasha told her she needed to.

Instead of doing the sensible thing, the thing she'd always done best, Berlin started saying everything she was thinking: "Sorry for what exactly? Whatever you did with Joe's wife? Or, like, having it go down at work? In the washroom? Or is it that you did it and I witnessed it? Is that what you're sorry for? 'Cause that was a shitty apology. Like you-don't-even-know-the-hallmarks-of-the-genre shitty."

He did that thing he did so well. He laughed. And then Cam

sobered. "Is all of the above an option?"

She was still weirdly angry, but she couldn't help it, she laughed too. Like her body knew better.

And there it was.

The small release.

It had been missing today in ELA, when Mr. MacDonald had laughed off his bruising, told stories about his prowess with bare fists.

Cam walked around the other side of the oven to pull the first of the finished pizzas, to cut and box them. Once finished, he faced her. "You've really done it, getting the community fired up, eh?"

"They are . . . yes."

Even if some of them were calling her a baseless idealist, a kid who didn't know any better, who'd learn to be silent, learn to follow, to fall in line.

"No, Bee, you're not hearing me. You've done this. They wouldn't have rallied like this for anyone but you."

It seemed important to him that she listen. He'd emphasized *you*.

"Thanks?"

"It was a compliment," he confirmed, boxing an order. "It's probably smart for you to assume that when I say something to you, it's meant in the best spirit."

She didn't know how to process that.

So she ignored it.

"It's not enough," she said. "The community rallying, that is. And things aren't one hundred percent positive. We don't have them all."

She was thinking of the *eliminate* comment again.

"The haters are gonna hate. You know this. You should know,

199

too, that it still matters. What you've done." He sounded serious, off. "It's not how I would have done it. But I'm no good at administrative stuff."

"I'm going to regret asking probably as soon as I open my mouth. But . . . what's wrong? With you?"

He laughed again. "Specifically? Or generally?"

Berlin rolled her eyes. She could hold space for him, challenging as it was. Sasha had done her a solid yesterday and today she could do the same for Cam. It was what one person owed another. Even if they didn't really like each other.

"Whatever," she said with a shrug. "Just answer the question."

"I'll proceed logically. The way you have to when discussing cosmically complicated shit like time dilation or faster-than-light engines." Cam held up a finger. "For one, I just did a very not-bright thing. And I don't know why I did it. Now I'm both regretful and kind of hate myself. A more-than-small amount."

It sounded like truth.

He held up a second finger like this was a speech and debate assignment. "Second, I'm having feelings. Unrelated to the not-bright thing. About specific things but also about everything. And I don't like feelings. I do best when I avoid them."

"You prefer to laugh about the world."

"Yes." His hand dropped, fingers curling into a fist. "I for damn sure do. But the wretched things don't seem to care what I like."

"Thirdly?" she prompted.

"Thank you for counting," he said. "Third, I miss my fucking cousin so badly I can't remember what it was like to love her.

200

That's . . . It's unbearable, Bee. And fourthly, or maybe this is sub-three, I can't stand that I don't know where she is. I can't stand it. I can't. I . . . I . . ." He didn't move, until his lungs forced him to inhale. And then he inhaled hard and long as if filling a void.

A black hole.

It was possible to carry black holes around inside of you.

As he talked about Kiki, Berlin had started nodding. She was still doing it, a tiny motion, didn't know what else to do. Didn't know how to comfort him.

And she was still angry.

For no good reason.

After a half minute, Cam recovered enough to speak. "Ugh, I need to ask you something. And I know you're going to hate it."

"That is not setting yourself up for success." Her tone was a shade north of lukewarm, just enough so he'd know she wasn't serious. "Eh?"

This time his laugh was freer, warmer. More like what his laughter ought to sound like.

"Bee, are you making a joke? At my expense, but, putting that absolute wound aside, I think that might have been . . . humorous."

It was subtle, but yes, it might have been. "Go on, then."

"I need your help," he said. "To search for Kiki. To figure out if you saw her, where she's gone to. And here's the part you won't like. I need you to talk to Quintana-Roo for me. And yep, according to the shift in your perfect eyebrows, that's exactly the part you won't enjoy." He paused. "There's another ask, maybe, too. But it can wait. I don't know if it's a fully formed thought yet. And I don't want to waste your time on nonsense."

The little golden bell Joe preferred to the mechanical ones most stores used trilled. A customer entered the shop, and Cam broke away to run the till. To do his job.

After they were alone again, he stepped closer. Not too close, but closer. "I don't know what's up with you two, which one of you broke the other's heart. But whatever it is, she'll still talk to you. You're her person. Her best person. You have been since forever. And I think . . . no, I remember . . . her and Kiki being weirdly secretive in the weeks before . . ."

He couldn't say it. Couldn't speak it into existence.

Even after all this time.

"I'll do it," she said. "Would you do something for me? Not in exchange. Just would you do something for me?"

She hadn't intended to ask. He'd done enough, was already helping. Online, Cam had reach with the nerdy Natives, plus the crunchy, granola stoners seemed to respond well to his brand of activism. They were exactly the people who didn't respond well to her. Who thought her uptight and judgy.

Cam nodded.

She wanted to restrain his floppy hair. Braid it away from his face. Not that she would—ever. A topsy-turvy world had been unleashed for a temporary time by the elk, by the storm, by their combined power. But it was only a blip. Only a moment one of the surrealists would have immortalized.

As soon as she'd steadied herself, Cam knocked her over again.

He said, "Of course. Anything."

He would do anything. For her. Not because it was owed. Because she asked. It was weighty, incredible. The very best thing.

Although she couldn't say any of that—could barely think it without blushing. So she said, "That's dangerous." And she expected him to laugh again, wanted him to.

"No, it's not. Berlin, I trust you."

She'd done nothing to earn it, and yet he saw someone worth trusting. So she rallied. Held herself together. And even though it meant Cam returning to a place she was pretty sure he had no desire to return to, he agreed. Without hesitation. They would meet at 10:50 a.m. at the start of Bee's free period. It was the only time she had to spare during the day. After free period, she had a special fundraiser lunch meeting with the FNMISA, then ELA in the afternoon, and even if Mr. MacDonald was going to ignore *The Tempest* again in order to have a class of seventeen-year-olds fawn over his ability to get pummeled, he'd expect her in the front row. Which meant she needed to do what she promised both for Cam and for the fundraiser now.

Opening a text chat she'd scanned a million times in the last few weeks, she typed, and this time, she didn't erase her words.

Can we talk?

After a minute, she added: **It's important.**

After another minute, she knew she needed to say it. **It's not about us.**

Three little dots appeared. They ghosted. Appeared again. Stopped.

"I'll report back." Berlin waved goodbye to Cam. She slipped into

203

the prep room, retrieved her winter gear. One of the things about being someone's (ex?) best friend was that you knew their haunts.

Bee could walk back to school and check the track over the basketball courts. It was worth a shot. She sighed, stepping outside, her muscles protesting. In her pocket, her phone buzzed.

You can have five minutes. If you make it here before I finish my grain bowl. I have other places to be. Get me?

At this time of the day, there were two options. Bowls, Bowls, Bowls was closer. But Berlin bet that even if Quinta had changed in some important way, and even if that change made them fundamentally incompatible now, Quintana-Roo wouldn't eat there. She agreed: the place was stale and corporate since the owners had franchised. Aster's, on the other hand, was cute and local, and in a plaza near the highway. It would be a long walk.

Berlin's body protested.

But she promised Cam. And that mattered. That was something she could hold on to. Something that could press against the numbness, and maybe, if she tried, if she continued trying, she could force it back and reclaim herself.

JESSIE

"Order up," the barista said from behind the counter. "I have a Winter's Wonderful grain bowl with extra sprouts and a delightful lavender latte with milk crumbs."

Sounded good, but Jessie was full. Her blood was sluggish. She had decimated her hummus wrap as petty revenge for the table manners her parents insisted upon. A little eff-you to the dinner guest Jessie was blowing off tonight. Dustin Patrick Granville thought he had her cornered, but she'd shown him. Now she wanted a dart. Even Aster's homemade spicy dill pickle chips did nothing to calm the craving for nicotine.

It was why Jessie was staring at the door.

A self-induced dare.

Go outside, dude. Get what you need, dude. You'll only sacrifice a few digits to the frost, only tip the balance toward early death a smidge further. And yet, Jessie's wretched body wouldn't budge from the chair. If she never ran out of chips, she'd survive. Like a fucking gremlin, she chomped another.

Her parents had invited that man into their house. Even after she'd told her mother about what happened in the owner's suite. A useless Hail Mary, that conversation.

The restaurant door opened. A rush of cold air invaded the café. But it was a rush of freshness too.

And there, in the doorway, stood Berlin.

Oof.

Bee was the last person on the whole flat earth Jessie expected to show up here. Aster's was crunchy to the max. White people in dreads, BO-and-patchouli-coexisting crunchy. And everything happened on slow time. The orders, the cooking, the eating. When she'd inhaled her dinner, Jessie had broken that unspoken rule. But no one would do anything other than rib her, remind her that

205

good things happened slow. The shop's reigning queen these days was none other than Berlin's little trouble-in-friendship-paradise bestie. Even asking on the down-low had done nothing to reveal the breaking news between those two.

Not that Jessie had been able to ask outright.

Gossips gonna gossip and Jessie's circle was profesh. Asking, that would have started something. And as much as Jessie wanted to know—more gremlin tendencies—she didn't want to harm Bee. Didn't want to hurt this girl almost as bad as she wanted a summer's day and freedoms from the things that held Jessie in chains—metaphorical or otherwise.

Standing in the doorway, Berlin banana-peeled her mittens off. The barista hollered a welcome. Berlin smiled, half waved. Once she finished scanning the shop, her face fell flat.

She hadn't come for Jessie. That was beyond obvious. But you could want a thing badly enough that wishes took over steering the boat. A sharp and bitter taste flooded Jessie's system. Like she'd been running. Or sucking on one of those old pennies, the kind that were going extinct all over this country, as if luck were too.

Bee approached Jessie's two-person table next to the self-serve water station. "Hey, have you seen—"

"She left. Ten minutes back. With the rest of the cross-country girlies." Jessie tried to keep her voice neutral. It had been delirious to hold on to a sliver of that bitch hope. Maybe, for Bee, it would always be about Quinta.

"Oh." Berlin's shoulders slumped.

Jessie softened. It was ridiculous to expect after a disaster kiss and two shifts together slinging slices that Jessie would become Bee's bosom bud on the tree. And when she found out it was Jessie's father ruining PMP, well, none of her colleagues would want a thing to do with her. This whatever it was, friendship or more, it was on its last legs already.

"Want a seat? I happen to have an extra." Jessie pushed the plate of chips across the table.

"Thanks." Berlin sank into the chair, her parka done up tight. "I love these. Even the weird flavors."

"Are you calling spicy dill pickle weird?"

"I very much am. One hundred percent."

"What's a normal flavor, then?"

"Ketchup," Berlin said, deadpan.

"Ew."

Bee ate another chip. "I'm trying not to dwell on it, but I wasted a lot of energy walking over here. She was probably on her way out the door when she texted. That's what I bet."

Her voice was melancholy. Low.

"Want a lift home? I was pretty much done here."

Though Jessie had no idea where she'd go after. She couldn't go to her house. Not with Dustin Patrick Granville at the dinner table. She was positive he sponsored the girls swim team just so he could put a decal of a bikini-wearing woman on his SUV. It wasn't the official school logo. He'd had it handmade, paid extra so it glowed in the dark.

The man was just awful. And after yesterday, she worried he would act out. Stake a fucking claim like Jessie was a gold mine.

The twisted dart-smoke-filled cavity inside her body got the sense that her parents were trying to set them up. Arrange a dynastic marriage. That it wasn't all in his head, his invited access to the owner's suite. That it was already agreed upon, a quiet, discounted sale for damaged-daughter merchandise. Like Jessie would be that kind of partner. A wifey. Wearing frilly aprons, dinner done by six nightly. Shake and fucking bake. Salt the only seasoning allowed on limp veggies.

"If you don't mind?" Berlin said. "I'd appreciate a ride."

Jessie smiled in response. "Sure thing, ketchup chips."

"Let's escape, spicy dill."

Jessie wanted to enjoy this. The banter. Because they had a rotten-after date stamped on their container. But she couldn't commit. Not all the way. Granville was still up in her head. His business, at least the legal side of things, was small fry. Which opened up the question: Why did Jessie's father like the man so damn much? Did her father believe this was the best she could do?

Jessie bused her tray and they exited Aster's silently.

She didn't even know if she wanted to get married or become a parent. She was seventeen. It wasn't the first thing on her mind. But she knew if she decided to go on that family adventure, she had options. A person didn't need to incubate a kid to be a parent.

It was a Russian fairy story, but Jessie loved it.

A couple longs for a daughter—not a son. They form her from the abundant snow and she's everything: independent and brave and as fully human as any boy.

But her parents screw up. They don't value their daughter and so they lose her.

Jessie wasn't made of snow, but if she ever decided to parent, she'd do better than that, than her own had done. And if she decided not to be a parent, that was okay too.

The future was always a thing without limits.

"Where to?" she asked once Bee was situated inside the Land Rover. "I don't think I actually know where you lay your head."

Berlin stared at the parking lot, worrying her mittens' pretty fur cuffs. With her pretty fingers.

"Bee? You okay?"

She didn't turn from the window. "Everyone keeps asking me that lately."

Jessie couldn't quite tell what was up. Was the girl's voice . . . wistful?

After a minute or so, Berlin shifted, making eye contact. "Do you really want to know? Or are you only being polite?"

Jessie smiled big and wide. "Maybe you don't know me well enough yet to be able to answer this one on your lonesome. But, Bee, I'm not really a polite kind of human. I don't ask questions when I don't seek answers." She waited a second. "Do you need me to inquire again? Would that prove I'm serious like lava cake exploding in the microwave?"

Berlin shook her head no. "I . . . need to talk with Quinta. Desperately. I promised someone I would. But she's . . . avoiding me." Bee's head dropped into her hands. "I'm worried she might, I don't know, hate me."

"I call impossible."

Berlin laughed. But it was flat. She thought Jessie's statement wasn't accurate. She thought it sarcasm. Worse, a dig.

Before Jessie could fix things, Berlin continued: "I don't know what I did. But I've done something. And my best friend, who has never not made up with me, ever, refuses to remain in the same room as me." She breathed deep. "You'd think I'd know what I did. Because it has to be something beyond the pale. It has to be huge. There should have been a screaming match. It should have happened louder. It should have been a clear break, visible to the naked eye, no X-ray needed. I shouldn't be all torn up, wondering. I deserve to know what I did."

Tears were falling.

Berlin didn't seem to notice. She stared at the Aster's sign, blinking rapidly. "I haven't told . . . anyone this," she said, a hiccup cutting her sentence in half.

The satellite radio was off. Inside the Land Rover was warm. Other than the faint circulation of air and the small sounds of Bee's breathing, of Jessie picking at the pristine steering wheel, the world was quiet.

Her hunger was practically content.

But Jessie's heart was beating so loud she was sure Berlin could hear it. "Want me to make it fair? Want me to drop something I haven't told anyone else either?"

Berlin sniffed, wiping her eyes on the sleeve of her parka. "You don't have to. Really."

And that's why Jessie wanted to. For once, this was mutual. Hey, she'd even asked for consent.

"I want to." She caught Berlin's deep brown eyes. Waited half a minute. Until Jessie knew she could speak without her throat closing on her words. "I know everyone says I'm fast, easy, what have you," she said in a rush, "but the honest-to-goddess truth is I've never had sex with anyone. I'm actually afraid to have sex. I'm a virgin who goes to second-base-plus a lot. Or I'm a virgin who takes the occasional dude to third? I don't know baseball well enough for this metaphor. Also I have strong feelings about the culture of virginity. Mostly, it's trash. But these are not the main points I want to make."

Berlin smiled a real smile. Finally. "I mean, I've only kissed one person."

A little bit of the hurt Jessie had been holding on to disintegrated. "Oh, I've kissed about a million guys. And a few genderqueer people. Just the one girl, so you know. But like, I'm . . . actually, completely, fully terrified of being in a relationship. Like a real one." Breathe, breathe, Jessie. It wasn't the end of the world. It was not. To say it. "Because . . . I can't replicate myself."

She was messing this up. But that's what happened, mostly, when you did something for the first time, you made a royals-on-a-bender mess of it.

"I can't have kids. Because when I was four years old, I had leukemia and, turns out, the treatments left me sterile."

The Land Rover's engine revved. And heat pushed out a little harder before everything relaxed. As if the vehicle, too, was exhaling.

Now that Jessie was saying this stuff out loud, it wouldn't stop coming. "I don't fit the narrative. You know the one girls around here are cast into. Marry, preferably your high school sweetie like your parents did, and then multiply. Go to church and raise your kids up to do this again and again to infinity. Yeah, we'll slut-shame

211

you on one hand and rush you to the altar with the other, and never see how fucking messed up that is."

Jessie needed a cigarette.

Needed the universe to rewind back to before she'd spilled herself open.

She needed—

"Thanks for trusting me with that," Berlin said, like it was that easy. "The story's different, you know, if you're not white, if you're trans or queer, if you're disabled. They don't want us to form healthy families because they think we're dangerous, threatening to their narrative, their way of life."

"True fucking story."

Everything relaxed. Every little bit. But she needed to make the confession make sense. The way she'd planned it.

"That's the thing, Bee. I'm sure that whatever is up with Quinta has nothing to do with you. Everyone thinks I behave the way I do because I'm boy-crazed or something. And maybe I am? Okay, yes, boys are gross, but I want to smash my face to theirs almost constantly. But I'm also the way I am to protect myself. To keep me safe. Do you get it? This isn't me dumping my shit on you. This is me trying to friend therapize you. And my way of thinking leads me to suspect that Quinta is acting the way she is because of Quinta. Not at all because of you."

Silence, again. But the quiet wasn't bad. It was space.

To think.

To rewrite her own narrative. Jessie was queer, yeah, but she was disabled too. The cancer treatments that saved her life had changed her body. And if the world didn't expect women to get pregnant *to be women*, then people like Jessie's father wouldn't see her as broken, as not enough because she had an impairment. There was power in knowing these things, in recognizing them. After all, it was society and systems that were fucked up, not people.

"Oh," Berlin said. "I've never considered it like that. In all the ways I've stewed over this, I've never thought of it exactly in this way." She brushed her bangs from her face, straightened. "I think I'm depressed. I mean, I think I have depression. Like the clinical kind. Maybe that's why? Why I couldn't see it like this?"

"Maybe. But, Bee, breaking news. There is a pill for that, eh?"

Berlin tried to smile but faltered. She shook her head, over and over. "At the same time, I don't think I've been a good friend. I'm caught in this never-ending numbness. Maybe Quinta got fed up waiting for me to realize that I wasn't being a good friend. That what happened between us happened slowly. Before I noticed it was getting colder, we were encased in an ice age."

"Want some more truth?" Jessie waited a moment for a nod, for something to say this was desired. "If she's truly your friend, she'll forgive you. And if she can't, don't blame yourself for something she's got control over. Notice the repeating beat here?"

"I hear you, yeah."

"Okay, good. But before she can forgive you, before you can give her the opportunity, before you can forgive yourself, you need to get right. Boost your happy hormones, dude. And while the best way to accomplish that feat is to let the power of modern medicine do its one job, I can also recommend another serotonin-boosting powerhouse . . . impromptu fucking roller-skating." It was a reach. But Jessie really didn't want to return to her house. "Calgary has a rink, and if we leave now, we can get in a couple hours of roller dance before they close up. You game?"

And she did want to spend time with Berlin. If she could see that Jessie wanted this, maybe even needed this too.

Tonight, they could save each other.

And wasn't that the best plot line? The one fairy tales never allowed. You had to be saved or ruined or eaten alive in fairy stories if you were a woman or a child. And in those stories, you weren't even allowed to line up to be eaten alive if you were queer, if you were disabled; you were simply disregarded.

Berlin smiled. "At this point, I'm ready to try anything. Even roller-skating."

CAM

When Mr. Banerji walked into PMP, still wearing his Fish and Wildlife officer parka zipped, Cam smiled with teeth. This guy was too much. In that good way. Cam fucking loved Banerji, and most days Cam was somewhat confident in saying that Banerji loved him back.

"Cameron! Watch anything good on the Netflix lately? The wife and I are ready for a new show."

"My mom's deep into a rewatch of *Battlestar Galactica*," Cam said, shrugging. "I've been keeping her company lately. When she's home."

Banerji nodded.

He got the subtext. That Cam's mom had introduced Kiki to the series during a girls-only weekend, ages ago now. That it was comfort to sink into the story, to feel next to his cousin in that way. That it was his mom's favorite, even before it became something she and Kiki had shared.

"The wife and I really liked the last one you recommended. That deep future stuff hits right for us."

The promise of a free pizza had drawn Banerji over to the shop, like Cam had planned. Normally, they ran into each other at community events or, in the Before days, at Cam's dad's all-night euchre tourneys. But those hadn't happened in a long time.

It's not that he couldn't stop over at Banerji's house, but then this wouldn't stay quiet long. It was too sensitive or too weird to text. Besides, there were certain things that a person didn't say in a text. Should never be said that way. Cam believed this at his core. The first time you said *I love you*. Goodbyes.

In-culture stuff.

Maybe this weird fell under that last umbrella. Maybe it didn't. Still, it didn't belong in a cloud somewhere. It felt like it belonged in the real space between two people.

"You might like *Cowboy Bebop*," Cam said while he finished prepping dough for the next order. "The anime, not the live action. I mean, you can watch the live action, but it was canceled. And in my humble opinion it needed to be thirty percent campier and/or thirty percent more noir to do the thing it was trying to do well. The anime, though? Solid gold. I've been holding that rec back until you were primed to appreciate it."

Mr. Banerji laid his hands on the top of the glass half divider breaking the room into kitchen and storefront. "Good, good. Have to keep the wife happy." He bowed his head and then smirked like he knew something Cam didn't.

Which he did. About a lot of stuff. But hopefully, today, about one specific thing.

Mr. Banerji seemed to sense that the fun talk was over. "So, why did you bribe me to come into town? Not that I'm complaining. This is the only pizza I'll eat within one hundred kilometers. And my best half is partial to the wild meats."

"I'll start on a Tashie's Uncle's Special, then? Bison pepperoni, deer sausage, black olives, our tangy red sauce on frybread base with mozzarella. Want a side of hot sauce too?"

"Extra hot sauce. Some goat cheese as well, I think. And add pineapple? For my wife?"

"Lactaid pills are in the cookie jar on the counter."

"That'll do it," Banerji said with a smile. "A perfect meal. Now what can I do for you?"

Cam hesitated. He wanted to tell a joke, to make this funny. But he wouldn't disrespect the wapiti that way. Not with a cheap laugh. "It's . . . odd."

"I like strange. Why do you think I work for Fish and Wildlife?"

"Them fancy government benefits?"

Mr. Banerji laughed.

"I can't explain it, this thing. But it's been driving me up a . . . wall."

Banerji just nodded, like, *Okay, okay, kid, spill.*

"The wapiti. The one hit Saturday morning? What can you tell me about her?"

"If you need to fill the freezer, I'll help. I know things are . . . tough for you and yours lately." Banerji's eyes were brimming with understanding. And maybe with a shot of sorrow. "But the elk, she was not suitable."

"She had the wasting disease, I know."

This time Banerji lifted his bushy eyebrows.

"I was there," Cam explained. "Not long after she was hit."

"I had wondered. You did a good job. She wouldn't have passed well. And the road guys didn't call us until late morning."

If Cam closed his eyes, he could call up her injuries like he'd spent hours cataloging them. "The thing is, what else can you tell me? She's—and this is where it gets real weird—she's haunting me? Or I'm obsessed with her."

He didn't need to say that there was something that made Cam want to connect the wapiti to his cousin. That was too far to speak aloud.

"Is this the kind of thing you'd be best asking my wife about? To everyone but Columbus, that long-dead colonizer, I am the wrong kind of Indian."

Banerji had married in. His wife was a relation of Cam's. But what Cam needed was to know more about the wapiti's physical self before he went the other way and started asking his mom or even his dad for stories. "What else can you tell me? Anything that stands out, seemed different about her."

"Well, yes. Because it was wrong for the season. Off by months. She was pregnant."

Cam blinked. He froze.

He didn't want it to make sense, but in his very messed-up brain it did. The wapiti had tried so hard to drag herself to safety. To protect her developing calf.

"And," Banerji continued, "this is confidential. I don't want this ending up on the group texts, eh? The asshole who hit her has been calling the office trying to convince us he deserves to claim her carcass, to have her taxidermized because she wrecked his vehicle. She owes him, he says. The man clearly knows nothing about taxidermy. Or Alberta Fish and Wildlife. We've sent her brain for processing. And by the time he decided we owed him something, we'd already destroyed the rest of the carcass. I didn't tell him that. Let him think I'm withholding, dicking him around. Let him think that."

"I know you probably shouldn't say . . ."

"You probably shouldn't be sending me home with dinner . . ."

Cam really liked Mr. Banerji.

"The owner of the new boxing gym." Banerji pitched his voice low. "Granville something. Three names, like fancy white families settle upon their kids. A serial killer kind of name."

Cam hadn't heard anything good about that gym. They'd been recruiting down-on-their-luck Natives to fight each other without gear for cash prizes. Cam wouldn't ever consider it. He was doing okay at PMP. And as long as there was a PMP in the undefined future, Cam would continue on okay. He could work his way up and on his off days drive one of his dad's taxis. But others weren't

218

as safe, as fine as Cam. "He's not a very good person, is he?"

Banerji chortled. "Not like you and me. We might not be perfect. We might offer and accept bribes. But we know what's right, what's wrong, eh?"

"I'd like to think so." Even if Cam wasn't happy with his dad these days, and even if Cam's mom was gone most of the week, they'd done their best with him and his sisters, and with Kiki, who'd ended up living with them for the worst reason.

They were still doing their best. All of them.

Even his dad.

Maybe Joe, too, was only doing his best.

"I know so," Banerji confirmed, and then while the pizza finished cooking, they talked about the next intertribal and how soon they could hold a reunion of the Science Fiction and Fantasy Nerdy Natives and its honorary married-in or otherwise adopted members.

When Banerji left all Cam really wanted to do was tell Bee what he'd uncovered. He wanted to watch her brown eyes behind those too-perfect glasses—wanted to know if she felt something resonate too. If they were synched up.

He only hated himself a little for agreeing to go back to school. But when Berlin had asked, he'd wanted to please her. Not only because of his very bad life choice, making out in the washroom at work with the boss's wife.

Earlier, Ira had arrived on time for his shift, and a few minutes after, Joe drove up in his truck looking for Emilie.

Cam had kept his head down, caught under a barrage of uncomfortable feelings.

Now Ira was in the prep room working on homework.

Even though no one was watching, Cam threw the dough he was stretching up in the air with that good drama. Tomorrow, he was sure someone would tell him he wasn't welcome on school property. That he wasn't wanted. And he didn't know what he'd say, what he'd do when it happened. Worse, he didn't know how Berlin would react. And her reaction mattered to him. What would he do, how would he hold himself up if she didn't take his side? Why did that seem the most important thing all of a sudden? Flour sparkling in the air, Cam laughed at himself, threw the dough higher.

Tuesday

Calgary Herald *newspaper clipping from mid-November:*
The RCMP officially closed the case of the missing seventeen-year-old Cree girl, Kiki Cheyanne Sound, today, citing a lack of evidence. Sound has been missing since September, when her family reported she did not return home after school. Canmore superintendent Malcolm Andrews offered this statement: "We have found no evidence to suggest anything criminal has happened. We are ruling out foul play. It is unfortunate, but sometimes young Natives run away from troubled homes. I'd like to commend my dedicated staff for the countless hours they put into this case."

CAM

He'd crossed the threshold and hadn't dissolved into dust like TV said vampires did in sunshine. This was the first of the day's good news. He hadn't slept enough to be bright-eyed, not after making sure his sisters were awake on time, had a breakfast that wasn't only sugar cereal, didn't miss their buses. Even considering Cam's absolute screwup, Monday's open-to-close at PMP had gone decent. He was a few nights' sales away from funding Sami's regalia supplies in full. And Berlin Chambers waited for him in the school lobby.

As if, miracle of all miracles, she wanted him here.

Like always, her glasses were high on her nose. Her hair was pulled into a perky ponytail. Her blunt bangs were perfect, as if the wind didn't muss her like it did the rest of them. Or she used that real good hairspray. When she caught sight of him through the busy lobby, she waved him over with her cute hand.

Cam internally cringed. Cute hand? He was in a bad way.

And there was nothing to do about it.

Walking around a group of younger students, done up like they were going to a party, for a second, only a blip, for Cam the room dimmed into sepia mode, a memory: Kiki here, surrounded by her swim team friends or the mix of them who were big achievers and ran cross-country, too, wearing a neon windbreaker, her hair in natural poofs. Even in sepia she glowed.

Cam wanted to hold on.

It hurt, yeah. But it was that good hurt.

The first bell rang. Across the lobby, Berlin backed up, to let everyone get to class. Cam stopped too. Fighting the crowd wasn't working.

Up until a few days ago, Berlin had disliked him. Now, between them, something new was growing. But there were reasons Cam could never do anything about this weird feeling she inspired. For one, he was her opposite in all things. Maybe even her one-sided nemesis.

He smiled.

Even if her aversion was dimming some, there was yesterday to contend with now.

The rock in Cam's stomach pulsed. This place where he'd never felt welcome, Kiki had loved. She'd been involved in everything. Academics, sports, the Native student group, even volunteering on Parents' Night—not for extra credit, but for goodwill. If Cam were to search the grounds, he'd find traces of his cousin all over. But he wouldn't do that to himself. Why had he agreed when this, just standing here, hurt?

Right, of course, Berlin Chambers, who could sell anything to anyone.

The lobby cleared. He cut across the distance. Berlin smiled like she'd said something.

"Pardon?"

"You're on time," she repeated.

He could do this. He could spar with her. "It's one of my talents."

She laughed, freely, warmly. "One of mine too."

He forced himself into the moment. Forced his memories of Kiki, so sharp here in the high school, his worries about yesterday, away. "I'm firmly on that colonial Mountain Standard Time," he joked. "Except when I'm late."

She waved a hand in the air co-conspiratorially. "There's always an exception. I learned that in French."

Her hand. Like most others, it was only four fingers and a thumb. It was small, like she was.

Being around this Berlin, it was easy.

If he tamped down this new noticing of her hands, her glasses, her perfect bangs. Her smarts. Her sharp edges. Even in a building that Cam hated, a building he might even go as far as to suggest

223

hated him back, Cam forgot that stuff, standing with her.

If only everything in his life could be this comfortable.

"Are you ready to do this?" she asked.

"Let's go crush capitalism with grassroots activism."

Berlin laughed again. "Good trouble, eh?"

Schools, their purpose was to socialize the good trouble out of the population. It was nice to be using one system to break another, even if the impact would be small in the end. One local business maybe saved. Quietly Cam wondered if it shouldn't be Joe's choice to sell his shop, even if it was a choice that would hurt Cam, hurt others. Not that this quiet thought would stop him from being Bee's copilot.

They canvassed, walking the halls, slipping into the library and other student spaces, gathering digital signatures and promises of letters of support and social shares. Still, he couldn't let yesterday go as easy as it seemed Berlin had. He wondered if he was owed an apology for what went down. If Emilie had used him. Because he'd been the only available person. And used for what exactly?

Yes, Emilie was hot. Like pretty much an exceptionally gorgeous, skinny, angry white lady. Cam's brain had shut down entirely when she'd grabbed him by the apron, dragged him into the washroom, and crushed her lips to his.

When she'd pulled the apron out of the way and unzipped his jeans.

Jesus.

Even now, he couldn't quite remember the event. That's what he was calling it. The Event. He couldn't quite remember what, if anything, he'd been thinking. He didn't know how long they'd been in the washroom before they heard the rear door announcing someone's arrival.

Ding.

Zip.

Emilie had stopped, withdrawn her hands, and glanced at herself in the mirror, as if coldly assessing the damage. As if she were looking through herself. Then she'd said, *That's good*, and giggled.

He figured he kissed about as well—or as badly—as any seventeen-year-old. That Emilie had *wanted* someone else to walk in on them.

"Joe and Emilie are divorcing," Cam announced, out of nowhere, as he and Berlin waited outside the faculty lounge. "And I think that maybe she wanted to get back at him. Yesterday. And that's why she picked me. I'm not excusing myself or anything."

If Emilie had a plan, Cam had ended up an easy pawn. When Joe had arrived at the shop he wasn't in any mood to help, even though they were swamped. He'd been looking for his wife, said she texted, claimed her car wouldn't start.

But Berlin and Cam had watched her drive off, easy as all that.

"That's what I'm thinking . . . ," Cam said. "I don't know what it's like for you, but my brain pretty much shuts down if someone kisses me."

Suddenly, the easy feeling dropped. Berlin's shoulders stiffened under her chunky-knit sweater. It was taupe or tan. He wanted to explore the texture of the knit. Discover if it was as soft as he thought. Not that she'd ever let him.

It didn't matter. Having started down this road, he had to finish the journey. To speak the feelings so they'd leave him alone. Because over the past five days with Kiki appearing, the wapiti haunting him, Joe selling, and Berlin's cute hands catching his attention, Cam had had enough of feelings. "Yesterday, my brain shut down. And maybe I'm thanking you for showing up when you did because I don't clearly remember what happened. Like I recall the general everything. I'm not claiming any of those soap-opera excuses. It wasn't my evil twin or amnesia . . . but I don't remember why I was kissing her back. Because I don't think I was. Like *me*, Cameron Sound. I think my treacherous body was kissing her back. Without permission."

"Why are you telling me this?" Berlin asked, her voice almost neutral.

But it wasn't. She was no robot. Even when she wasn't acting aloof and better-than, she held her cards close. Because her cards, they'd reveal her. And she didn't want to be an easy read, didn't want to be opened up by others.

Cam didn't want to be opened up either. He wasn't a can of tomato soup.

"Kinanâskomitin, Bee," he said simply.

"You're welcome, I think."

He laughed at her tone. Wary, but also warm. "You do think, don't you? Like all the time?" He didn't wait for her to respond. Only wanted her to know that he knew. She couldn't hide behind those bangs and her straitlaced attitude any longer. "So, Bee, you tell me what you're thinking."

She spoke in a measured way, word by word, without tone or inflection. "About whether we should knock on the faculty lounge door? You know, what we were discussing before you changed the topic. Or about yesterday?"

"Both?"

"We should wait for someone to come out," she said, glancing down the hallway at the large wall clock. "The period ends in ten minutes. When a teacher emerges, we can ask permission to go inside and tack up a poster, chat with whoever remains."

He nodded.

"And about yesterday? Cam, she should not have done that. I mean, you shouldn't have done it either, but Emilie's legally responsible. At least until you're eighteen. After that, age-of-consent stuff changes. You're seventeen and basically her employee." Berlin exhaled loudly. It fluttered her bangs. "Young men . . . their brains don't actually stop developing until like twenty-five. Did you know that?"

"Bee," he said, entirely bowled over by her knowledge and, frankly, how much she cared. She might think him empty and frivolous, but he'd be honest with her. He wasn't going to wear a mask or hide. Even with the disaster that was yesterday in his backstory, Cam still mostly liked himself. "I watch the History Channel not so much for the Nazi-hunter stories; I mean, I'm on that anti-fascist train, obviously. But I watch the History Channel, really, for the space stuff. Not whatever CBC special you caught late one night on brain development in the youths."

"The History Channel is pretty awesome," she said, deadpan.

"Not *Ancient Aliens*, that shit's problematic."

"Never watched it. But I believe you."

They stood a few feet down from where, last year, she'd, very much on accident, slammed a door into his nose. There had been blood everywhere. His T-shirt, ruined. The floor, flooded. Later, as she'd tried to help stanch the bleeding, the stuff was smeared on her hands. That day, she'd been so horrified, at least once the blood started to gush. Fully animated. Totally alive. But in the seconds before the blood, when he had felt only sharp, bright pain, she'd looked like she'd been sleepwalking.

And in all the time since that incident, even when he'd caught sight of her riding around in Quintana-Roo's topless Jeep, upbeat pop hits blaring, or wandering around the summer intertribal in Calgary, wearing beaded hoops, her hair in two short braids, she hadn't looked nearly as awake as she did right now.

He didn't want Bee to go back to sleep.

For her to lock herself away again. He only hoped he didn't need to bleed like a faucet to keep her here with him.

"So," he hedged, "speaking of aliens . . ."

Her straight face broke. Berlin laughed, like he'd hoped she would. "Sorry, sorry, n-no. Continue," she stammered, trying to rein the laughter in.

"I've always wanted to use that as a narrative transition." Cam checked the hallways. That big clock was ticking down the minutes before Berlin's study period would end and Cam would have to leave. Who knew when they'd have time to talk like this again? And since Friday night, the two of them had been gathering things they shared, things they needed to share. "I found something out. About the wapiti."

"Wait, you've been asking about her?"

Cam nodded.

"I have too."

His skin broke out into gooseflesh.

"I—I can't stop thinking about that night," she whispered.

He stepped closer. "I'm worried she's haunting me."

"I wouldn't use those words exactly. But something like that, yes."

Cam exhaled. "That makes me feel way better. Like nobody wants to be the only target of a slightly off-base haunting by a very large cousin of the deer."

"I had . . . nightmares. Really awful nightmares."

"She was carrying young," Cam said. "Pregnant."

Berlin let a little exhalation escape. "Oh." It was filled with sadness. "Oh," she said again, quieter.

Cam didn't know what else to add. His heart hurt. For the wapiti, for the tiny one who would never be born, for Kiki, always, and even for Berlin—who he was starting to realize was hurting bad too.

Her falling-out with Quintana-Roo, certainly. But Cam would bet his original still-in-the-packaging VHS of Star Wars trilogy that something else topped that.

She crossed her arms over her chest, hugging herself. "I know who hit her, who killed her."

For a second Cam heard *her* as *Kiki*. For a horrid second. But no, they were talking about the wapiti.

When they spoke, it was at the same time. Both at a whisper now.

"Mr. MacDonald's friend."

"Dustin Patrick Granville."

Cam had looked the man's name up last night.

The bell rang. Doors swung open. Students flooded into the halls. Berlin pressed herself against the wall.

"This is the wrong place, the wrong time. But, Cam." Berlin leaned close as the bell finished sounding. "We should talk about Kiki later too. I have some . . . I don't know. I won't call them suspicions. I have thoughts. And I want to think them through with you."

Was there ever a nicer sentence? Berlin Chambers wanted Cam for his thinking prowess. "You could cut?"

"I can't. I just . . . cannot do that. I'm sorry."

"Don't apologize. It was a stupid idea."

"I hate that word," she said.

"So do I."

"Then don't use it."

He laughed now, properly chastised. "I'll work harder. Sami would kick my butt if she caught me calling someone or something stupid."

"I miss seeing her. Your mom doesn't bring her over much anymore."

"University," he said, like it explained everything. "Can you do after school?"

Bee nodded earnestly. Exactly like the girl who hadn't cared to have anything to do with him since kindergarten, when she'd won their last battle by stabbing him in the hand with a pencil.

Even if she had disliked him to the point of violence, she had

230

seemed to care about other people so deeply. Everyone but Cam. Something had shifted.

Cam couldn't be sure when.

"I'll pick you up," he said. "Red LeBaron? You might know it? Barely produces heat but refuses to retire to that junkyard in the skies?"

"After school," she agreed, laughing again—as if she thought Cam were funny. "And I should be honest. It wasn't the CBC. Where I learned about brain development. I don't know why I'm telling you this. But I am. It was vintage episodes of the *Sunday Night Sex Show*—" She stopped herself, then shrugged and continued: "We streamed them. Because for a while in Grade 9, Quinta and I found that show more fascinating than any of the learning we were doing in this building."

She held herself tight, waiting for him to mock her for revealing she'd done what half their class had that year. He was starting to be able to read Bee. To see when she was anxious, when she was vulnerable.

"I'm not going to laugh at you. You're brilliant. If I knew about brains and kissing, I might not have ended up in the washroom at work with Joe's wife. And our sort-of boss. I've never really understood if she qualifies as our boss or not." Cam shrugged one shoulder, mirroring Berlin's earlier body language. "Wait, wait, hold up. Are you saying my brain not keeping pace with my body when someone kisses me is science?"

This time, Berlin didn't laugh, but she smiled.

It slayed him. But damn if he didn't want more of this . . .

whatever it was. Even if it was a feeling. And feelings were dangerous.

"I'm saying it's probably science," she offered. "But I'm also saying that there's a reason consent laws exist. And maybe part of that is the brain not keeping up with the body when lips are involved? And that kissing someone back isn't wrong. But some people shouldn't be kissing you in the first place."

The halls were emptying as students made their way to lunch. Only a few stragglers remained at their lockers, dragging out the seconds where they didn't have to be in the cafeteria or a classroom.

He sent Berlin a look. "I followed eighty, maybe ninety percent of that."

She tried not to react. But Cam could read her now, and this time when she smiled, his entire brain stalled out like the LeBaron sliding on ice when he forgot to engage the clutch quick enough. And it didn't start running again until the faculty lounge door finally opened and out walked the worst teacher Cam had ever had in a long history of shitty experiences with teachers.

He wanted to tell Berlin about the time, that first week after Kiki went missing, when MacDonald cornered Cam during one of the community search parties. They were both getting a slice from the boxes Joe was delivering every few hours.

Cam had taken a bite of the only food he'd had all day when MacDonald had started talking: *Why don't you leave this to the professionals? It's not like you're making any progress here. It's been five days, Cameron. You tried. But you're not doing yourself any favors, out here, when you're already failing my class.*

This hour with Berlin had been the best moments Cam had ever

232

spent in this building, and like things went when you lived with sideways luck, here was the worst part about the school, showing up, as if to keep the universe properly balanced.

BERLIN

She knew they had the same free period, but she hated that it was Mr. MacDonald who left the faculty lounge first. Anyone, most literally, other than him would have been preferable. Even Mr. Roper, who refused to give Berlin higher than a 90 on any assignment, no matter what she did. Especially after what Mr. MacDonald had said on Sunday. How he'd talked about her. How he'd spoken to her. It was harder and harder to pretend she respected him in the ways you were supposed to respect teachers and other knowledge keepers.

But she tried. "Good afternoon, Mr. MacDonald."

He held a Styrofoam cup in one hand, wore a fitted pink-collared shirt. The kind people wore in the summers to go golfing at Silvertip, but fashion.

"It is a good day, isn't it?" he said, a grin on his still-bruised and totally battered face. "I'm ready to hear you're officially joining the curling team."

A greasy, uncomfortable clench gripped her insides. She hated fake ice, the taste of ammonia.

Then it happened. Mr. MacDonald spotted Cam standing slightly behind her, and the shift, it was instantaneous. Her teacher dropped his faux friendly act and pivoted. His cup tilted, spilling coffee onto the floor. He wiped at his hand briskly and cursed under his breath. "What are you doing on these premises?"

It was instinct. Berlin threw out an arm to hold Cam off, at least until she could explain. Technically, campus was closed during school hours. Visitors needed to stop by the office and declare themselves. And, yes, technically, Cam wasn't a student any longer.

"I invited him," she said. "He's helping gather support for Pink Mountain Pizza? I'm—"

"Is this what you're wasting time on instead of your schoolwork? Shakespeare won't read himself."

She'd finished the play.

She'd told him she finished the play.

Always, even when all she wanted to do was lie in bed and be empty, always, she did her readings. And every other assignment. She was, as he'd said, *technically perfect.*

She stared at the coffee on the floor. "I wouldn't call it a waste of time."

"I just did," Mr. MacDonald said. "We talked about your next move. If not curling, what about track?"

"I didn't agree."

"And I thought you were smarter."

Cam stepped closer to Berlin and in the process closer to Mr. MacDonald. "Don't talk to her like that."

Cameron was defending her. The greasy feeling retreated and she could breathe without choking.

"Don't make me call down to the office and have you escorted off the premises." But Berlin's least favorite teacher wasn't done. He

234

looked her in the eyes, as if this was the most important thing he would ever say to her, and here was what he said: "If this is what you took away from our little chat on the chairlift, then you've gotten the answer wrong. About your life, but about living in general as well, yeah? You can't fight progress's forward march. Nor should you. I wish you Natives could see that. You'd all be better off if you could see that."

Her vision fizzled with red, a moment of rage, a moment of grief.

He hadn't.

He had.

Berlin refused to show her feelings. To fight back. Not because she couldn't risk him tanking her grade and ultimately screwing her very planned-out future, but because she didn't argue with anyone who used the phrase *you Natives*.

She said nothing, pretended to let it go.

"Get to class, Ms. Chambers. Your performance in ELA is slipping. You hardly participated yesterday. And if I ask around, I'm sure I'll find my colleagues reporting similar behaviors."

The spill on the floor was bleeding into the hallway.

"It's. Lunch. Period."

And she was late to her FNMISA meeting. In his classroom. And she'd failed utterly in her attempt to speak to Quinta about fundraiser donations. She'd have to report that to the group.

Cam grabbed her hand and gently pulled. "Let's go."

His was warm. Bigger than hers.

She shouldn't have said anything. But it seemed important. In a real way. "Aren't you going to clean that spill?" she asked.

Some things mattered. Enough to take the risk.

Mr. MacDonald stared her down. "The janitor will get it when he passes through later. It's his job. Mine is enlightening young minds."

It was a dismissal. A statement as loud as *you Natives*.

To believe that you should clean up after your own mistakes, you had to care about others. Acknowledge your privilege. Use it for the common good and not for your own benefit.

Mr. MacDonald thought himself too good to gather paper towels from the faculty lounge and get down on his knees.

Prickling with heat all over, she squeezed Cam's hand and turned. She wanted to tell Mr. MacDonald that he was a terrible human and that even if he was fooling a bunch of high schoolers now, he wouldn't fool them forever. He was an elitist, irresponsible . . . a colonial, capitalism-loving settler and a generally awful person. That's who he was.

Cam was guiding her toward an exit.

It was the right plan. The exact right plan.

Mr. MacDonald's voice carried down the hall: "Cameron isn't welcome back, Ms. Chambers. If you aren't careful, you'll end up following his path all the way to that pizza shop permanently. And then where will you be? Working for minimum wage making overpriced food with kids from the high school for the rest of your life. Wearing an apron and a hat."

It was an attack. From someone who was supposed to support students. And it was cruel.

"He's an asshole," Berlin whispered, for Cam's ears only.

Behind them, Mr. MacDonald began to whistle.

"Let's talk," she said. "Cam, only for a second."

"I—I should go."

"Let's talk," she said again. "He's a grade-fucking-A asshole."

"Not here," Cam said, shaking his floppy hair in the negative. Rallying enough to take control, he changed direction, dragged her toward the gym, and before she could even lodge a protest, yanked open one of the janitor's closets, pulling her inside. He closed the door, set the lock, but didn't release his grip on her hand.

Finally, Cam spoke: "That was about me, not you."

"That's not entirely accurate. He's been on my case lately. I don't know why. But thank you."

"I do. Know, that is." Cam brushed his fingers against her palm. "Haven't you noticed? It's business as usual around here. Most of the teachers keep their garbage prejudice to themselves, at least during school hours. MacDonald never has."

It's not that she didn't believe Cameron. Only, her experience of the world had been different.

"Until this week, he's never been that way with me."

Cam dropped her hand. He leaned against one of the metal storage shelves and let his neck fall back, exposing his throat.

"He has, Bee, you just didn't want to see it. I remember last year. Before I . . . He mentioned your work with the Native student association as if it was lesser than track or swim or whatever extra-curriculars he endorses as real, as important. Like it was a frivolous social club. And not a group of dedicated people who want to make this place and this community better for those coming up. Who volunteer their time at the hospital and with the elementary schools.

Like all you did was bitch about settlers and what you were owed on the school's dollar."

His cheeks were reddening, his hands clenching.

"And he hates Ms. Ducharme. She'd be a better faculty advisor for you all. But no, MacDonald is waiting for Abbott to retire—Kiki always said the only reason *he* sponsored the group was because it got the administration off his back for some historical chess club trip debacle."

They didn't bother Abbott and he didn't bother them. It worked. But it would be nice to have a real faculty sponsor. And having Mr. MacDonald in the role would be hellish.

The closet she and Cam were in was a storeroom. The year she started high school, the FNMISA, spearheaded by Kiki's enthusiasm, had petitioned the school to switch to eco-friendly cleaning supplies. Around them, the shelves were stocked.

This was what they did. One of the things they'd accomplished.

"I mean, we do complain some," she said without much inflection. But there was enough. She wanted him to smile, to laugh.

He didn't—couldn't yet.

"How did you know we did all that? You never joined us."

"Berlin," Cam said, "it's like cosmic-level hard not to notice what you do. All that you do."

"Your mom?" she asked. "I'm sure Kiki talked about everything too. Before."

"Yeah, she did. That's how I knew how to get in here. The week these supplies arrived she dragged me down for show-and-tell." He pushed his hair off his forehead and finally smiled. "Bee, you're completely and totally a part of this community, here in town, but a part of the wider Indigenous communities that stretch across the prairies online. What you do isn't unnoticeable. You're kind of loud. In that way."

"Oh."

"You don't see yourself very clearly, do you? And I don't mean in the mirror. Because Creator knows you know how to use a comb and that fancy hairspray that keeps your bangs so shiny and flat."

He wasn't kidding.

This wasn't a joke.

"I could teach you the hair tricks."

He laughed.

So did she. But she owed him more than that too. "You are right."

"Finally," he said, nodding to himself. Like this was a big deal.

"I'm starting to think I don't. See myself that well. But you can't tell me that Mr. MacDonald doesn't hold a bunch of ire for you as well."

"Oh yeah, he hates me." Cam sighed. "And don't ask what I did. The man acts like I've personally wronged him in the worst way. Just by breathing the same air."

"He's always had his favorites."

Neither of them mentioned how he held up anyone who joined one of his teams as the best of the best. How it was obvious they were beloved. How he'd give them extensions he didn't offer anyone else. How he made time before and after school to consult with those students.

"He's probably the reason I dropped out."

"What a total, complete asshole. And like no offense to assholes. But fuck him."

Cam laughed again, a low-down rumble. "Oh, Bee, thank you for that."

"For what? Saying what's true?"

"You're adorable when you curse."

And the room suddenly got too hot. Her heartbeat echoed in her temples. "I didn't know," she said cautiously, as if changing the topic would be enough for her to find her calm again, "that you have a learning disability."

He scoffed. But it was good-natured. "What did you think? No, no, seriously. That I was incompetent? Careless? Lazy?"

"Um . . ." She nodded sheepishly. "All of the above?"

This time his laughter was louder and sharper.

They weren't all the same. Like a language, his laughs had different meanings, inflections. Cam was more complicated than she'd given him credit for.

"Wow, Berlin Chambers and the ableist bullshit, eh?" he said.

"I'm sorry. I—" She stopped herself. "I've always been incredibly hard on you. For no good reason."

"And I thought your reason was you've been sore all these years over losing our kindergarten fight."

"I did not lose."

"You totally did."

"I stabbed you," she said. "With a pencil."

"Right, that was an illegal move. You weren't allowed anything but soft markers for the rest of the year. And I got to spend the

240

afternoon in the nurse's office. So, by default, I won."

She sank down to the floor, leaned against the shelf's support beam. "I am sorry, for that too. I have no idea why I stabbed you that day."

"Brain development, eh?" He sat next to her. "I don't think you're a stuck-up perfectionist anymore."

"My reputation will never recover," she said dramatically.

"Honestly, Bee? I hope it doesn't."

"Oof."

She was picking up Jessie-isms. After only a few days. A few hours in each other's company, skating round and round, bathed in neons.

"You know I mean it in all kindness, right?"

"I do."

He straightened against the shelf. "Let's get out of here, like out of this cursed school, and try to get more support. I'll drive."

Berlin wanted to. She did.

But she couldn't.

"It's as easy as walking out the front door." He was looking at her funny. "I have plenty of experience. I'll be your guide. We can pretend the exit is a river we need to ford. No one will get dysentery, I promise."

She rested her chin on her hands. "I'm already late for an FNMISA meeting. I have a test in bio, a team project to work on in World Religions, and Mr. MacDonald will crush me like a pop can if I don't show up this afternoon. Not after . . ."

"I get it," Cam said, pushing himself up from the floor.

He offered her a hand.

Outside the closet, the hallways were empty, the only noises coming from the cafeteria. Berlin wasn't sure, but she thought she might be hungry. "Let me walk you out."

"You're, ah, gonna defend my person against the other horrible humans in this building, are you?"

"Yes."

She would.

He smiled and laughed. This one made the hairs on her arms buzz.

"We still on for after school? We can approach Quintana-Roo together?"

"I cannot believe you still call her that. She only ever tolerates me using her full name."

"She said I could."

A wave of irrational jealousy tried to knock Berlin off balance. Her very best friend. The person she thought she'd been closest to in the wide-as-eternity universe, that person who would no longer talk to her, who had her trek into the cold yesterday and hadn't stuck around, that person let Cam, who wasn't even her friend, call her by her legal name. "Doesn't sound like Quinta at all. Maybe you don't need me."

"Bee, trust we all desperately need you. Even Quintana-Roo."

"I want to believe that."

"Go eat. Tell your activist club that I kept you. The rest of the world can wait until the next bell."

"Is that how life works?"

"It could, if you let it, Bee," he said as they stepped into the lobby again.

242

The day had clouded over.

"See you," she said.

"I'll be there."

She hurried to the ELA classroom, thinking through what she'd tell Tashie and the others. How she'd make it up to them. She had tried but she hadn't tried hard enough. She'd fix it, buy the supplies herself.

Whatever peace she'd found, for a hot second in a storage closet with Cam, would probably be the best part of her school day.

And that was fine.

She stepped into the classroom, ready to take whatever the other members of the FNMISA had to throw her way, but they'd already finished. The circle was gone. The desks were back in perfect rows.

Closing the door for a little soundproofing, Berlin screamed until her lungs emptied of air.

JESSIE

The witching hour approached. She was inside Berlin Chambers's freakin' house, sitting on Bee's dead-cowskin couches. Drinking her silky and spicy hot bloody chocolate. Jessie had even spotted a three-legged rescue cat. Ye gods, a tripod! She shoved another pastel marshmallow in her mouth. One of the little ones. The almost-too-cute-to-eat ones. And she was surrounded by the people she was quickly deciding were probably going to become her friends.

Not like her school buddies.

These people were going to be her real friends. If, and it was

243

asking the wide and wisdom-filled universe for a massive boon . . . if when she finally told them her father was the big bad behind the ruining of Pink Mountain, they didn't loathe her.

Berlin had her laptop out with its Save the Bats sticker on the casing, and she was counting responses on social media, making a chart to present to Joe tomorrow. Next to her, Sasha was doing the same with another platform, and every once in a while they'd read out a particularly poignant or funny response.

"This one's good. buriedinpages says, 'Praying to the pizza gods for y'all. Sacrificing a round of mozzarella for the cause,' and then right below it, laura_rueckert_writes comes in with this knife to the belly: 'Come on, Joe—you're better than this, my friend. There are always other options than selling out.'"

"Hopes and prayers and a good dose of sharpened guilt," Cam said from his spot across the room on the other couch.

He'd been voice-texting friends who hadn't followed through with promised support while Jessie made a final push, taking steps to block her brothers from seeing her posts. That would be an unsinkable-ship-is-sinking-and-we-don't-have-enough-safety-gear-level oopsie.

"What do you think"—Sasha paused dramatically, staring straight at Berlin—"be'Hom 'IH?"

She pursed her lips and started shaking her head. "I don't even want to guess."

"Was that Klingon?" Cam asked from across the living room. "I didn't know you were a *Star Trek* fan."

Sasha laughed. "I got you, Berlin! Finally!"

"Yeah, you got me, all right," she said. "With a fictional language from TV. How sporting. Did it take you long to think that up?"

Sasha shrugged. "Not that long."

And then they laughed. Jessie wanted to join in. But tomorrow, fifteen minutes from now, would be the last full day they had to change Joe's mind. And an entirely unwanted, unneeded disaster-level sinkhole loomed.

Berlin wasn't the only one worried that Joe wouldn't be moved by their #SavePMP and #KeepPMPLocal campaign. Though they'd gone for it, and really tried, like they were pulling an all-nighter, they didn't have a rat's chance against the rat catchers. Jessie's father never lost.

As many scrapes as she'd gathered in her life, she'd always believed in ripping off Band-Aids real fast. She chewed a handful of marshmallows methodically. Jessie had to tell them. Even if these things were kept all hush-hush until deals were finalized, she knew exactly who was buying PMP.

"Oh, this is a good one." Sasha interrupted the quiet again. "bhootbabe says, 'If PMP goes corporate, I'm quitting pizza.'"

Cam half yawned and then put his phone down. "Hey, I have a thought to share or a statement to make. I'm not sure which yet. But are we kinda bullying Joe? I'm starting to feel like this is next door to bullying."

Berlin shrugged.

Sasha threw a hand out but didn't speak.

Jessie didn't have answers either.

"No one else?" Cam exhaled loudly. "All right, I'll go back to not bullying my friends and foes into not bullying our boss into not selling his shop to a bunch of bullies."

The Poseidon Group were that. And you needed a united front to win against that level of bad. But the whole PMP crew wasn't even fully committed. Quinta and Ira were closing, to give the rest of them a chance to work. But that's all those two were willing to offer. They didn't believe in the cause.

And worse was coming. What Jessie had trolled out earlier, snooping through her father's at-home office, had solidified things. And when she told these people who she so desperately wanted to be her friends, they'd probably turn against her.

"Why did we decide on hot chocolate instead of something with caffeine?" Cam yawned again.

Berlin smiled in his direction. "Want a Coke?"

"Are you offering?" he volleyed back.

"No promises, but check the fridge. At the bottom, behind my dad's collection of hot sauces."

Cam whooped.

Over the rim of her mug, Jessie studied the room like there was a test next period and she couldn't fail. Bee didn't sprawl on the couch like Cam. Instead, her shoulders were posture perfect. She had a lap desk with a reading light attached. It was so hot. Not only her posture but her give-a-care.

"Let's take a mini break," Jessie said, fast. She needed to hold on to this goodness a little longer before she did the brave and broke the spell. "Let's see who can shove the most marshmallows in their face."

Cam returned from the kitchen. "I'm in."

From their place next to Bee on the couch, Sasha raised an eyebrow. "What does the winner earn themselves?"

"You three decide on stakes." Berlin put her laptop aside and stood. "We'll need the jumbo marshmallows for this or it will take all night."

"How about five bucks and bragging rights as the one with the biggest mouth," Cam suggested.

"Perf," Jessie said.

Returning with the fancy vegan premium-sized marshmallows, Berlin tore the bag open with her teeth.

Ye gods and oof all in one.

"Okay, go," Berlin said, and they started.

By three it was getting hard to speak.

At seven, Berlin tapped out. She extracted the last two marshmallows from her mouth carefully.

By eight, Sasha was turning red.

At nine, Cam laughed and almost choked. But he held on.

Jessie couldn't take another. She held up a hand. And then she said, "Dudes, I have something to tell you all."

But it came out garbled.

"Come on." Berlin smiled. "No talking during this part of the competition."

Cam went for ten. But Jessie knew it was time. The clock turned and whatever this was, now it had to survive Jessie's father. And not much escaped his attention unscathed. She spat as many of the marshmallows out of her mouth as she could and blurted: "I said, dudes, I have something important to tell you."

Wednesday

capitalislife0003451: Communism failed for a reason. All you minorities need to stop living in the past.

proudddbois: It's these Indians always complaining about what's good for society.

fuckPMP: The CPP should lower the student minimum wage again if these kids have time to get up to bullshite.

CAM

All he could taste was the sticky, too-sweet confection. Even though he'd won their challenge, some cash he wouldn't accept, and bragging rights, which he would, it didn't feel like a win. Not once the marshmallows reminded Cam of his cousin's s'mores pizza, and not once Jessie's words registered.

"That's fucked, Jessie," he said.

Yes, Cam was tired.

The kind that settled in the bones and took up permanent residence. The way settlers had. All over this land. And he knew how that had turned out. It was not a good sign. For things to come.

Neither was this news.

"I know, I know," she said in the least Jessie voice Cam had ever heard from her. But she recovered. "It's fuck-a-duck-level suck."

"North Americans tend to catastrophize." Sasha leaned into the couch. "But yes, can confirm, this is bad."

Berlin seemed a lot calmer than Cam felt. One of her eyebrows peaked. That was the extent of her reaction.

She said, in that forever deadpan tone of hers—the one Cam was starting to crave like sour candies—"It sure explains some things."

Like she'd been hit with friendly fire, Jessie recoiled.

That's when the door to Berlin's house opened and in walked the most unexpected of all unexpected guests: Ira, and behind him, Quintana-Roo.

"We talked it out, closed a few minutes early," Ira said. "We want to help."

Quintana-Roo shrugged, keeping her eyes averted. "What he said. And we brought some more uninvited guests to this party."

Theatrical SarahLynn and her older sister Tashie, who had only ever worn black since Cam had known her, entered the house, gabbing as they took off their shoes in the entryway. Behind them was Vincent—the guy was ace on the drum and had a great voice—and a Métis girl in a onesie a few grades behind who Cam didn't know by name but knew by sight.

That wasn't it.

Nico Vasquez stepped inside, looking awfully uncomfortable.

"We figured you could use all the help you could get. And at least, now, you'll accept it when things don't go your way." Quintana-Roo was talking right at Berlin.

It wasn't warm, but it was support-like. And now they didn't have to track her down. They could have their talk with hot chocolate. It might smooth out Quintana-Roo's edges a smidge. Or it might be handing her a weapon.

Hot chocolate to the face would hurt.

But it would be a good story to tell.

While the newcomers shed their winter gear and got settled in the living room, Berlin continued staring at her best friend. And then, as if she'd made a decision about something life-changing, Berlin stood, placed her lap desk on the floor gently, and walked out of the room, taking to the stairs.

For a minute, no one spoke. Not even Jessie.

"Well, that went exactly fucking how I thought it would. Whose good idea was this?" Quintana-Roo asked, walking off toward the kitchen to help herself to the fridge.

As he scanned the room once more, it was obvious what Cam needed to do. He followed the prickly, hurting girl. First up one set of stairs and then up another to the attic. There, she curled against the wall in a window seat. Probably called it a reading nook. Snapdragon, the three-legged cat his mom loved so much, sat on Bee's bed, chirping. He cooed quietly back at the cat, lowered himself slowly onto the other half of the window seat. A fluttery curtain tickled his cheek.

Berlin's hands were wrapped around her legs, her feet tucked close to her bum. Her socks were chunky rainbow knits. Reaching out, he ran a finger along the strip of red. Then back to orange. Her foot tightened, but when he traced yellow, she relaxed into the sensation. He worked his way to where the pattern restarted and reversed.

The cat meowed from the bed. It was friendly, curious.

Berlin breathed in and out, to calm herself. To find footing on the ice. She faltered. Heaved.

Cam continued tracing gentle waves against her right foot.

Downstairs, the PMP crew and assorted guests' voices were muffled. Berlin's parents had gone to bed hours ago.

"I'm sorry," Cam said eventually.

It was true.

This was too much, too awful. The way every word dropped seemed to scald her. And though Cam knew it, he still needed Bee to talk to Quintana-Roo with him. He needed her to do something that hurt so badly, it sent her fleeing from her own living room.

Berlin wasn't the kind to retreat.

To run away.

She held her ground. She was inflexible in so many ways, only this time, because she couldn't bend like trees did in hard winds, she'd snapped.

"Stop," she said. "You have nothing to be sorry for."

He continued tracing the rainbow. "Well, I asked you to talk to QR with me. And that can't tickle."

Horrifyingly, Berlin started to cry. Two constant rivers rolled down her cheeks. She didn't make much sound. Was holding back. As much as she could.

Cam didn't know why her tears hurt him so much. The way they hurt when his sisters or his mom cried. Like his insides were being ground up into hot-dog filling.

Next to him, Bee hiccupped. Wiped her face on the sleeve of her sweater. The same one she wore that morning at school. The one she wore when he picked her up at the final bell, when they'd decided not to return to PMP—to talk to Quintana-Roo on neutral territory—and instead pushed harder on their final attempt to save the shop.

"You need a Kleenex. You're going to scratch yourself, doing it like that." Cam spotted what he wanted. Gathered the box from atop a dresser and handed it to her.

She took a tissue and blew her nose loudly. When she finished, her nose was red and her eyes were still brimming, but she turned to sit again, her back to the window, her feet settled on the carpet.

Cam held out a hand.

"Ew," she said, and a broken laugh emerged.

She pushed herself up, got rid of the tissue in a small wicker trash can. When she returned, she sat next to him, close. Looked his way for a second. Then, in a careful move, one slow enough he could have stopped her if he'd wanted to, she leaned into him, resting her head against his shoulder.

"What are we going to do? We've been running around all day long and we've been working so hard. And none of it matters, does it?"

His throat clamped down. Heart thumped like it wanted to run. And what if they were hurting Joe with all this hard work? What if everyone was hurting now?

Feelings sucked.

Cam smoothed out his voice. It was what she needed from him.

"It does. I promise you, it matters."

"But what if we're trying to save something Joe wants to get rid of? What if he needs to leave this place? Not wants to, needs to. What if he's running from something? Something terrible. And what if it's his own guilt?"

In the entirety of their relationship, which, if family lore was to be trusted, meant they'd known each other through their pregnant mothers, in utero, Cam had never before heard Berlin utter so many terrified, speculative sentences in a row.

"This is a bit shadowy for me. I'm no good at word games." He didn't push away from the tickle of her hair against his nose. "But I want to hear what you have to say."

"What if . . . ," she said, "Joe . . . what if he was the one . . . what if he hurt—"

Cam's chest tightened until he wasn't sure he could speak. But he had to. "No. Impossible. How could you suggest that?"

They were still pressed against each other. Touching.

It was the most intimate thing Cam had ever done with someone who wasn't related to him. Because intimacy was different than making out with someone in a washroom.

"I don't know," she said, and started crying again, against his long-sleeve shirt.

Cam was angry. Not at her. At the world, at feelings. He was scared too. But he was still her friend. Sort of.

He handed Berlin another tissue. "Do you really need to tell me?"

She nodded.

"Okay, I'll listen. But I'm doing this for you, so you can get it out."

"There was a photo. On the wall. At work. And it seemed important."

"In Joe's office?"

"Yes. One of Kiki. She's not wearing her apron or her ball cap."

"I know it," Cam said carefully. He loved that photo, the way his cousin's eyes seemed to be laughing but her face wasn't giving away the play. "Why does it matter?"

What had Berlin, who saw the world so differently, seen that Cam couldn't?

She moved away. Far enough to look him in the eyes. Not so far that he couldn't still feel her thigh pressed against his. "Not a single one of the other pictures on that wall are like that. Every other one of us are wearing the PMP logo in some fashion. Aprons. Ball caps. Those hideous pink plastic name tags from back in the day."

"But it's not proof. Not against Joe. It's that causation and correlation thing from science class."

She nodded, then shook her head in the negative. Nodded again. She was fully fucked up.

Welcome to the club, Bee.

It was something Cam had known Before—how the universe became smaller, how the hole left behind consumed light at an unknowable speed. How a missing auntie found, a lost cousin, hurt in the infinite. How the hurt didn't compress but expanded. How that expansion was forever.

"But, Cam, I looked at that photo and I knew, immediately, in my body, that it meant something. It means something. I have to trust myself. If I stop, if I don't, I . . ." She didn't finish her thought.

She didn't have to.

He understood. Still, he had to be sure she knew, that something, it could not be what she thought. "I believe you. There's a thing there, yes. But, Berlin, it doesn't mean Joe . . . hurt . . ."

"Okay, okay," she said, picking at her sleeve.

He reached out, stilled her hand. "You're going to wreck your sweater."

"Quinta bought it for me."

"Ouch."

"Yeah." She stopped shredding the knit. "What do you know about Nico?"

"The guy downstairs right now?"

"Yes."

"You don't think . . . ?"

"I don't know," she practically yelled. "But he lied to me. Made it seem he was in the shop the day the police interviewed Joe. As if he worked at Pink Mountain. That's the only way he would have been there. And if he wasn't there, why is he telling stories and why do his stories make me doubt Joe? You don't try to punch a hole in a brick wall after the police interview you over your former employee going missing unless you're guilty. So Nico's spun up in this somehow. He's still . . . sore about Kiki. But he's not family. He wasn't one of her people."

Cam laughed. "Bee, for like a year that guy was head over his ski boots for her."

"But following her to work every night, isn't that stalkerish? Couldn't it have gotten . . . out of hand? He lied to me! Told the story like he witnessed it. How else would he know the details?"

"Did you confirm it with anyone?"

She shook her head.

"Maybe he was in the shop that day? You know, we do sell pizza and most people are obsessed with it. Maybe he called the police on Joe? Maybe Nico's just a gossip?"

Berlin grumbled.

"Nico gave her the sweetest Christmas gift. It was so Kiki."

"What was it?"

"A little notebook. Neon orange. With a set of those fancy archival pens. For her poetry." Cam lifted his arm, swung it around Berlin's shoulder. He needed something to hold on to too.

"She loved that book. Carried it everywhere." Berlin sighed like she couldn't let it go. "Cam, he lied."

"People lie, Bee. They protect themselves, they make themselves seem more important in the story, bigger than they were. It doesn't mean they're capable of . . . that."

"If you think so, okay."

"Is that it? Or do you have anyone else your awesome brain has filed under suspects comma Kiki?"

It was becoming easier and easier to say his cousin's name.

Berlin pulled her little hands up against her chest. "If you're certain, like solidly, about Joe."

Cam did the most outrageous thing. He leaned over and pressed his lips to Berlin's forehead, in the space between her bangs and

256

her incredibly perfect glasses.

She squeaked but didn't move.

"As sure as you can get about a person. Joe thought of her . . . almost like a daughter."

Berlin laughed. "Because they're both Black? Come on, Cam."

"No." He chuckled. "Joe . . . he thought for a while he had a kid, a girl. But it turned out not to be a thing. And his daughter-not-daughter would have been older than us, around Kiki's age."

"That's sad," Berlin said, falling quiet against him for a minute. "What are we going to do? How can we fight Jessie's dad and his coalition? The Poseidon Group owns half the province. And a whole mountain."

"One named after your ancestor, eh? Didn't he side against Louis Riel?"

"That he did."

Cam laughed again. Because of how she said it. He couldn't call it flirting. But he'd call it warming. Berlin Chambers was warming to him.

"Well, first . . ."

She raised a finger, counting on his behalf.

"We're going to go back downstairs. And second . . ."

She raised another finger.

"We're going to get louder. Call them out. No more letting these guys hide behind Joe. It's time to draw Darth Vader and his minions out in the open. We're going to name them, call them out for everything we can uncover. Because Joe might be doing business with these guys, but he's not one of them."

Cam folded her fingers down. Then wrapped her tiny hand in his.

He expected her to hesitate about their campaign going dirty. Cam didn't love it, not how they'd hung Joe out for the entire community to comment on his life choices. But Cam didn't like Joe partnering with those men either.

Without hesitation she said, "Downstairs, they all need to agree. Everyone."

Cam nodded. She hadn't asked the first time. It had come as a little bit of a surprise to him when Berlin had posted to social media. But that was how news spread in Native communities and Cam knew almost no one who didn't use social media in some way. But this time, she wouldn't decide for them. Bee would offer everyone a say. To get on board or to get clear of the coming explosion. Even the girl who broke her heart, was still breaking it. Berlin didn't fit as a leader, the one at the helm, making solo decisions and ordering others to follow. She wasn't suited to that role. But she was exactly right for this. For holding folks together. For asking others to join in collaboration.

"Let's do this, then," she said.

From the bed, the cat chirped again. Cam had been right. Bee's bedroom was tidy. Almost obsessively so. Except for the stack of books piled on one of the bedside tables. Those piles continued onto the floor. Salvador Dalí. Frida Kahlo. René Magritte. Pablo Picasso. Books upon books about artists. The kind that fussed reality with twisting, twisting things.

A nice surprise. Unexpected. Tamping down a glut of unwanted feelings, Cam followed Berlin back into the fray.

BERLIN

The walk from her bedroom to the main floor had never seemed so impossibly long. But she couldn't retreat. For one, Cam was behind her. If she tried to run, he'd think less of her.

In the kitchen, Vincent stood next to Tashie and Darcie and the tea-making stuff. They'd never been in her house before, but they looked comfortable circling the island. "Hey, Bee," they said in unison.

Berlin's phone was filled with unanswered texts. It sat on the living room couch, next to her laptop, where she'd left it when she fled. Most from Tashie:

> **Did you ask Quinta yet? We needed to get that poster to art yesterday!**
> **Yo, where are you?**
> **Berlin? Did I miss spring forward or something? Did you go home sick?**
> **Okay, then, we're done in here. But text us, yeah?**

Tashie leaned against the counter. "Missed you this afternoon."

"Yeah, you don't ever skip meetings." Vincent added sugar to his tea.

"So we knew it was serious."

This from Darcie, who was wearing her PJs.

"But since I saw you after school, getting into Cameron's car . . . ,"

Tashie said, in the way only someone who was an older sibling could, all care and slight annoyance wrapped together, "we knew you were okay."

In the other room, Quinta was laughing with SarahLynn.

It sounded so normal.

Tea in hand, Darcie shrugged. "I tracked down her schedule and followed her to World History. I couldn't wait and see."

"Don't scare us like that, Berlin." Vincent crossed his arms on his chest. "Yeah?"

It wasn't the right moment, but Berlin started tidying the kitchen. She moved the kettle back to its corner and replaced the lid on the sugar caddy. Then she stopped. "I am so sorry." She couldn't look at them. "I let you all down and I didn't ask Quinta about donations. It's—"

"Chill, Bee." Tashie reclaimed the kettle, filled her mug with hot water. "You didn't let us down. You're busy, yo. So I had SarahLynn do it. She dropped by PMP and got Quinta to agree to send over a bunch of baking supplies. We're good."

One attempt and it was done. When Berlin had walked across town only to be blown off. "That easy, eh?"

"Like bear grease."

Berlin couldn't help but laugh quietly. "Thanks. For the assist."

"Yeah, always." Tashie pushed the sleeves of her sweater up to her elbows. "Don't you get it yet? We're your friends. Or we could be your friends if you let us."

Darcie and Vincent nodded.

"And after my sister chatted with your bestie, of course," Tashie continued, "it was basically midnight and SarahLynn's calling me talking about how tonight is this whole last stand against the end of a good thing. I've been crushed all week about Joe leaving. So I dialed Vincent and we video-chatted Darcie. Now we're here. Put us to work."

Before, when Berlin had Quinta, she hadn't needed other people—hadn't thought of anyone else in that way. What she'd had was enough. Or it had seemed to be, the way at first glance Duchamp's *Fountain* appeared simple.

Berlin hadn't bothered to explore if there were other ways of seeing, of knowing. She'd just accepted it: that Quinta was her one and only. That Quinta could carry all of Bee and that in return she could carry all of Quinta.

Which wasn't true.

It had to start somewhere. Relying on others. And Pink Mountain was running out of time.

"I'd like us to be friends," Berlin said.

Vincent smiled. "Then it's official."

In the living room, everyone divided the labor. Calling out Mr. Hampton, Dustin Patrick Granville, and the other members of the Poseidon Group. They reminded the community that if Joe decided to sell, these weren't the right people.

"He sets up a pot, like two grand. And then sends out fancy invites." One of Nico's friends had tried it for the fast cash; that's how Nico knew.

This time, Berlin had asked for his source. She was still a little upset with him, the way his stories seemed first person when they weren't. How a person could hide so much in that gap.

The buddy lived in Calgary. But Nico's friend sent pictures. They were #NSFW. Brutal. All that violence for a possible payday.

Not that Berlin didn't understand how two thousand dollars could be life changing. Even if she worked because she wanted to, not because she needed to. Two thousand dollars could do so much for so many people she knew, could fund the No More Stolen Sisters' self-defense program for years.

It seemed so simple, when before it was about Joe leaving them. Now it was about finding someone who could carry on the good work Joe had been doing, so that if he really wanted to, the boss could retire.

"And if local business titan Kyle Hampton is willing to work with someone whose entire model for making cash money is baiting those who are in need," Nico said, warming up to the room, "then how can the community trust Kyle Hampton?"

It was a rhetorical question.

No answers required.

But it was a question from a liar too. Berlin couldn't shake that, couldn't trust Nico's motives. Tonight, he'd been at Pink Mountain minutes after SarahLynn, as if that was how the universe worked: by accident rather than by design.

And Berlin was only just learning how love could go bad. Or maybe it hadn't been love at all between Nico and Kiki. Maybe it was obsession. How you could consume a person and name it love.

"Hell's flaming red bells, run the other way!" Jessie said, but she was torn up, too, her hands, her knees shaking.

She'd left the house to smoke in the backyard, returned a minute later to say something, only to flee again. At the roller rink, they'd talked about nothing, about everything. Jessie's father didn't know that his daughter wanted to be a welder. That his daughter wanted to build things, things that would drive the world, things that were functionally beautiful. It was three years of school and Jessie swore up and down that her parents would never pay.

"They weren't going to pony up before this, so it doesn't matter," Jessie said, standing near the front door, her hands clutched, still imbued with a tiny tremor, as they said good night to everyone. "And, Bee, I should have told you sooner. About my father."

"When did you find out?"

"Last night when I went all *Archer* on his home office. But I've had Spidey-senses a-tingling for a week or so."

"You're forgiven."

"Yeah?"

"Why not."

Everyone else but Cam left, climbing into cars and trucks. Jessie hesitated at the door, clutching her tote bag. "I should go too."

"No, stay. You do not need to be in your house when he finds out."

On the landing outside what had been Berlin's childhood bedroom, she told Jessie that she could stay as long as she wanted. As long as she needed. Even if that meant forever.

Because wants and needs were different things.

Bee *was* learning.

A while later, Cam, who refused to leave until he'd finished pinging his list of contacts, fell asleep on the couch. Later, much later, Bee

263

did too, her lap desk on the floor next to an empty mug and more than one opened bag of mostly devoured marshmallows. She'd quit working when Cam started snoring, too caught up reliving the fraught conversation she'd had with Quinta to tidy things.

They had worked for hours. Putting everything on pause to focus on Pink Mountain. But when Quinta rose to go to the kitchen, Berlin followed.

Staring out the window over the sink at her bee boxes, Quinta rinsed her mug. The bees had lived in Berlin's backyard since the day Quinta got them—because Quinta's family's apartment over their store didn't have a yard. The bees were clustered, staying warm. Not hibernating. Only waiting. No one would know until spring if they'd survived the cold.

When Berlin entered the kitchen, Quintana-Roo attempted to walk away, muttering, "Excuse me."

It might have been the late hour or that Berlin had finally let tears come. And with the tears came the hurt. And the hurt was feral. She exploded: "Isn't this enough? Haven't I been punished long enough? Is this a game? Are you playing with me?"

"I can't, Berlin. Not now." Quinta's voice was hardened.

"When?"

"You don't understand."

"Make me!"

"Not now," she'd said again, but not as hard, softening, even as Quinta pushed her way out of the room.

They'd been loud. In an open-concept home, there was no chance the others hadn't heard. Wouldn't hear what was coming

264

next. "I miss you so much."

Quinta didn't turn around. "I know," she said, low-key.

Not *I miss you too.* Not *Say you're sorry!*

I *fucking* know.

Sometime after three a.m., Berlin stewed on the couch, listening to Cam's quiet snoring, until she eventually wore herself out.

She woke, her mouth dry, covered under her mom's Pendleton blanket.

"Rise and shine, my little anti-capitalists." Berlin's mom appeared, carrying coffees. "It's a school day."

Bee dragged herself to a sitting position. "Too early."

They hadn't had one of those afternoons in forever. She and her mom hanging together, not doing anything but drinking tea and watching a documentary. For as long as Bee could remember, every minute between the two of them had been rushed, as if time itself were melting like it had in that Dalí painting.

"Morning is always too early," Cam said.

He couldn't grow facial hair. Not really. But he looked delightfully mussed, sitting in her living room, drinking black coffee, his hair extra disordered.

Hers was a mess too. She patted her bangs, trying to flatten them.

Berlin's mom leaned on the arm of the couch, ready for the day. "Did you make progress? I fell asleep after your dad but didn't hear much. I'll remind my colleagues too. We live off pizza when we're on call. Let's not pretend otherwise."

Cam laughed, one of his light laughs. "We did okay. Things might explode today."

"I trust you're safe?"

"Yes, Mom," Berlin said as if it rankled. But it didn't. It felt good to be loved, protected.

"Cameron, how's Sami doing? I know not seeing her in my clinic is for the best, but I miss her pocketing pens, tongue depressors, and whatnot every time I turn my back."

He tensed, looked down at his phone first, then answered, "She's great. You should come visit."

"I need to make time," Berlin's mom said, and then shifted her gaze to stare at her daughter. "I'm proud. Of you both."

Cam fidgeted with his phone case. "Can I ask you something? Get a grown person's perspective?"

"Of course."

Berlin knew and also didn't know what was eating at him. But he wouldn't break her confidence, wouldn't tattle, share anything about what happened last night in her bedroom. That she trusted completely.

"So, I . . . ugh . . ." Cam hesitated. "I keep thinking we're sort of bullying Joe with all of this."

Berlin's mom shifted to sit on the couch. "He does have the right to sell his business, yeah."

"But, Mom, shouldn't it matter who he sells it to?"

"It does. But like many things, there's no easy answer here. I remain proud of you both for the attempt, whatever happens. Know that."

Cam tried again. "Maybe it's not bullying. But it's something like it? It's that . . . we have a bad history of blaming Black people,

266

of hating on them sometimes loudly and sometimes very quietly, when we should have solidarity between us."

Berlin's esophagus burned and it wasn't from the coffee.

Her mom nodded. "That's a really smart assessment, Cameron. I hadn't thought of it that way. Maybe you need to talk to Joe about this? Both of you?"

And that had been it.

Moment over.

Even if Berlin had wanted to, there wasn't space in the room to say how it was hard to get out of bed, hard to push through the day, so difficult to simply exist. Or to say that she might have been wrong in how she'd approached Joe's leaving.

Her parents kissed each other in the entryway, like they did every morning before going to their clinics.

"Want to shower?" she asked Cam once they'd left.

His eyebrows spiked.

"Not with me!"

He cackled. "I have to pass. Tanya and Callie aren't texting me back. I need to make sure my sisters got onto the bus. If not, I'll have to ferry their butts to school."

Of course, Cam's mom was in Calgary. Studying Indigenous law. Which was brilliant. But it also meant she wasn't here as often as she used to be. Here, as in town. But also here, as in, in Berlin's kitchen, drinking nasty kombucha with Bee's mom. But where was Cam's dad that Cam had to get the girls off to school? That seemed the real mystery.

Cameron, it turned out, wasn't one.

He was a good brother. Responsible, kind. Truly funny. And he could see the complexities of the world in a way she couldn't without his help.

She'd judged him. Judged him so very badly.

That, along with the coffee in her empty stomach, the fluttering nerves from what she was going to do today, and how she'd approached the Joe situation mimicked the roll of seasickness. Berlin wanted to throw up but knew it wouldn't make things better.

The nausea would build again.

Her near-perfect attendance record was a weird point of pride. But today, after three hours of sleep, she was cutting. There were more important things than Bio, ELA, and World Religions. Finally, it made sense. Something Quinta had said months back, in early spring, sitting in her Jeep, staring ahead at a red light.

Even though it had been too cold to go topless, Quinta insisted they unscrew the six bolts keeping the roof on. As they drove into the city for an afternoon of thrifting, Bee had gotten caught up in the blaring music, the way it echoed in her chest exactly like the universe used to do. And for the drive, even though she was freezing, even though they weren't talking, Berlin felt almost okay.

At the time, Quinta's statement didn't make sense. *There are more important things than high school, Bee.*

This morning, in the shower, Berlin understood. It was revelatory.

And so, Berlin Chambers was cutting. With Cameron Sound. Her, what, frenemy? The boy she'd stabbed with a pencil in kindergarten? For who knows what lost reason?

Last night, tracing slow rainbows on her socks, he'd been so careful with her. He hadn't tried to turn her or her pain into a joke.

"Fuck," Berlin swore softly in the steamed-up room. She reached out, sketching her obsession on the mirror. Maybe that's what she hadn't seen in Magritte's pipe? It was about possibilities, about yes and no at the same time. About an unfixed option. Other options.

The universe was always expanding.

In her bedroom, she checked her phone. Cam was picking her up in ten minutes. She pulled on today's socks. They were knit, plain brown. Nothing to trace here. To distract herself from nerves at ruining her perfect attendance record, she fed Snap and the other three- and four-legged rescues. In the afternoon, she'd return to care for the bats. Maybe she'd even nap. During ELA. A delightful silent protest.

At that, she smiled.

CAM

While he backed out of the Chamberses' driveway in his LeBaron for the second time today, Berlin was abnormally quiet. She brought with her that pomegranate scent on her still-damp hair. The quiet between them suited his mood.

Funereal. That was it. He'd been to too many funerals in his life already. His auntie, three friends in a row that awful year when he was thirteen and suicide seemed the only option for so many. This mood brought Cam around again to thinking about his cousin and the funeral they never held. Because his family needed to believe she was, more than five months later now, still out there.

Even if it made the RCMP right. That no foul play, she'd run off.

It was bitter, this hope. Like the coffee Bee's mom had served. No wonder Berlin was judgy and uptight, drinking that stuff for breakfast.

Hope was bitter, but necessary too.

And that was why Cam loved speculative stories: aliens and spaceships and good Native horror films. But Cam truly loved that possibility, how anything could happen. In those stories, hope was alive, even when things were most bleak. A part of Cam that knew he needed oxygen, yeah, but he needed that possibility just as much.

At a stoplight, his passenger sighed. It was unlike her. But it wasn't a conversation starter, the way Tanya or Callie would have used it. The silence continued.

So many things in Cam's life were about shutting down possibilities. Maybe that's why he'd left high school. Why he was okay with his self-imposed PMP call sign being The Dropout. Because that had opened things up. And Joe was trying his best to close them all down again. Even if he had the right to do it, it was hurting Cam. How could you build a future on a shifting foundation? Cam had only just realized last night that while he couldn't do the admin stuff a business needed to run well in the regular way, he could do those same jobs his way. Voice to text was a tiny miracle.

Slowing to make the turn, Cam pulled into the shop parking lot cautiously. It was a full hour before he was due for the day shift. They parked next to Joe's truck, turned off the ignition. Neither of them made a move to exit the LeBaron.

"How do you want to do this?" he asked, his voice shaky. The coffee had been a bad idea. But Cam hadn't wanted to turn down food and drink. That would have been rude, against the spirit of hospitality.

"How do *you* want to do this?" Bee volleyed back.

He laughed. "No one gives me that kind of power, Berlin."

"I'm not giving. We're sharing."

"Sharing." He swallowed against the heaviness in his throat. "I think I like that."

They sat in silence again. Like she was waiting him out.

Cam had to want it, had to step into the space on his own or it would never be true sharing. He'd have to really want to maybe co-own a business for the dream to ever materialize. When he did speak, it wasn't what she expected. He could tell in the way Berlin shuddered against her still-buckled seat belt the littlest bit.

"You know," he said. "I was sure you were an elitist. Nose up in the air, rule-following because rules, not because you believed they should be followed. One of those hypocrites who looked down on everyone else so you could get yours." Still that coffee upset him, made it hard to speak over the pressure in his chest. "But you're not. I was wrong."

Berlin unbuckled and reached for the door. "Let's go in," she said. "See if we can get Joe to change his mind too."

It's not that Cam expected her to echo his sentiment. But he'd hoped. And that was the crux of it all. Feelings were too much, and Cam was drowning in them today. No, he'd been drowning in them since last night, since Berlin's bedroom. Maybe, if he were willing to give feelings their due, since the wapiti.

The bell to the staff door rang. Joe's office was open. It was pure luck that Joe was out front, singing his version of Queen's "Somebody to Love" in a deep, melodic voice.

Cam itched to see the photo of Kiki now. The one in Joe's office where she was out of uniform. To view it the way Berlin did, through her eyes. Even though he'd never been in the room without Joe, he stepped inside.

Berlin followed, practically on his heels. Resting an elbow on the desk, she leaned forward beside him.

They stared at Kiki.

Kiki smiled back.

Cam brushed his fingers against the picture's glossy surface.

"You feel it too," Berlin said.

"Yeah." He'd never drink coffee again, the way it was sitting in his body, heavy with pressure. Cam exhaled. "He loved her."

"Oh," Berlin whispered. "That's what it is."

They were caught up, in whatever—in feelings—when Joe's shadow overtook them.

"Can I help you two with something?" He wasn't angry. He sounded resigned.

They had hurt him too.

"Can we talk?" Berlin asked. She backed up until she was pressed against the far side of the office. Then she pushed her little self upward to sit on the extended arm of the desk.

Cam joined her in the corner. He wasn't sure the desk had the structural integrity to hold both of them.

"Do I have a choice here?" their boss asked, and Cam's guilt gnawed at his insides, like a wapiti who had grown predator's teeth.

"We all have choices, Joe. Always."

There she was. The girl Cam had assumed was elitist, spoiled, and maybe even a little unkind. He'd misunderstood. He really had.

Berlin didn't couch, hide, or pretend. She talked straight. And in this world, in this maddening world, it came out wrong when a person didn't have the context. When they didn't know Berlin's heart. Even if they hadn't been friends before last Friday, if they'd baited and taunted each other, whatever they were, they weren't that anymore.

Joe huffed, taking a seat in his chair. "Why do I always feel like I'm back in the kitchen with my mother, all of two feet tall, getting reprimanded over some slight, when you talk at me, Bee?"

"It's my superpower?" She pulled her arms close to her body. "Disappointed mom talk, that is."

"All right, say what you need."

Berlin glanced over at Cam.

He stared back. Even with almost no sleep she still had a rosy glow. Her glasses sparkled almost as bright as the rest of her. Her brain, her heart, her honest, sharp mouth. "You should say it," he offered.

She smiled and he was awestruck. "Okay."

Eventually, she turned away. She had to. Cam wasn't alone in this room with her. Wasn't in a position to trace nonsense patterns on her skin. Here, it would be too real.

And even if there were other pressing things—his cousin for one, saving PMP next on the list, and making good with Joe, too,

273

eventually—feelings were needy bastards. And his, they wanted to spend time with Berlin, be the only one she smiled at in that too-bright, too-loud way.

Cam felt sick. Fevered.

"Joe, the whole community wants what we want," Berlin said, pulling the printouts from her bag. "The whole community wants you to stay."

He nodded, flipping through the pages carefully. It was a great fat stack. He'd need hours to read the comments.

Not all of them were kind. Some were downright angry, positioning what they wanted in the world over what Joe might want for himself. But all the responses were passionate.

Berlin continued: "This place, it's not only good pizza. You know?" she said, smiling at Cam.

"I mean," he added, "we do make damn good pizza."

Joe let out a rough laugh, and then, horror of all horrors, he hunched over and began to cry. He clung to the stack of papers. "Don't you think I don't know all this already? Pink Mountain is my life. The most important relationship I've ever had."

With statements like that, Joe's wife had reason to be a little ticked. Primed for retribution. Though Cam was sure he'd been used, and he hated that he'd been so easy to manipulate, he understood where Emilie was at, facing that kind of heartbreak.

"Then why are you leaving us?" Berlin asked quietly. "Why are you breaking this place apart?"

Joe wiped tears from his face with the back of his hand. His breathing was ragged.

Feelings. They fucked you up well and proper. But the thing with feelings was, even if it was your own body they were ravaging, a person wasn't always sure what to call them, how to name them.

"Is this. . . ," Cam said, breaking the silence. "Is it about my cousin?"

"Jesus," Joe said. "It's . . . no . . . and, Jesus," he said again, "it's yes."

In the background, the dough mixer was running. Funny how Cam hadn't registered it before this moment. The mechanical whir was comforting. That machine, and Cam believed this fully, in the depth of his nerdy self, that machine had known Kiki, remembered her touch, her voice. And it would remember Cam's too. After all, all things were alive. Cam didn't know if in the language they'd use animate verbs for the dough mixer, but he would.

Joe rested his graying head in his hands. "Did you know I knew your . . . ah, aunt Delphine? Back in the old days. When we were young. During the summers I spent in Winnipeg rollicking, pretending I was going to make it big, a pseudo Freddie Mercury on the prairies. Delphine was at every show, at every after-after-party in someone's shit rowhouse."

Cam's knees got weak. He leaned against the desk, against Berlin. Never once had Joe mentioned Auntie Delphine. But in most of Joe's stories, the players were nameless.

"Delphine, she was vivacious. A great dancer. Epic kisser. A little too in love with being youthful. Fearless even in Winnipeg where things weren't safe. She was like her daughter in a lot of ways." Joe cleared his throat. "She had a drinking problem back then. We all did. It was part of the package. Beer, yes. Whatever hard liquor we could afford—that too. There were a lot of clouded nights. And even more that were whiteouts, when the snow comes at you so hard, so fast, you can't see half a foot in any direction."

Cam had to ask. "Is she . . . ?"

"My daughter?" Joe shook his head. "I don't think so. Anymore. Um, Delphine said it was so unlikely that it wasn't possible. She insisted enough that I had to trust her."

"But you love her? Kiki?" Cam asked. He needed to hear it. Needed to.

Berlin pressed a hand against his thigh. And traced gentle patterns.

"I loved her," Joe said. "And loving her fucked up my marriage—or my marriage couldn't handle my loving her, my grieving her."

Cam understood that.

His dad wasn't ignoring his family; he was grieving, anticipating when the grief would solidify, when they'd have the kind of proof that stopped hopeless hope from growing. And even if Cam got that, with his underdeveloped brain, he got that his dad also should know how the rest of them were stuck in the grieving, the hoping, too.

Sami still cried herself to sleep surrounded by her stolen treasures. Tanya and Callie couldn't mention their cousin's name, as if invoking her would bring down pain on the ones they loved. Cam knew his mom was trying to hold it all together. That she wasn't sleeping much.

And Cam, well, he was screwed up too. In so many terrible ways. And he couldn't stop feeling them all. Every small, sharp bite.

Next to him, Berlin hadn't quit tracing shapes on his leg.

"I appreciate what you and the crew have tried to do," Joe said, having regained his composure. "But it doesn't change things. It can't change what I have to do. Maybe you understand now? Maybe I should have told you two this. Maybe I could have saved us all some time and heartache. I very much could have gone without being lectured in the Safeway by a pair of white ladies in Lululemon leggings over business ethics. And that was one of the nicer public set-downs I've lived through this week."

The patterns stopped.

"Your buyers. They're bad people," Berlin said, doubling down. "They don't believe what we believe. Don't act how we do."

That was it. Actions mattered. Cam could only imagine the stories Joe wasn't telling about his encounters this week. The way in Canada someone could carry on with their insidious niceness as they spoke hurtful or harmful words. Bee and Cam and the rest of the Save PMP crew had encouraged people to be that kind of nice to Joe.

"Berlin." Their boss said her name calmly. "We're all bad people. In one way. Or in another."

She sucked air into her lungs fast. Retracted her hand, tightened. And Joe pushed out of his chair, excusing himself, saying something about a root beer. The dough mixer ran, its motor squealing now, the way it did as it finished the cycle, and Cam couldn't help but compare that sound to the one he remembered from the night where snow had come at him, when the wapiti had breathed her last.

JESSIE

While she worked on building crusts for orders, Jessie's father's fancy-ass Mercedes cruised into the lot. The mood in the shop was dour. The report was the boss hadn't taken what they'd done well; he hadn't changed his mind. So Jessie had been keeping her head down. After all, she was kin to the enemy. She hadn't returned to the house all day, and she'd been screening her father's calls. But it didn't make the tree shake out any different.

He emerged, pulling his peacoat tight, everything about his body language fully POed. She'd never seen him this ready to blow an artery.

Fuck a fucking dead duck.

It could not get worse. And it was going down at her work. In front of her would-be friends. As if Jessie was a bad pupper needing to be reminded who the man of the house was before she piddled on the overpriced, ugly-as-burnt-toast carpet.

He burst into the shop, and even though there were customers waiting for their orders, even though he was making a scene, he hollered: "Jessica Gloriana Hampton, remove that apron and get yourself to your vehicle. You will be going home. We are going to have words."

"We're having the words right now," Jessie said, pretending that everything was completely copacetic.

She stood behind the sneeze guard. Far enough away that he couldn't reach over the top, wrap his hands around her throat. Or anything high drama like that.

He'd never breach the swinging half door.

Kyle Hampton did not do kitchens.

That's what wives were for, eh. And in a pinch, when the wife was out, a nanny would serve. To fetch, to brew coffee, to clean granite counters, occasionally to screw in the guest bedroom.

"I won't ask a second time, Jessica."

"No. Thank you," she added, because as much as she wanted to rile him, she also knew further aggravation wasn't smarty-pants.

Quinta abandoned the cutting station. Sasha stopped what they were doing too.

"Mr. Jessie's Dad, I think you should go," Quinta said as if she were bored. "As in exit. As in leave. And never come back."

He opened his mouth, but Quinta interrupted, holding her index finger up in the air: "Don't you have a shady business partner to console? Or collude with?"

Jessie had been predisposed not to like this girl because Jessie was clearly on Team Berlin, but nope, this was the best. Quinta had a protective streak and when she used it, wham bam!

"Who do you think you are? Your parents ought to be ashamed of you. I'm taking Jessica with me. Go ahead. Call the police. That"— Jessie's father pointed—"is my seventeen-year-old daughter, and I'm in control of everything she does. Including where she works. And as of this moment, she does not work outside of the home."

Sasha laughed. "Oh, we'd never call the police. We're not that kind."

Quinta put an arm around Jessie's shoulders. "Besides, you probably have the RCMP in your pocket. Or is it your shady business partner, you know, the one running those horrible underground

279

fights? I heard he was so drunk that night when he totaled his SUV he couldn't walk a line. And yet there was no mention of a DUI anywhere in this town, when we talk about everything that happens here. Strange, right?"

"I don't need to stand and listen to these . . . accusations."

"Yeah, you don't," one of the customers said. He was older but looked familiar, like Jessie had seen him around school on Parents' Day. "Go home. Take a breather. Let your kid get back to work. There's pizzas backing up in the oven."

"Oscar," the woman next to him admonished with a gentle smack on the arm. She wore a red winter coat. "We don't care about the pizza. We care about the man who's attempting to intimidate a group of teenagers. For shame."

Jessie smiled. It was nice when folks had each other's behinds.

"If you do not return home this instant," Jessie's father said, his forehead all creased up, "you're not welcome back. You'll never see your brothers or your mother again. You'll find the payments on that vehicle stopped and that none of my employees will ever help you. With anything. Is a menial food-service job worth all that?"

Jessie didn't have to think. At all. "It is, yep. Would you, most kindly, eject yourself from the store now?"

It took a moment.

He stared. The way he'd stared across the dinner table since she'd gotten boobs, like he couldn't care less about her, like those boobs were useless if she couldn't have children. And yet, like he was planning something, some way to recoup his investment.

He backed away, thrilling Jessie. That he hadn't been willing to turn, to make himself vulnerable. He feared her, a tiny little bitsy bit.

The woman in the red winter coat clapped.

Quinta said, "Fuck," and went off to rescue pizzas.

The printer started spitting out orders. But Sasha ignored it, stepped closer so they wouldn't be overheard. "You okay?"

She'd only worked here for a titch less than a week and already these people cared about her. "I'm great," she said, absolutely meaning it.

Like she had no clothing. No place to sleep. And her family was supposed to treat her like she was dead. And still, Jessie was great. As soon as she got the chance, she would smoke a whole pack in the Land Rover. It was underhanded. But her father would have the hardest time getting the dealership to take the thing back when it reeked of teenage rebellion.

"You," she said to the older couple waiting for their meal. "Your food is on me tonight."

The man smiled big. "Hey, free supper!"

"Oscar," his companion said again, but she was smiling.

"Was that the Poseidon Group guy?" Oscar asked. "I saw something online on the group chat about him trying to buy this place?"

Jessie nodded. "He's bad news. But you all were wonderful. So your pizza's free."

The woman said, "Oh no, you don't have to do that. We can pay."

It was Quinta who backed Jessie up. "Aren't you Vincent's grandparents?"

They nodded.

"Your money's no good here, at least today," Quinta stated. "We'll take your money next time with a smile, sound fair?"

They capitulated.

And throughout the night, as the crew closed shop, both Quinta and Sasha checked in. Sasha offered their couch as a resting place. Quinta was already making plans to set Jessie up in the annex to her family's health food and Chinese grocery store. And Jessie knew, too, that Berlin's offer of a bedroom in her parents' house for as long as it was needed, even if it was forever, wouldn't expire. It was good strange to be cared for, to be wanted.

Jessie wouldn't fight it. She'd defile the Land Rover, park it on the front lawn of her parents' mini mansion, and then she swore to the gods of great pizza and good fellowship that after she'd quit smoking forever, she'd put her energies entirely back into trying to save this unexpected place.

CAM

Even though Tanya and Callie said they'd watch Sami tonight, it was hardwired into his brain to need to check on his sisters after work. They were in the kitchen, cooking Kraft Dinner and hot dogs with a boatload of ketchup on the side. At least the hot dogs were from a Native-owned butcher in Calgary and not full of that commercial junk.

He climbed the stairs.

In the shower, cleaning the day shift from his hair, Cam forgot the world—until the twins started yelling at each other. They had been doing this a lot lately.

The second he stepped out of the shower, towel wrapped around his waist, Sami pounced. Already pushing it to get back to town and pick Berlin up on time, Cam couldn't play mediator for his twelve-year-old sisters. But he couldn't ignore Sami either. Not when she looked at him, all mischief in her eyes.

"Hey, Sami! What's up?"

She giggled.

"What's good?"

She giggled again.

It was a game they played.

"Tânisi kiya?"

This time, she signed, "Ham!" and jumped up and down.

"Ah, Sami, I can't."

Ponyo was her all-time favorite movie. They'd watched it a hundred thousand times.

"Ham," she said seriously. "Please."

"Ask Tanya or Callie to watch it with you. I have to go out."

"All they do is fight!" she signed, and then pouted.

"Come on," Cam said, dragging Sami back to his room while he changed. He set her up with YouTube clips from *Ponyo* and other Miyazaki movies on his phone.

Downstairs, his sisters were still at it.

"It's your turn to do the dishes!"

"Is not!"

"I did them yesterday."

Sami followed him into the kitchen and shrugged one shoulder, like, *See, told you.*

"Stop it, you two. Leave the dishes. I'll do them tonight." Cam was late now. "You told me you'd watch her, eh? And instead you're arguing?"

283

They both put their hands on their hips. They looked at each other and then Callie, the oldest by six minutes and usually the more reserved sibling, spoke: "Dad said we didn't have to do the dishes if we didn't want to."

Cam tried to keep his voice flat, level, but he failed. "Dad's not here."

"You're not here either," Callie volleyed back.

"I'm here all the time!"

In the last day or so, Tanya had done her hair up in tiny braids. It must have taken hours. "Not lately," she added, getting brave.

It was true. He'd been gone because he had a job. And for the past few days, he'd been gone even more, running around town with Berlin.

"Let's watch *P-O-N-Y-O*." Sami finger-spelled the last word. "Ham, now!" she said loudly, in case they didn't get it.

Callie grabbed her phone from the kitchen counter. "Yeah, let's watch it!"

"Come on, Sami," Tanya said, flicking her hair as she turned. "We'll watch the movie with you."

They were frustrated with him, yeah. It was in the girls' body language. But Sami was happy. As his sisters settled on the couch and the living room speakers came alive, Cam scarfed down leftover KD. He was late, but he was hungry too.

Stomach full, Cam was outside PMP in the LeBaron talking with Berlin—again. They stared at the shop. Had parked so they had a view of the front windows. "This time we've got her cornered.

What's she going to do? She's got to close."

"You don't know Quintana-Roo that well."

"She's not going to run, right? I'm not wearing good chasing shoes."

"She only runs on the track."

Bee had napped, smelled all sweet-sour. He wanted to infuse the scent into the upholstery of the LeBaron. So when this was over, when he returned to his regularly scheduled programming, he'd at least have a keepsake. "You're right. I don't know her that well. Since for our entire childhood you wanted nothing to do with me, neither did she."

Berlin thought about it. He could tell by the way her eyes almost looked up, like she was checking her memory files.

The Time You Bit Him Hard Enough to Bruise on the Playground.

The Yelling Summer.

The Kindergarten Incident.

Berlin swallowed. "She's got to like you. At least some. She lets you call her by her legal name. Haven't you wondered why?"

So Bee was going to deflect. That was fine. It's not like he wanted an apology because he carried that little scar on his pointer finger even now. "Not really."

"I do. She's categorically against that name. Like it's not even hers. We used to make fun of her parents and their hipster granola-crunchy-meets-colonial naming practices all the time."

"Yeah, but her swim team, cross-country, and curling buddies all call her QR. I used to go sit in the spectator seats," he said, remembering the Before Times. "My whole family used to go. To support Kiki."

"Really?"

"Didn't you attend your best friend's sports meets? Her curling tourneys?"

Berlin shook her head. "No," she said sadly. "Maybe that's what she's upset about?"

"Maybe," Cam said, but he didn't think either of them really thought so. Tonight, they couldn't quite be honest with each other. The other times, they could have been aberrations.

"What's the second favor?" Bee asked, as if out of nowhere.

"I didn't ask for a favor."

"Cam, *this* is the first favor." Berlin waved her hands around. "It was days ago now. But you said, *There's another ask, maybe.* Like you wanted to say it but weren't sure you could trust me with it or something."

"Oh, that. I need your help," he emphasized. It had only been a thought, maybe it had been a dream Cam couldn't speak, but something was telling Cam this was his chance. "To put together a business plan. I want to give Joe an option. He seems to think there aren't any others. Do it or don't do it. But here's Option C. And you know that writing and reading are . . . impossible for me . . . and they're not for you, and, well, you got a ninety average in Business last year?"

"Ninety-eight," she said.

"Yeah, I need Ms. Ninety-Eight Percent on my team. And maybe this is how we work with Joe, instead of barraging him into doing what we want."

"Is this what you want, Cameron?"

He'd put so many obstacles in his own way. Maybe Cam didn't need to drive a taxi to serve his community. Maybe he could do this in his own way too. "Yeah, it is."

"Then I'm on your team," Bee said, like she meant it. Like she hadn't deeply disliked him a few days ago. "But let's get this disaster over with first."

As soon as Quinta spotted her best friend stepping into the storefront, she reacted: "Nope. Not tonight. I don't have the energy. We've already dealt with one asshole. I'm tapping out."

Berlin sucked in air.

She turned as if on a pin, pushing through the door again to escape. "I'm sorry," she said, almost hyperventilating. "I cannot do this." Her voice was breaking. "I'll wait in your car."

Once Bee was safely back in the LeBaron, Cam finally lost his cool. "You do not have to be so unkind to her. Whatever she did, she doesn't deserve this. From anyone. But from you, it's worse."

Crossing her arms on her chest, Quinta exhaled. "I know. And I didn't mean that she was the asshole. Just that I was tired from the earlier incident. Berlin Chambers has never been a true asshole a day in her life. Even when she might want to be one. She's too good."

"Stop treating her like one, eh."

"Why are you her knight in broke-down armor all of a sudden, Cameron?"

"Why have you cut your best friend off without a word, Quintana-Roo?"

She defused.

It might have been invoking her full name. Or that someone was calling her on her behavior. It might have been a hundred things.

But Cam jumped on the silence. "I need you to tell me what you and my cousin were whispering about seven, eight months ago. When you weren't glued to Berlin's side, you were constantly in Kiki's company. At school, at those summer track meets."

"Cameron." Quinta stared at him as if it was important he listened. And then she said: "You have to let her go."

It was the wrong thing, the worst thing, she could say. The way Quintana-Roo's voice got sad, heavy, blanketed by her own pain. But for Quintana-Roo there was no hope left. Hope had exited the building, evacuated itself from the whole fucking town.

"You have to let her go," she said again, quiet and careful.

Caught in an ugly storm, Cam turned, crashed out the door, ignored Sasha calling his name. He leaned over a frozen snowbank, gagging. He didn't expel anything. But his throat burned.

Because he knew it now. He knew.

He'd been holding on to threads, and the threads weren't connected to anything. They'd been severed. Kiki, his vibrant cousin, was gone. The universe had let her go.

It was so final. His body worked on autopilot. Returning to the LeBaron, where Jessie spoke to Berlin through the open passenger window in hushed tones. Watching Jessie wave goodbye. Driving the LeBaron out of town to his house. Helping Berlin cross a wicked patch of ice, his body cold, his body needing hers. Even though he'd already eaten, cooking up the last of the Kraft Dinner in the pantry. Eating again. Compiling a fairly decent plan to slowly buy the business from Joe, a kind of rent-to-own scheme with sliding-scale buyout payments that would increase over time. With Berlin's help, managing to get the girls in bed, to do the dishes, to start a load of laundry, to run the dryer, to fold small socks and sweaters and his dad's pajama bottoms. Bee was there, steady, as if she understood he couldn't stop. To think. To feel.

She didn't ask questions.

At one point, she called her parents, telling them she was staying over—making an excuse, without making Cam the center of the story. She'd spoken about Joe and Pink Mountain and how she was needed, how school hadn't been an urgent priority and so she'd cut, how tonight, they were at Cam's. How it was important to her.

She stayed close. When he needed to ground himself, he grabbed for her hand. She let him. Even more, she held on like she needed it too.

Hours later, looking around the kitchen, she asked, "What's next?" They had cleaned the fridge, organized the cupboards, even Kiki's spices. It was time.

"Dishes. Laundry. Sisters in bed." As tired as he was, Cam almost added homework to the list.

He walked into the living room and sank into the couch.

Closed his eyes.

Felt the couch shift as Berlin settled too.

Later, much later, when Sami came downstairs, rubbing her eyes, complaining of a nightmare, she found Cam on his side, curled up, his head on Bee's lap. Neither of them talking. Or scrolling on their phones.

They were only breathing.

Sami's bottom lip quivered. "Bad, bad dream," she said out loud, for Berlin's benefit.

Under him, Bee shifted. "You rest. I'll help her back to bed."

"No." Even Cam's voice hurt. Ached like he'd been crying. "She's my responsibility."

"Sit with Bee," he signed before going into the kitchen to put the kettle on.

With a mug of freshly brewed Sleepytime tea in hand, he followed his baby sister upstairs. Sami settled into her bed. She signed her thank-yous and sipped her tea.

The trundle was half pulled out, the sheets mussed.

Cam moved off the bed to stash it away. He didn't want Sami tripping when she got up to pee.

"No," Sami signed. "Put the book back."

"Which book?"

His eyes were gritty. Like he had sand beneath the lids. He wanted to return to the couch, curl up as small as he could and let the feelings roll over him, where he was safe, Berlin close by.

"Kiki," Sami said.

"Kiki's book?"

Sami passed off the half-gone tea. She crawled across her bed, pulled her huge stack of pillows apart, and smiled a bit sad. "Yes."

Cam took the neon-orange notebook from his sister. He held it until Sami finished her tea, until she returned to better dreams.

Like a sleepwalker, he carried the notebook downstairs, and when he didn't find Berlin there waiting, he found her at the kitchen sink, doing dishes she'd uncovered somewhere in the house, and he pulled Berlin, her hands soapy and wet, into the living room, pulled her onto the couch, gathered her closer until she was settled against him. Hip to hip.

He held the book. "It's hers. My cousin's."

Then he opened it like the universe was about to shift and started reading aloud.

A Little Over Six Months Ago

The Rules

> *Always pick up*
> *your phone*
> *Text back—don't*
> *leave him on wait*

You know you can't do that risky stuff
anymore, Kiki. Smoking will kill you.

His house—
it's yours too, he says.
> *His couch,*
> *it's taking in your shape.*
> *His bed*
> *is crowded these days.*

Keep the curtains drawn. Stay
inside. Follow the rules.

Date Nights

take us into the city, where we're not known, where to anyone
    we're two people who can't get enough

of each other. Into the city where we don't have to pretend
    like we do in the halls, at practice, when we find each other

in the same restaurants in town. Into the city, where I pretend
    harder than he does, where I imagine a different future

for myself. But those are misty dreams & here in this world
    some of us only get so much. In the city, I tell him about you

& he cries. In the city, he promises us forever, makes us promise
    in return. We'll do it in the morning. Nobody can know.

It's not safe, he says, they'll take him away from us, they'll take
    him away

& just like that he convinces me.

Little Bean

That's what I call you
when we're alone.

I want to call you
Delphine, but he thinks
the name is too big,
too bold & who's to say
that you're a girl?

I know, little bean,
already many things:
a girl needs a father
more than a mother needs:
a high school diploma
or a cousin who hums
little songs without words
tucked into the trundle bed
next to my changing body.

Little bean, I dream so many things for you, so many things I never
had. To start, a dad. & this man loves us so hard it bruises. A hard
love is better than no love, than no father. This I know. Little bean,
little bean & this I swear, if his love ever hurts you, we'll leave, but I
can take it. I'll take anything. For you.

Dear Mr. X

I suppose I should thank you
for every encouraging word

I suppose I should thank you
for the rides to practice

for the early morning
coffee, sweetened just so

for each kiss, for clarifying
what happened that long-ago day
at the pool, for your

patience, for your kitchen,
for buying eggs & flour & vanilla

I suppose I should thank you, too,
for poetry

Ars Poetica

      or the last poem

Poetry requires a nimble mind; time & time & time; delight, fancy & feeling all right; the lark's call & someone to appreciate its splendor against the pines; a composition book & a pen, gifted & the patience to cross out every word—

When this started, I was young & angry & didn't understand poetry at all

Thursday

Inscription inside Kiki's notebook: Now you have your own small book, one you can carry in your pocket. Now you have your own small book, one where you can keep your secrets safe. And the pens write like a dream too. Here, let secrets coexist with dreams. Happy Christmas. —Nico

BERLIN

She was cutting school again. It was becoming a habit. And it wasn't because she woke up on Cam's couch, pulled hard into Cam's arms. It wasn't because she'd gotten like two hours of sleep. It was because if Berlin went to school today, she'd fucking damage Mr. MacDonald. Do him worse than he'd been on Sunday, recovering from a nasty head-on collision with the elk.

After Cam had found the notebook, after they'd read three years of poems, it was sickeningly clear.

Six months ago, Kiki was alive. Six months ago, Kiki was newly pregnant. And only days ago, Berlin witnessed her climbing into a taxi outside a twenty-four-hour convenience store.

In the middle of the night, gripping that neon-orange notebook as if it were a lifeline, they'd texted Quinta. It was a hunch. Only that. And miracle of all miracles, Quinta replied.

Q: How did you find out?

B: I'm calling. Pick up. If you don't . . . I'm never speaking to you again. Never, Quinta Adams-Wang.

Q: Yeah, call.

"I have you on speaker. Cam is here."

"Don't hate me," Quinta said, her voice sleep-heavy. "I—I—fuck," she said. "Don't hate me, Cameron."

He shook his head. Like he couldn't even speak.

Berlin understood. She took over. "Tell us everything. Every little thing."

The phone line crackled. "I don't know when it started. Not really. Maybe last spring? This wasn't the first time he'd tried this with one of us. The semester before . . . he'd paid attention to me. Not that I would ever. I shut him down. But last spring, we were traveling to Calgary, Lethbridge, a lot for meets. Prince George that one weekend."

Cam clutched at his stomach, still holding the notebook. His fingers drained of blood.

"We need details."

"I only know so much. I got myself dragged into their drama . . . maybe a week before school started in September. I saw him holding her wrist. Real tight. Rough, almost? Like it was . . . I don't know . . . personal? And then he saw me, told me to get on the bus like I was the one in the wrong. After, I tried not to pay attention, you know? I didn't need that. Didn't want that to be something I had to carry around." She cleared her throat. "But like then Kiki

298

corners me. Because of what I witnessed, she thought I could hear her out. And so I did. I listened. That's all."

Quinta sighed into the phone, stopped storytelling.

Berlin was infuriated. "But you didn't help her. You helped to hide her!"

"I did not!"

Cam was crying now. Very quietly.

"I didn't think she'd fucking disappear. Like who thinks that's a valid exit plan from a relationship?"

"Quinta."

"What?"

"You didn't tell anyone."

"I didn't know. Not really. He . . . um . . . cornered me, told me not to say a thing about the two of them. That he broke it off. That she'd probably run away. And that sometimes horrible things happened when Native girls ran away. He got all choked up. And he . . . I don't know . . . threatened me? Or warned me? Or something. Not to look for ghosts." Quinta was dispassionate, almost like this wasn't completely horrible, wasn't a betrayal stacked upon a betrayal. "Later, months later, I ran into her. Waiting in his car, wearing drab, oversized clothing, outside the Walmart in Cochran. He was buying Pedialyte because she couldn't stop throwing up. She's in town. At 1742 Oak Lane. Her car is parked in his garage. The backpack, it was planted. I don't know if he did it himself or if he got a friend to do it. That's it, all I know." Quinta cleared her throat again. "Don't hate me, okay? I didn't know what to do."

"You're not allowed to ask that," Berlin said, and hung up.

Eyes filled with rage, body overflowing with a need for action, Cam had wanted to leave immediately. "Let's go. Get your parka."

Instead, she convinced him, lying down, facing each other on the couch, that the best chance they had of talking to Kiki was waiting until Mr. MacDonald left for school. And lying there, Cam calmed. He needed someone to ground him. He'd said it more than once, touching her. That she grounded him. That he could feel things when she was near. That he could handle those things better.

After another sleepless night, it was time to execute the plan. Jessie and Sasha teamed up, waited in Sasha and Ira's truck for Mr. MacDonald to park and head inside the building. Once he did, they'd text.

And then it would be time.

And then, maybe Berlin could get some good sleep. Her whole body wanted those uninterrupted hours. But she wouldn't let Cam do this alone.

In the LeBaron, he was tense, quiet. He'd helped all three of his sisters get dressed and on the bus like it was any other day. But he'd covered their toast with honey, drenched it in sticky honey.

"Why have you never learned to drive?" Cam asked, breaking the silence.

"That's what you want to talk about? While we're on our way across town to the house of one of our teachers, where your missing cousin has been living for the past six months?"

"Yes." His hands were at nine and three, exactly like the driver's education class Bee had taken said you were supposed to do.

She'd taken the class and done great on the practice quizzes. But she hadn't ever planned on going through with scheduling a test.

"Okay, fine." She knew it was a silly reason, in some ways. But it was hers. "I've always needed Quinta. Always. From the very first day we met. In a solid way."

"Maybe that's your problem?"

Berlin rolled her eyes. "Do you want to hear the rest of the story? Or do you want to interrupt?"

He shrugged sheepishly. "I'll hold back. For now."

"But Quinta, she never needed me. That girl fought her own battles. Didn't need help figuring out which universities to apply to next year. Or how to handle her overbearing mother. Or what to wear to impress a crush. She didn't need me to sit in the viewing area during curling tournaments to feel special."

They were passing the spot where they'd found the elk. Passing fast, the only snow in sight frozen into banks on the edges of the road. Berlin would carry that night forever. And if she had to bet on it, so would Cam.

It was theirs.

A part of their story.

"So, if she didn't *need me* need me . . . well, I had to need her enough for the both of us."

He turned up the heat. "You've gone completely space-bonkers if you think Quintana-Roo doesn't need you."

"She's done fine on her own the past few months, hasn't she?"

"No, she hasn't. The first thing she did after discovering my pregnant cousin was not missing and was being kept at her coach's house was to drop you like you were a liability. That's one in a series of terrible decisions."

Berlin hadn't thought of it that way yet. She hadn't considered the two things were connected. "Why are you being so nice to me?"

"Why are you being so nice back at me?" he countered.

"I don't know," she said, pained.

"Yes, you do. You basically held me together yesterday, last night, this morning." He glanced at the GPS as they drove into town, turned into a subdivision.

It was only blocks from Pink Mountain, from the convenience store. Not quite walkable. But close.

"You like me," Cam said, as if it was obvious.

"Do not," she responded, in the way that someone might if they were all of six and a half years old: grab the closest thing and stab the person who infuriated them the most with it.

He laughed like he didn't know exactly how to do it. It came out stilted. "I don't believe you."

"Okay," she said finally, patting him on the shoulder once, twice. "I like you. I don't want to be mean to you."

"That's nice." He was staring at the road ahead. "I like you, too, Bee."

"And I was wrong," she said haltingly. "About you. What I thought too. Before."

He didn't answer right away, and it made her proper sick.

"I'm glad you've admitted it," he said a beat later. "Now we can be best friends."

Even though they were driving to a teacher's house, a teacher who had taken Cam's cousin from her life, like her life hadn't mattered, Berlin had to laugh.

It felt so good.

To release the tension.

"Whoa, this is moving too fast," she said, teasing him. "I said I like you. Not that I want to be your best friend forever."

"Can't take it back, Bee. You like me. We're BFFs. Those are the rules in this car."

They turned onto Oak Lane. Cam slowed. They watched the GPS count down the meters. Both of them quiet until the LeBaron stopped in front of a plain house, single level, double garage, with the curtains drawn and a sign in the window: Go Wolverines!

"I'll wait here?" She had no idea what to do. Hadn't studied for this, for how to do something like this.

Cam unbuckled his seat belt, then reached over to unclip hers. "That's silly, Bee. Friendship isn't about needing people. It's about having them next to you when you do scary, awful things. Wonderful stuff too. But this morning, we're in the scary, awful category."

She nodded like she understood, like this was a realist painting and not what it was.

"I want you next to me when I ring the doorbell. And if, when we get up there, if I can't manage it myself, you can grab my hand and help me do it."

"I can accomplish that."

"You're excelling at this best-friend thing."

She laughed even though she didn't think what he'd said was funny. Not exactly.

They climbed the icy steps.

Cam reached for the door, faltered. Berlin understood. She took his hand in hers. He basically told her she might have to. She was ready. Prepared to assist, as required, even though she was terrified.

They rang the doorbell.

The curtains peeled back the tiniest bit. Berlin caught a glimpse of maroon ends, hanging from the remains of a two- or three-day-old topknot.

When the door opened, all Cam did was step forward, pull his very pregnant cousin into his arms, and say, "It's so fucking good to see you, Kiks."

CAM

They were in MacDonald's kitchen, sitting at his table. And Cam wanted to smash all the man's glassware, but he also wanted to get his cousin out. Away. Where she could be safe. There was no way he was leaving her here.

"I'm fine, Cameron," Kiki said.

"No, you're not," he roared back.

He'd been yelling a lot.

"Cam," Berlin reprimanded him.

She wasn't at the table. She lingered by the kitchen doorway, as if she worried they'd need to make a quick escape. It was 10:40 in the morning. And even though MacDonald had his prep period now, he hadn't left campus.

Jessie had promised she would watch his vehicle all damn day long.

304

Cam's cousin sat across from him at the kitchen table. Kiki's cheeks were fuller. She wasn't wearing any neon. That made him sad. Kiki loved bright, saturated colors. The kind that didn't fade, that didn't give up their brightness wash after wash.

"It's his baby, Cameron," Kiki said. "This is where we belong. I'm . . . sick over it. For letting you think something happened to me. I can't stop throwing up."

"You're sorry?!" he yelled. Berlin's hand clamped down on his shoulder. He mediated his tone. "Do you fucking know what you've put us through?"

"I—I . . ."

"Do you know what you've done to us? To your family?"

"Cam," Berlin said again. "Stop it."

Kiki crumpled inward, her hands resting on her belly. "Do you understand now? How once I ended up at Alex's place, and after a week had gone by, and then two, and then four, how I couldn't change my mind? I'd already ruined everything! It was done. Do you get it? Do you understand?"

"Jesus," Cam said. "You can always come home. Always, kinisitohtowin?"

"I don't have a home. This is it for me." She rubbed her belly. "This is good enough."

Cam's heart broke open. Splayed itself, and then it was beating again. A new wound to carry etched into the muscle.

"You can, cousin. That's the point of family. We're always here for each other. We have your back. And"—he smiled—"your front too."

Kiki laughed, then burst into tears.

"Shit, I'm sorry, Kiks."

"It's not you! It's this baby. All I do is eat and throw up and fucking cry!" she yelled. "And get all rounded. And crave things in the middle of the night that I don't have in this really sad fridge."

Berlin, always the sensible one, said, "What he did, what Mr. MacDonald did to you, it's abuse."

"Don't try that on me, Bee. I'm eighteen. I have been for months."

"But you weren't eighteen when this started. And he was your teacher. He wasn't supposed to seduce you. After, what, a cross-country meet?"

"Come on, Berlin," Kiki said. "Of course it was swim practice."

Finally, his cousin's spark was in the room. Cam felt better than he had in months.

"And how do you know I didn't seduce him, eh?"

"Quintana-Roo told us," Berlin said. "About . . . Mr. MacDonald. About what he does. What he's done to others. Not just you."

Kiki rolled her shoulders inward. "I was . . . a complete fool, yeah."

"We all make mistakes," Berlin said. "In fact, we make lots and lots of them. All the time."

And coming from Bee—the uptight perfectionist, it seemed—these were the words his cousin needed.

Kiki looked his way. Her eyes were full again, but the tears didn't drop. "How can they ever forgive me? For that pain? He didn't exactly lock me in this house. He leaves every day for work. I could have left too. My car still has gas in the tank. And I didn't, I didn't . . . leave."

"That's not how he got you here. It wasn't a kidnapping." Berlin paused. "But you know he forced you to stay in other ways. Or made it really hard to leave. To think about leaving. That's what I bet."

The kitchen, it was shabby. Yellowing plastic blinds. Glossy black furniture that didn't fit the room. No jar of honey on the countertop.

"Cousin," Cam said. "They're going to be so happy to have you home. And yes, they're going to be hurt, probably angry. But they love you. We love you. And I can tell you that this abusive man, the one you're living with, doesn't, and he won't love your baby. And the longer you stay, the harder it will be to leave. And, Kiki, you have to leave this place."

For a minute, she was quiet, too quiet, not like the old Kiki, the Before Kiki, at all. And then she blew air from between her lips, loud and long, and said, "Help me fucking pack."

"Tâpwe, cousin."

Cam wanted out of this house as fast as possible. When he excused himself for a minute to calm his anxiety, that still-grumbling, still-hungry fear, unable to stay in that bedroom without throwing up, Berlin followed him. She opened a window in the kitchen, in the middle of winter. And then she stepped right up into his space and wrapped her arms around him.

He hugged her back, standing in the winter breeze, for a long time.

JESSIE

She leaned on the counter next to the cash register. It was all over town, that Kiki Cheyanne had been found at one of her teachers' houses, very preggers with his kid. And the other thing all over town like bad spaghetti coming up again: the Poseidon Group, the conglomerate of men who were planning to buy PMP, were involved in an illegal boxing ring targeting the unhoused and other folks down on their lucky charms.

Someone had slipped that the garbage teacher was best friends with the boxing baddie, and now several hundred people were outside of Pink Mountain Pizza, straight-up protesting the sale.

It was snowing. Big dramarama flakes. But active snow meant it was warmer outside than you might think. The crowd in the parking lot overflowed around the corner, across the street, as far as Jessie could see. It was a massive win. Joe couldn't sell. Not to the Poseidon Group. Not after this.

But he could sell to Cameron. Over the course of the next ten or fifteen years. Slow and steady like good food, like good friends.

Cam was in the back end with the boss.

Nobody was buying pizza. Not even the tourists in the hotels. Tonight, it wasn't only a local story. It was being picked up nationally. News had spread that far.

The crowd outside, it was better than nicotine. It was all wondrous things. Jessie peered out the window again. And the only thing that could make this day better was walking inside.

"Bee, hi! Wow . . . it's beyond words, right?"

"Jessie Hampton, beyond words? Is the sky falling?"

Jessie stood tall. "I mean, it's not like today I didn't assist in helping a girl free herself from a monster and incite my first-ever town-wide riot."

"Protest," Bee said, taking a seat in one of the chairs in the lobby. "Please don't call it a riot."

Now they were eye level.

"So," Berlin said. "About that kiss?"

"Oh, are we doing this tonight? Is it spring already?"

"It's not. But can we?"

Jessie left the kitchen and claimed another chair. They looked out the windows, not directly at each other.

"I'm not really sure how to think about it," Berlin said, slowly tracing something on the foggy glass. "To be honest. I've only had one crush in my life. And now one kiss. But even if I don't think about the kiss, I know that . . . I really want—no, need—a friend more than a girlfriend."

It should have hurt. At least a sting. A mosquito bite Jessie could crisscross with her nails. But it didn't. "That's fair," she said, and it was.

"And you're basically living in my house. That's a consideration too." Berlin finished her drawing. It was . . . like an old-school Sherlock Holmes-y pipe.

Another unexpected thing.

"I've been thinking on that. I'll pay rent. I'm not freeloading because you're my friend."

"My parents would never let you. They'll want you to save money for your welding program. Or for whatever it is you want."

Berlin stared out at the crowd, so Jessie did. They were chanting. Their voices were mellowed inside the shop. But they hadn't quit, not for hours now. The pizza oven was empty, running at a low hum.

Slowly the pipe faded from the window.

"Bee?"

"Yeah?"

309

"Maybe this is a good thing. The kiss that shall not be repeated."

"Tell me more, friend."

Jessie liked that. A lot.

"So, I was thinking about how in fairy tales, they have that kiss, right? Snow White, Sleeping Beauty, that poor frog. True love's kiss, it's everywhere. But what if . . ." Jessie paused dramatically. "What if . . . the fairy tales are dead wrong?"

The girl sitting on the chair, watching the snow flit down, burst into laughter. "Let me get this straight. You've been basing your life choices on the poor girls in Disney movies?"

"Only a very little. And sometimes I take my life lessons from the bloody chop-off-your-heel-to-fit-into-a-shoe stories."

"Oof, Jessie."

"So I was thinking." Now she was flat-out smiling. "Maybe it's time to chop that like a lumberjane. Put kissing aside for a bit. Figure out a new model for approaching life. Something more solid."

"Less patriarchal?"

"That too."

"Sounds good to me. Want some help?"

It was perfect. Not fairy-tale perfect, with the trappings, the too-heavy burden of true love's kiss. But real-life perfect. And Jessie was sure that was kilometers of twinkle lights better.

BERLIN

All throughout the day there had been this weight. It was something Cam said, the way he seemed truly upset about how they'd gone at

310

Joe. It wasn't what Joe said—people in town did that all the time, got up in someone's business or told a BIPOC person how to live their life. But it was how he'd said it. Like it had been worse. And maybe it was how looking at Quinta's absolute fuckup had forced Bee to consider her own. And once Berlin's dad had said something like *Sometimes, sometimes, it's better to beg forgiveness than ask permission.*

He'd also suggested she think first, before acting.

Berlin could admit it to herself, as she walked through the kitchen, into the prep room, and toward where Joe and Cam were stashed away talking in the office, that she didn't do that often enough.

Instead, she leapt and got things done. But she didn't always think through the complications first. How it was a little wrong to go at Joe as if Joe hadn't made a strategic choice. How too many Black people had been treated as if they were no better than children, had often been treated worse than that, how the same thing happened to Indigenous people all the time, how Berlin should have considered this when she decided she would be the one to save Pink Mountain.

That if she'd figured out what the pipe was trying to say sooner, maybe she'd have found another way to keep this place from changing, to keep the people here together, to keep Joe in their lives in a healthy way.

She stopped, lingering in the doorway. "Can I interrupt? I'll be fast."

Joe and Cam were sitting close, peering at Joe's laptop.

Kiki's picture didn't shine as bright anymore. In fact, the whole office looked old, ragged, as if this week had taken a toll on it too.

"I wanted to say that I'm realizing, thanks a lot to Cameron, that I went at this the wrong way, and I'm sorry, Joe, because I disrespected you and hurt you and I hope you don't take anything I did and then look on Cam's proposal badly. That's it, what I wanted to say."

She didn't like how it felt to have to apologize, to have been wrong. Because she'd gone about this in a twisted way for the right reasons.

Still, those things battled inside her.

"I already told this one that I don't believe you've bullied me. In this relationship, I'm the adult, the one with the power."

Berlin nodded. He did have power in a lot of ways.

But so did she.

"And don't believe for a minute that if I had wanted to stop you, I wouldn't have stopped you. You would have backed off, right?" he asked, but didn't pause for her to confirm or deny. "But it's impossible to stop the internet when the internet gets going. How many comments did you leave out of that package you printed for me?"

She waited to see if it was a rhetorical question.

It wasn't.

"Um, enough."

"And why did you leave those comments out? Why didn't you add them in and boost the numbers?" He paused again. "You didn't think, did you? That you would embolden those voices by matter of putting a Black man's decision up for public comment?"

"I did not . . ."

Cam interrupted. He pressed a hand against the shoulder seam of her sweater. "It wasn't just Bee."

"Yeah, you had a whole team working on this. But we all know

312

who the ringleader was." Joe wasn't done. "And though sometimes, Berlin, you're more like a bull in a china shop than you realize, that's what Pink Mountain is about, making mistakes and learning and knowing that even if a thing is hard, even if you don't win, even if you eff it up badly, that you tried."

"I think," Berlin said, nodding on repeat like it would show Joe how serious she was, "that's something I'm going to have to study longer, before I stop breaking the dishes."

Joe swallowed. "Did that teacher ever—"

"No."

"Good." Joe relaxed into his chair. "Now, I know better than to use my fists to bring down justice, but that doesn't mean I wouldn't have rethought my approach if he'd hurt another one of you."

"Thank you," Berlin said. "I'll try to do better, I will. I won't forget."

Joe offered her a hug. She needed it. After, Bee walked out of the staff door and into the night, ready, maybe, to break another dish or make another mistake. But not to make the exact same one.

She found Quinta across the street in the crowd, but somehow standing apart, holding a sign: Capitalism Kills.

"Nice one," Berlin offered.

"Oh, this? Someone handed it to me. But it seemed . . . not in the spirit of a protest against degenerate teachers and bad, bad business dealings . . . not to carry a sign."

It was more words than Quinta had willingly offered her in months.

Months!

Her best friend hadn't talked to her in months. To protect a predator.

"How could you not have told me?"

Quinta didn't waver. She still thought she was right. "It was Kiki's story to tell. Or not. It was none of my business. She decided to stay with him. I didn't decide for her."

"You know how much BS that is. Blaming someone for their abuser's actions. But that's not what I mean." Berlin put her hands deep in her pockets. Her mittens were somewhere else. In Cam's LeBaron? At his house? In her own home, being used by one of the cats as a comfort item? Who knew?

All of her, she was coming loose.

"I mean, how could you not tell me that Mr. . . . that he had tried to groom you first?"

Quintana-Roo rolled her eyes. They were all done up in moody eyeshadow capped with perfect winged eyeliner. "Don't make me cry. You know I hate crying as much as I hate people who leave voicemails. It's fundamentally unnecessary."

The crowd started a new chant. The snow drifted down.

"I'm serious, Quinta. Why didn't you tell me? You've told me everything else from the minute we met each other. That you thought your mom was a witch, that story about what happened at summer camp the year we were apart."

They'd gone to different camps. It had been horrid.

"I couldn't," she said eventually, putting her sign down, leaning it against her leg. "I was . . . embarrassed."

"You've told me plenty of embarrassing things. It never stopped you before. I was your best friend!"

It was cold, but Berlin didn't feel it. She knew she was messing up again, blaming Quinta for something that had happened to her. Because there were reasons not to tell, reasons to keep your secrets inside in order to hold yourself whole. They weren't good reasons, but that didn't make them any less compelling. Life was complicated, messy.

And then Quinta said it simply. Like it was a fact: "You were having a hard enough time yourself. You didn't need more."

"What?"

"You were having a hard time, Bee. Struggling to I don't know . . . pull off happy. You didn't need my bad drama on top of your own."

Berlin repeated herself again. This was the sticking point. Where it all ended up. All her anger. "I was your best friend." Past tense. Berlin had said it twice. In the past-fucking-tense. She enunciated every word: "You should have told me."

This, this was what she needed, right now. To be heard. To be hurt.

"Probably," Quinta said in that surly way of hers.

God, Berlin had missed this. Her totally grumpy friend.

"What now?" Quinta asked, the sign still resting at her feet.

Berlin ignored the question and asked one of her own: "How many people do you think are here tonight?"

"Five hundred? Maybe more? Half the school is out here all aflutter. We so love to watch someone fall. And a teacher? Even sweeter."

Most of the crowd's chants were about Mr. MacDonald and the Poseidon Group. People were happy to make an ethical stand against a corrupt teacher, some shady businessmen, and, of course, a Black man.

Berlin could see it now.

How she'd been okay if the community canceled Joe when Berlin hadn't even known the full story all because she was hurting.

"Do you remember how many people showed up for Cam's auntie?" she asked.

"A handful."

"And for Kiki?"

"A few hundred."

"Those early days, yeah, before they found something else to do," Berlin agreed. "And look at them here, angry over pizza and that a high school teacher got caught doing what so many white men do all the time. It's not like this is new. But they pretend it is. That it's out of the ordinary. It's sad, no?"

"It's sad, all right." Quinta's breath emerged in a cloud. "I didn't say it clearly last night. But you need to know. I didn't find out Kiki was at his house until . . . months and months into this. I believed him. I shouldn't have. But I believed him." She rolled her shoulders, cracked her neck. The kind of thing she did when she was anxious or before she tore the roof off her Jeep. "I didn't know. Not when everyone was looking, when we were grieving. I need you to hear that."

The crowd was getting rowdy again. Berlin tuned them out. Cam was still inside making his pitch, and Jessie was supervising

316

the empty till, and somewhere in this crowd, Tashie and the rest of the FNMISA were teamed up with Sasha and Ira, thanking people for showing up. For their support.

Bee knew already. But she needed it spoken. "When did you find out, then?"

"Christmas break, duh. Outside the Walmart in Cochran."

"Is that the only reason you stopped talking to me?"

"Yes, you Tofurky, you're my one and only." Quinta sounded angry. "Can you forgive me?"

What a question.

Was it possible to let go of this hurt? Could Berlin paint this hurt onto stretched canvas? Could she force the pain to live there? In a world unhinged from this place? A world apart?

"Maybe, after a while," Berlin said, even if she wasn't certain yet. "But not tonight."

"Will you forgive me tomorrow?"

"Don't push it, Quinta."

"Yep, got it," she said.

Berlin knew she ought to leave, find Cam or try to repair some of the damage she'd inflicted on Joe's reputation. Instead, she asked another question, one that had been irritating her most of the week: "Why exactly do you let Cameron call you Quintana-Roo?"

"Honestly?" She laughed. "I like the way he says it."

"You like the way someone pronounces your horrid, colonial AF legal name?"

"Weird, eh? It's not that it will ever grow on me, and who names their child after the state in Mexico where they met on vacation? I mean, my parents could have named me Cancún."

"Or Isla Mujeres."

"Tabasco. Or, even more hipster-y, Nuevo Tabasco."

Berlin laughed despite herself. "So many terrible options."

"My parents made a critical mistake that I will never stop being infuriated by. But Cam makes me not hate my name as much."

"Some things change after all."

"Some things," Quinta said meaningfully. "But not all of them. And certainly not the things that have been set in stone since we were six."

They did have a history. But history was garbage a lot of the time. Sometimes, history was a scar on someone's finger from when you stabbed them with a pencil. Sometimes, history was stolen sisters, stolen over and again.

But if they couldn't change history, then what were any of them doing? What was Berlin doing?

"I don't know if I can forgive you yet. But I know I don't want to not forgive you at all. So, maybe in the spring, come by the house sometime," she said. "To hang out with your bees. Or whatever."

"Will do." Quinta picked the sign back up. "If you'll excuse me, I have a protest to join."

Everything, even the falling snow, felt lighter. Berlin walked away. She still had a really hard conversation in her future with her mom and dad. But tonight, she was pretty sure she'd survive it. That spring would come. After all, as tough as things were, as hard as things had been, would continue to be, some moments still

318

shined brightly enough, even while they hurt, the way a healing bruise, when you tested it, could remind you of the pain and the joy of flying down a mountain.

CAM

Joe was in Cam's family's living room, sitting next to Kiki, telling stories. It was a parallel universe. That was the only explanation. But Cam checked, and he wasn't in space or untethered. He could laugh at the stories, could feel them in his body.

After hearing out his proposal, Joe had closed the shop. And he'd followed Cam home.

Berlin was in the kitchen making tea with his dad.

Cam's dad was home. In the kitchen. Helping to make tea.

Yep, a parallel universe. Entirely.

"And you know what your mom did?" Joe asked, his voice booming. "She turned around and she gave that asshole a facer."

Everyone laughed. They laughed around the hurt, with the pain. Because, yes, there was hurt and pain sitting in the room too.

"He said sorry after that, and your mom, she said, 'Now, if you'd gone and apologized first thing, you'd be eating steak dinner tonight, not laying a fresh cut on your eyeball.'"

Moments like this were when this place was most like a home. On euchre tourney nights, movie nights, when they were sitting around telling stories. This was exactly right. And pain was part of a good life.

His cousin sat on the couch like she'd never left. Exhausted, clearly, and she kept running off to toss her cookies because turns out she was sick with something called hyperemesis gravidarum—basically excessive morning sickness that for some people never stopped the whole pregnancy—but she refused to go upstairs to the trundle bed. The doctor she'd seen that day said the medicine should help but it didn't matter: as long as Joe was telling stories about her mom, Kiki would stay.

It was nearing midnight.

"That wasn't the only time your mom taught someone a lesson."

"Yeah," Kiki said. "She was good at those."

"She was . . . I have stories, too, eh?" Cam's dad said, half-perched on the arm of the couch.

Tanya and Callie were asleep now. Sami had crashed early. She'd curled herself around Kiki's belly, and she'd whispered secrets to it until she nodded off. Joe might have been weird. In this living room. Out of place. But that wasn't true, not in the parallel universe.

And Berlin was becoming a fixture. In all timelines. She'd held on to him in sleep and now she was making tea, listening to stories with his family.

Kiki, she'd returned. And Kiki's baby would grow up loved. Probably a lot of Kraft Dinner, hot dog, and ketchup meals made in burnt pots in that baby's future. But lots of honey too.

In another universe, the wapiti had given birth. The little wapiti was okay. And here, in this place, Cam would keep their memory alive. That wherever this ride ended, when the universes collapsed again, collided, there would be good things alongside heavy ones.

Berlin carried a loaded tray. "Refills, anyone?"

320

"It's decaf, right?" Kiki asked before taking more.

"At this point," Berlin said, "we should all be drinking decaf."

Kiki laughed. "But when do we do what we should?"

"Not often enough." Joe spoke like this was something he'd learned the hard way.

He hadn't signed. And he hadn't agreed to Cam's proposal either. Which was fine.

Cam could wait.

Everyone deserved time to think. That's what Joe had said. Before he called it a night, thanked the protesters for doing the good work of keeping him and the rest of the community accountable, and turned the neon Open sign off.

"Joe." Cam's dad sat next to Kiki. "I shouldn't ask. But I'm too tired not to ask and I should have a long time ago. My sister, she was a lover. Are you—?"

He didn't finish his thought.

"Uncle!" Kiki said. "Seriously!"

"I wish it were true." Joe ran a hand against his close-cropped hair. "But Delphine said no."

Cam remembered something like Joe saying it was close to impossible. Joe describing the drinking, the nights like a winter's whiteout storm. How that wasn't no. That was possibility. "That's not what you told me. Not exactly."

That in another alternative universe, tonight, it could be truth.

"I'm too young to be a grandfather," Joe said with an easy smile. He reached for Kiki's outstretched hand.

Cam's dad laughed. "That's what we all say."

"It's up to Kiki," Joe said eventually. "Cam's right. Your mom said it was close to impossible. In those days, well, there are a lot of nights I don't recall. If you want me to, I'll take a test. Happily."

Kiki nodded.

"But whatever the test says . . ." Joe smiled. "You know I told you this when you quit making pizzas, but I'm always here for you, kid. Whether you're my blood or not, you're one of mine."

The whole room inhaled, exhaled, as if in unison.

The whole room lived in this good moment.

"Thanks, Joe," Kiki said, shifting the mood. "I spent the last few months with only one person, and he was trying to make sure that I only had one person for a long time before I . . . left. And it's so hard, living that way."

"Niece . . ." Cam's dad was trying not to cry. "You've never had only one. Even when he told you that . . . you always had more."

Kiki pushed herself up awkwardly and hugged her uncle.

Hugged Cam's dad.

Cam's dad was present.

It was enough to upset the balance. Because Cam was still angry with his dad. Still not ready to forgive and forget. But Cam yawned, needing to sleep. He had to drive Bee home first. Having her camp out with him on the couch was one thing. But not a single person in the room would be okay if he dragged her upstairs to his bed, even if all he had planned was to sleep next to her, maybe hold her, so that when morning arrived, he'd wake in a universe of the possible. Where Kiki was safe and the baby wapiti was too.

"I can drive her," Joe said, stretching. "I should be going soon."

Cam smiled. "Thanks, but I want to."

Bee slipped into her gorgeous handmade parka and stepped onto the porch. When he told her they were best friends, he'd been joking. At the same time, Cam hadn't been joking at all. Standing here, in this place, next to Berlin Chambers and her magnificent glasses, her perfect bangs, he laughed.

Those were the best jokes, the ones that were and weren't. They provoked the best kind of laughter.

That was the thing about laughter. It healed what hurt, balmed the rough moments until they were steady again.

That was one good, good thing about laughter. And it turned out, in this life, it only took one good thing to feed possibility, to stifle fear, to invite more goodness inward and onward.

Friday

BERLIN

It was cold outdoors. But it was fresh too. The snow had laid down a blanket on the roads, on the land, something to keep everything insulated, even warm, throughout the long night.

When Cam joined her, she stepped to the side, making space. They stood on the porch, breathing in the winter air. It tingled, sparked in the deep reaches of her lungs. Like they were expanding fully, open, for the first time in too long.

"What are you thinking, eh?" Cam asked.

He'd been so quiet tonight. Smiling, but watchful.

"About PMP. And my proposal, I mean."

She didn't hesitate. "Joe will agree. It's not about the money with him. It was never about the money. And it's the right sale, this time."

He shrugged. His floppy hair moved. "How do you know?"

She turned to look Cam in the face. She had to stand on her tippy-toes to try. "Because."

She just did. The way she knew that spring was on its way.

"Because?" he echoed.

"Just that. That's my answer."

"I'll accept it," he said, staring down at her glasses.

At night, they would be wine-dark. But in daylight, they were Coke-red and sparkled like stars. She hadn't intended to buy Coke-red glasses. But they'd called to her.

"Berlin?"

"Cameron?"

"This is strange. But . . ."

What hadn't been weird this week?

"Go on," she prompted.

He looked nervous. "Oof. I'll just ask, and if it's wrong, you say so, okay?"

"I can do that."

"Can I kiss you?"

She thought about it, shrugged, and with a little laugh said, "Okay, sure."

His lips were warm like winter couldn't touch them. The warmth was welcome. He tasted like tea and good heat.

It was odd.

Too, too strange.

And this time, Berlin had been ready for it. Or she thought she had been ready for a second kiss. That second kisses would be easier than firsts.

Cam pulled away, a mischievous grin on his face. "We tried, eh?"

He was still holding her. Not tightly. But he hadn't let go.

"We did."

"It was too much for us, right?"

"I think so?"

But she wasn't sure. How could you be certain? About anything? But about kisses, specifically? The pipe wasn't a pipe. But it was too. And maybe the pipe was more.

She'd already figured this out.

But she hadn't figured out kisses.

"You'll just have to be my best friend, then," he said. "It's settled."

They turned away from each other. Berlin thought about walking down the steps, climbing into the LeBaron, fastening her seat belt. But she didn't do any of those things.

She hesitated. And he caught it.

"Wait a minute. You said, *I think so*. Not *I know so*." Cam smiled. His too-pointy eyeteeth were fully present. "Should we try it again? For science?"

Already she was moving back into Cam's arms. "Couldn't hurt. For science."

This time, she pulled at his parka to steady herself. This time, she tried to lean into the kiss too. Third kisses were like freak snowstorms and broken friendships that shouldn't break.

He pulled away, brushed hair behind her ear. "Kiss me back,

Bee," he said against her neck. "Just kiss me back."

This time, she did.

And the snow came down faster, landing in Cam's eyelashes and in his too-long hair. She dizzied. She tasted him, beyond the tea and the heat. It was Cameron Sound, playful and complex and too much in the way that laughter was too much, that joy was too much, that hurt could be too much too. This time, when Cam broke away to breathe, he laughed. That laugh said he was happy. That he was okay. Berlin couldn't help herself—she joined in.

She was out of breath like she'd been running. Maybe it took three times for kisses to start making sense.

So she pulled him back down. And kissed him a fourth time. She didn't have to tell him to kiss her back, because it was like he couldn't help himself. Like he needed her. But even better, he wanted her too.

Eventually, her fingers got cold. Where were her mittens?

Cam pulled her hands into his and rubbed them. "That settles it. Best friends who kiss. That's what we are to each other now, Bee."

Berlin laughed again.

Every time it came easier.

She was still learning how to feel again, still learning about kissing. Still had to face her parents and tell them how she'd been numb for so very long. And Berlin knew if she needed someone to hold her hand when she had that talk, she had a bevy of good options.

The wind was cold but right. And now she could sense it. Quiet and careful. In her chest.

The hum of the entire universe.

She stood on the porch, her hands warming under Cam's careful attention, and listened. He brushed her bangs from her face like he couldn't stop touching her, and she let her eyes close. He didn't do anything else, only offered little reassurances.

It was still there.

Still waiting.

Still hers, as much as the universe's song could belong to anyone.

What fucking relief.

What glory.

. . . .

A Note from Jen

. . . .

A few weeks before my thirty-fifth birthday, amid a global pandemic and a recurrence of major depressive disorder, a friend broke up with me. Now, this hurt—still hurts, to be honest. They were one of a small handful of people I trusted with early drafts of my writing, and with the other deep, red, messy parts of myself.

All of this is to say, Berlin Chambers and her very stiff, rule-following personality—one that cannot come to terms with the concept of *depression* as someone who *gets things done*—is familiar to me. And so is the absolute trauma of her platonic relationship with Quinta coming to an end, as if fate or the universe is trying to make a very sharp point. So while Berlin is prickly and flawed, I can't help but love her and want to take care of her messy parts.

If I look back, the representations of clinical depression I was exposed to as a young adult and in my twenties were rare enough that I can't remember any; or, if they did exist, they must have felt as if they were not relatable to my experience because they didn't stick, didn't help me to identify depression when it showed up in my life. Perhaps, on my part, that's a flaw in imaginative empathy. Berlin's story, after all, is only *one* narrative about how depression manifests, it's not *the story*.

If living with depression or other mood disorders is familiar to you, and you recognize a part of yourself in Berlin, I want to remind you there are resources to help. Friends, family, teachers, medical professionals, and organizations like the Kids Help Phone (Canada), Talk Suicide Canada, the National Alliance on Mental Illness (USA), the Crisis Text Line (USA, Canada, Ireland, UK), the Trevor Project (US), the 988 Suicide and Crisis Lifeline (US but also coming to Canada in late 2023), and others are the netting around you, to catch you when you're falling.

I believe that we need more characters who experience depression and other mood disorders represented in our books and other media. One of the ways we recognize parts of ourselves is by seeing our reflections out in the world.

I also believe that as a community we need to talk about friendship breakups so much more than we do. Platonic relationships deserve as much attention and care as romantic ones.

If you believe these things, too, let's together change the world a small, radical bit.

This book centers on Kiki Cheyanne Sound, a biracial Black and Indigenous teen, and her disappearance: one day she's in school, participating in extracurriculars, and the next she's gone. It also tells the story of Kiki's mother, who was murdered while driving along what in Canada is called the Highway of Tears because of the significant number of Indigenous women, girls, and Two-Spirit people who have disappeared there.

These are two stories of the Missing and Murdered Indigenous Women, Girls, and Two-Spirit (#MMIWG2S) human rights crisis. It is ongoing, currently happening across ancestral Indigenous lands in the colonial nations of Canada, the United States, and Mexico, and this book is as much about this crisis of #StolenSisters as it is about teens on a mission to crush capitalism. Like everything else, these things are interconnected, sometimes so much so that the relationships between them are assumed to be natural rather than a series of deliberate choices, upheld and reaffirmed over and over.

My first experience with depression coincided with the publication of an article in the *Winnipeg Free Press* titled "New database lists 824 murdered, missing native women in Canada." By this point in my life, I already knew that Canada's legal and policing systems were deeply flawed, that they didn't value the lives of BIPOC community members. But the article's database detailed a level of violence that had not before been compiled and presented to the public at this scale.

What had been information shared in whisper networks—a dangerous part of the road, warnings of "starlight" tours care of the RCMP, where Indigenous people are driven many kilometers outside of town and abandoned in the cold by the police—or stories in communities, of aunties and sisters and nieces and cousins and friends gone missing, became a visible wound on the land. And the wound was larger than many of us could have imagined. Some of us knew the wound was there all along.

My heart was broken open.

In hindsight, I can see that this was the moment when I could no longer perceive Canada as an entity that did both good and bad things. I couldn't rationalize my understanding of being both Canadian and Métis any longer. This was the moment when I was radicalized, when I had to acknowledge and deconstruct colonial ways of thinking in my heart and head and body if I was to continue being.

Kiki isn't the first character I've written who is immediately affected by this human rights crisis. I always knew that she would save herself—with the help of her friends. And while the procedural aspects of Kiki's story aren't central, it should be evident how many different systems fail her. In this, Kiki's story isn't fiction.

The problem is ongoing and travels across colonial borders. #MMIWG2S activists remind us to stay small, to get involved in local action. That's where we have the most effect. To find a local-to-you action network, check out where these hashtags are used in your city or town: #MMIW, #MMIWG, #NoMoreStolenSisters, #MissingAndMurdered.

It's up to us to make a world where Kiki's daughter, and others, can thrive.

In the same way that #MMIWG2S is interconnected with capitalism, they are both also connected to anti-Blackness. It was important to me that Kiki was a mixed Indigenous and Black teen and that Joe, Pink Mountain Pizza's owner, was a Black Canadian with a historically long family history on the Canadian prairies. Both of their stories are rooted in different kinds of anti-Black sentiment and action.

Cam seems to think what the PMP staff are doing to Joe is bullying. But that's not exactly it.

What Berlin and Cam and the rest of the PMP staff cannot see is that taking public action against a Black man, without knowing the full story behind Joe's choice, is insidious anti-Blackness at play. Berlin gives everyone else in her life this consideration—including Quinta. That is, Berlin offers complex and full humanity to other people who hurt her, but not to Joe.

Representing how anti-Blackness functions, how it happens in seemingly unconscious ways, how it takes these caring and activist-savvy teens too long to understand what they've done, is absolutely intentional. They might comprehend a lot of things about racism, misogyny, and other gender-based violence, as well as privilege, but they do not understand how anti-Blackness exists within them and in their communities.

The ways that Indigenous people, people of color, and other marginalized groups inflict violence on our Black friends, family, and neighbors must be rooted out. It is a poison. Eliminating anti-Black thought, feelings, laws, and actions in our communities and our nations is what we owe each other.

It is what we owe each other now, not later.

This is urgent.

Oof.

I recognize I've just told you the world is on fire and we're running out of water, and some people have no water but more fire, and some of us have fire and also fire tornadoes.

I know all of this is a lot. The world is a lot. The wide-spinning universe is a lot—even if you don't believe in alien life, even if you can't laugh at hurt the way Cam does.

In my heart of hearts, these are things I believe: that we are better in community, that we deserve strong and healthy communities, that with friends on our side we can do anything. I believe that we each have strengths and weaknesses and that's why communities are strong—we have a variety of ways of looking at the world, and the more ways of seeing and of knowing we can bring together, the more unstoppable we are against a tide of immediately critical issues.

We need all the Cams, the Berlins, and the Jessies, the Sashas, and Iras, and Quintas, the ski and snowboard devotees, the crunchy hipsters and the powerful teens running FNMISAs across the continent to come together and work for fundamental change. Good pizza can only help.

Controversial food opinions incoming: I believe pineapple belongs on pizza and that pizza is an open-faced sandwich.

I know some of you are cringing.

Let us remember this: pizza is good, but it's not critical.

So let's order many different pizzas and come together. It's the only way to heal, to bring a better timeline to life.

That and laughter.

············

Jen's Absolute Favorite Pizza

············

Meet the Pineapples

If I can have only one topping on a pizza, it'll be pineapple. To me, it's foundational.

These people are the pineapples to my bookish pizza: Rosemary Brosnan, whose editorial vision helped me to shape this book into something more than it was to start; Cynthia Leitich Smith, who is always looking out for my writer's heart and for teen readers; Patricia Nelson, who is the first person to challenge me and also is supportive AF when I need to vent about the state of the universe and/or this business; and everyone else who was involved in small and big ways in getting *Those Pink Mountain Nights* into the hands of readers, including Courtney Stevenson, Suzanne Murphy, Kathryn Silsand, Laura Mock, Patty Rosati and her team, Susan VanHecke, Mark Rifkin, Katie Shepherd, David Curtis, Sabrina Abballe, Anna Bernard, Nicole Moulaison, and Annabelle Sinoff.

Thank you so much for what you do for me, for books, and for readers!

Meet the Green Olives

If a pizza menu has green olives as an option, I know I'm going to leave satisfied. Green olives complement pineapple. Together they are a delicious experience, one where salty meets sweet.

I can't say this enough: big thanks to everyone who has played a supporting role in my life while I was writing this book. But especially, maarsi to Katherine Crocker for many, many phone calls and texts in which they helped me understand what I was truly trying to do with this book; to Edward Underhill for being my person with whom I can complain about Goodreads and other evils of the universe; to Jamie Paction for being there and always checking in on me and celebrating my wins; to early reader Susan Azim Boyer, who told me to keep writing and who is one of the most optimistic people I know; and to my fellow 22Debuts, 2K22 Debuts, and my PW15 class—collectively you are my best book people.

Meet the Hot Peppers

A pizza without a kick just makes me sad. It might have something to do with how hot peppers and hot sauces are always in high demand on my family's table.

Thanks to Natalie Leif (who won the naming rights to a character—Nico!) and to Bridgette Hoshont'omba (for being the mind behind Tashie's Uncle's Special!) for donating to Books for Palestine.

To my colleague LaTanya McQueen for telling me her theory on postcards being basically time travel—thank you, that stuck in my brain big-time!

To Michelle Sound, who graciously offered up her last name for Cameron's family, and to Danielle Lorenz, who named Snapdragon when Snap was still a raccoon—maarsi for coming to the rescue on twitterdotcom when I sent out the signal for help.

To everyone else whose names I borrowed for secondary

characters—SarahLynn, Callie, Tanya, Dr. Banerji, Mel—I am much obliged. Also, big love to friends who let me use their Instagram handles in the book!

Teachers, I know I was hard on you in this book—but every story needs an antagonist. Most of you are incredibly dedicated to your students' success and you fight every day with your hearts and heads against systems that do harm from within one of those broken systems. My thanks for what you and librarians and all the other educational support staff do!

Uncountable thanks in the infinite to my family and friends. My dad keeps trying to sell my autograph to his neighbors. My aunties and uncles are always celebrating me. My sisters aren't big readers, but they are always my biggest fans. My niece and nephews don't know how cool it is that their auntie is an author yet, but they love me anyway. My friends far and wide, across time zones, are consistently so excited for me and support my author journey. You show up and you keep showing up, and I see you, and I love you.

Meet the Goat Cheeses

Tangy, creamy, and always surprising, goat cheese just does it for me! It's such a perfect complement to the other ingredients, rounding out the perfect pizza experience.

Thank you, dear readers, you're the GOAT.

A Note from Cynthia Leitich Smith, Author-Curator of Heartdrum

Dear Reader,

Are you finishing *Those Pink Mountain Nights* with a slice of pizza? I like mine with a thin, crispy crust and marinara, grilled chicken, mozzarella, and mushrooms. Maybe you're more of a thick-crust fan or prefer the toppings piled high. Maybe you don't even like pizza.

Ironically, the one quality we all share is our fierce individuality. It's informed by our life experiences and emotions. It's reflected in our specific perspectives.

Consider how in this story Berlin, Cameron, and Jessie misunderstand or underestimate each other—and other key people in their lives—and how that causes conflict, heartache, surprise, and, ultimately, leads them to rethink their assumptions. Mixed signals, high-stakes secrets, and the ripple effects of trauma get in the way of our heroes making sense of their world. I bet you know something about interpersonal dynamics like that too.

Our individuality is also reflected in our degree of power (or lack thereof) in relationships and how we navigate them. If only we could automatically trust authority figures in particular to keep our best interests at heart. But too often, young people—like Kiki—are abused or marginalized by the very people who are supposed to guide or protect them.

Meanwhile, it's tough trying to gauge others' intentions, especially when you're doing the hard work of growing into your true self. If you've been harmed by someone you trusted, that doesn't make you foolish. If you're hurting, that doesn't mean you deserve to suffer. Hopefully, you already know that. But sometimes it's helpful to have it said clearly and outright.

I'm wowed by author Jen Ferguson and how she creates nuanced, flawed, yet inspiring heroes as well as by the care she takes in crafting emotionally resonant stories that nurture empathy and understanding. Have you read many books by and about Indigenous people? Hopefully, *Those Pink Mountain Nights* will motivate you to read more. The novel is published by Heartdrum, a Native-focused imprint of HarperCollins, which offers stories about young Native heroes by Indigenous authors and illustrators. I hope you found reading this novel to be entertaining, cathartic, and, if needed, a healing experience.

Books and pizza are good medicine.

Mvto,
Cynthia Leitich Smith

In 2014, We Need Diverse Books (WNDB) began as a simple hashtag on Twitter. The social media campaign soon grew into a 501(c)(3) nonprofit with a team that spans the globe. WNDB is supported by a network of writers, illustrators, agents, editors, teachers, librarians, and book lovers, all united under the same goal—to create a world where every child can see themselves in the pages of a book. You can learn more about WNDB programs at www.diversebooks.org.

In 2014, We Need Diverse Books (WNDB) began as a simple hashtag on Twitter. The social media campaign soon grew into a 501(c)(3) nonprofit with a team that spans the globe. WNDB is supported by a network of writers, illustrators, agents, editors, teachers, librarians, and book lovers, all united under the same goal—to create a world where every child can see themselves in the pages of a book. You can learn more about WNDB programs at www.diversebooks.org.

ABOUT THE AUTHOR

JEN FERGUSON is Michif/Métis and white, an activist, an intersectional feminist, an auntie, and an accomplice armed with a PhD in English and creative writing. Her debut novel, *The Summer of Bitter and Sweet*, was named a William C. Morris Award Finalist and a Stonewall Honor Book and won the Governor General's Award. Her go-to-number-one-absolute-favorite pizza topping is pineapple. Visit her online at jenfergusonwrites.com.

ABOUT CYNTHIA LEITICH SMITH

CYNTHIA LEITICH SMITH is the bestselling, acclaimed author of books for all ages, including *Sisters of the Neversea*, *Rain Is Not My Indian Name*, *Indian Shoes*, *Jingle Dancer*, and *Hearts Unbroken*, which won the American Indian Library Association's Youth Literature Award; she is also the anthologist of *Ancestor Approved: Intertribal Stories for Kids*. Most recently, she was named the 2021 NSK Neustadt Laureate. Cynthia is the author-curator of Heartdrum, a Native-focused imprint at HarperCollins Children's Books, and serves as the Katherine Paterson Inaugural Endowed Chair on the faculty of the MFA program in writing for children and young adults at Vermont College of Fine Arts. She is a citizen of the Muscogee (Creek) Nation and lives in Austin, Texas. You can visit Cynthia online at www.cynthialeitichsmith.com.